Hitch

Hitch

Kathryn Hind

HAMISH HAMILTON
an imprint of
PENGUIN BOOKS

HAMISH HAMILTON

UK | USA | Canada | Ireland | Australia
India | New Zealand | South Africa | China

Addresses for the Penguin Random House group of companies can be found at
global.penguinrandomhouse.com/offices

First published by Hamish Hamilton, an imprint of
Penguin Random House Australia Pty Ltd, 2019

Cover design by James Rendall © Penguin Random House Australia Pty Ltd
Cover photographs by Getty Images and Shutterstock
Typeset in 12/18 pt Minion Pro by Midland Typesetters, Australia

Printed and bound in Australia by Griffin Press, part of Ovato, an
accredited ISO AS/NZS 14001 Environmental Management Systems printer

A catalogue record for this
book is available from the
National Library of Australia

ISBN 978 0 14379 434 9

penguin.com.au

MIX
Paper from
responsible sources
FSC® C009448

For my mother, who laughs loudly
and loves fiercely

The posts on the Stuart Highway were white with round, red reflectors attached at the top. Most of them reached to the middle of Amelia's thigh, but post three hundred and forty-eight, counting south from Alice Springs, stuck out of the ground at an odd angle, clipped by a car or a truck. Or kicked over by someone like her. If she narrowed her eyes till her vision blurred, she was not alone: the posts ahead became red-eyed stick-aliens awaiting her arrival on their stretch of desert road. She stopped walking and touched the fur on Lucy's head in a signal for her to do the same. Something rattled in Amelia's pack and took a moment to settle, and then there it was: the buzz of a vehicle in the distance.

Lucy stood on guard, ears pricked, her nostrils twitching as she sniffed the air. Amelia looked down the highway to the quivering horizon, left then right, but saw no sign of life. Her pack towered above her like a high-backed chair, tugging her shoulders back. She tightened the strap around her waist for what seemed like the hundredth time that day, then ran her finger beneath the rubber bands around her wrist, clearing out the sweat. She walked on. Lucy panted along beside her, the tags on her collar clinking.

Post three hundred and fifty-one was striped with green paint from base to middle, a feature she hadn't noticed on any of the others that morning. Red sand lay flat around her, ripped in two by the highway, and the long threads of cloud above were of no use, leaving her exposed to the December sun. Trees and bushes were scattered across the land, bonsai versions of the flora growing closer to the coastline; they provided no shade. A month had passed since she had been in the little town on the east coast. As she walked, she summoned the sea breeze, wished for its coolness against her burning cheeks. She'd spent a couple of weeks in that town, in a studio apartment with stark white walls. The nights were warm, and she'd lain on top of the bed in her undies, window open. A breeze lifted the sheer curtain and brushed the material against her skin. She'd grown used to the rumble of the ocean, to the way the slap and sucking back of waves delivered her into sleep.

She was thirsty again. She swung her pack off her shoulders and let it fall to the dust. There was no hiding her neglect of it: a tear ran the length of the side so that a layer of lining oozed out, and the green canvas was stained with dirt and rings of salt.

She longed to spend time sponging its creases and sewing patches over the injured material.

She stretched, rolling her shoulders back, pressing in hard on the lumps in the muscles around her neck. Her old Mount Franklin one-and-a-half-litre bottle was wedged in the side pocket of her pack, a few mouthfuls left in the bottom. She yanked it out; the plastic popped and snapped as it caved in and reshaped itself. The water was warm and tasted chemical, having stewed with the inside of the bottle. She held a sip in her mouth, then let it seep slowly down her throat.

She lowered to a crouch, a knee cracking on the way down. 'Here you go, girl.' She made a bowl with her hand and poured water in. Lucy lapped it up, then gave Amelia's fingers an extra lick. Her dark fur was hot to touch, its flecks of auburn lit up by the sun. The light brown ovals above her eyes wiggled like beetles as she followed Amelia's movements, asking for more. Amelia made another pool in her hand, careful not to spill a drop.

She tracked the buzz of the engine, guessing the direction of its approach, wondering if she should change her course, get out of the desert, perhaps head back to the coast. Lucy had loved it there too, especially the mornings, when sunrise bruised the walls pink. They got up early to walk along the cliffs, past the barrier threaded with notes and flowers: messages for the lost souls who had jumped. One morning she'd sat on the cliff edge, legs dangling, counting the seconds between waves of white water smashing the rocks beneath her. A woman had called out, asked if she was okay. Amelia tucked up her legs, eased back from the edge to placate her. Once alone again, she moved forward, imagined being obliterated below, joining the collision of salt water on stone.

The buzz was now louder, transformed into a drone; she squinted her eyes against the glare, looked up and down the highway, but there was still no hint of the source. She hoisted her pack onto her knee, then twisted it around and over her shoulders, heaving it as high as it would go. Her back twinged after a few steps so she took hold of the shoulder straps, shifting the pack's weight forward. This provided some relief, but without a free hand she was at the mercy of flies, unable to shoo them away; they landed on her lips and nuzzled into the corners of her eyes. She cursed herself for not being tougher in the heat, wished she was back at the coast, swimming beyond the breakers. She had floated on her back out there, watching the sky flare into day. It was a good place for Lucy and her for a little while, until Zach appeared in the faces of the townsfolk. She'd see him in flashes on the main street, but sometimes he emerged when she dived beneath the waves, an underwater predator. She couldn't keep him at bay while she lingered in the white room.

A drop of sweat ran between her eyebrows, slid down to the tip of her nose; it hung there for a moment before falling, leaving a tiny crater in the dust. She stomped on it and carried on, blowing at damp strands of hair that stuck to her face.

It was almost midday. Both truckies and tourists travelled that highway so, setting out at six in the morning, she'd been confident of a ride. Too confident, it turned out, since she had by now walked too far out of town and was almost out of water. But that sound was getting closer; by post three hundred and sixty-two, it could be there beside her. It would probably be a white car. White was more common than red, black or silver. She'd begun counting with Sid when they were kids, up the hill that divided their suburb from the next. The first time they'd counted, she was so sure red was the safe bet. But after an hour white won with thirty-seven compared to red's feeble twelve. She wasn't used to losing, not then, and especially not to Sid, all skin and bones and insecurity.

She gained a visual on the vehicle: a red road train. Not white after all. And it was headed south: her way. 'Lucy, heel.' Lucy moved in close, her body radiating heat, fur tickling Amelia's calf. She took three steps away from the edge of the road. The last thing she wanted to do was spook the driver. Road trains were the gods of outback roads; they had taken her huge distances, and she had learned to respect the brute force of them and the endurance required to drive them. She stuck her thumb out.

The truck moved closer, about twenty posts away; the size of the monsters surprised her each time. She listened for any acceleration or deceleration of the engine, however slight, gauging whether the driver was considering picking her up. But the engine belted along with a roar that quickened her heart. She raised her arm higher and stood on her tiptoes just to be sure. She managed to catch the eye of the truckie as he passed; he gave a short nod and lifted his index finger off the wheel. She swapped her thumb for a wave as the truck zoomed by. Its wake slapped her in the face, the thunder of it ringing in her ears. She pressed her lips together and closed her eyes against a spray of grit. Lucy sneezed.

Amelia took a deep breath through her nose and exhaled, then turned and continued walking down the highway. Though her arm ached in protest, she put her thumb out again in an invitation, as if it might conjure the next vehicle.

Post three hundred and sixty-three. Her heart was too fast and the skin on her chest was pulled taut by the straps of her pack. The air was thick, difficult to push down her throat. She concentrated hard on the details of each post: white paint peeled in different patterns; one was streaked with dried bird shit, another sprouted a dandelion at its base.

At post three hundred and eighty, she stopped for more water. She couldn't help but be disappointed in her usually loyal Mount Franklin bottle for being nearly empty, but immediately regretted the feeling. Her thighs trembled as she squatted at Lucy's level, struggling to balance under the weight of the pack. Lucy drank from her hand, dry nose pressing her palm.

There was another vehicle. She stood – this one was already close, a modern engine sneaking up on her. It was white and looked like a ute, which was a good sign the driver might be dog-friendly. She faced the vehicle, arm out, thumb straining as high as it would go. Lucy barked once, her tail swaying slightly, as if she was unwilling to celebrate too soon. The ute passed and, through a haze of exhaust and dust, the brake lights illuminated: the shining red of salvation.

She paused for a moment to savour the view. Sometimes a stopped car was only a mirage, broken when a family piled out because a kid was about to vomit. Or she approached the window only to find some grey nomads squabbling over a map. But this was the real deal, she was sure. Gripping the shoulder straps of her pack to steady it, she ran towards the ute; a quick approach minimised time for the driver to change their mind. Lucy ran too, getting ahead then turning in excited circles while she waited for Amelia to catch up. Amelia's pack jangled and a length of rope attached to a side strap whipped her in the ribs as she ran.

The driver's forearm rested along the open window. There was something relaxed about it, at ease, as if its owner were kicking back in a lounge chair. She tried to flatten the knots in her hair as she approached the passenger side of the ute. The window was open, and when she peered in the driver lifted his sunglasses onto his head.

'How you going?' she said.

'Good, good.' His smile was slow and lazy. 'Where ya headed?' His eyelashes were impossibly long, the kind her mother would comment on, and they softened his face, an outdoors face. She tried to interpret her instinctual response to him; there were only a few seconds to decide if she trusted this man.

He waited for an answer, drumming his fingers on the passenger headrest. Lucy jumped up against the door, resting her paws on the windowsill. The man clicked his tongue and stretched his arm across the car towards her. After a quick sniff, Lucy accepted his pat.

'Adelaide,' Amelia said. A lie, but she had to appear purposeful, as if someone was expecting her.

'Righto. Well, I can take you part of the way. A good part of the way. I'm goin' to Port Augusta.' He flicked his head towards the passenger seat and made a short whistling sound, which sent Lucy's ears up and then back against her head, tail wagging. 'Jump in.'

He was young – Amelia guessed late twenties – and she stood for a moment more, transfixed by the triangle of sweat that darkened the blue fabric of his T-shirt just below the neckline, and the few chest hairs that poked out above it. He swatted at a fly near his face, and the movement snapped her out of the trance. His smile was different then, and she knew he was laughing at her; she'd been staring too long. Sid was always telling her off for that.

'Thanks,' Amelia said, her hands gesturing wildly out to her sides under his gaze until she found a place for them on her straps. She walked to the back of the ute and hefted her pack into the tray. At the passenger door, the man was moving things to make room for her, jamming CDs into the glove box. She climbed into the cab, into a smell of hot chips and tomato sauce. Lucy scampered in on top of her, then found a seat in the middle behind the gearstick. As she got comfortable, Lucy's tail whipped the driver in the face; he gently pushed her out of the way. After a quick head check, the driver steered the car onto the road, spinning the wheel with the heel of one hand.

'I'm Will,' he said. He extended his hand across his body towards her, keeping hold of the wheel with his left. A detailed tattoo of a curling wave took up most of the inside of his right forearm, the blues and greens vibrant. Lucy sniffed his hand and Amelia shook it briefly, the skin rough, the fingers thick around her own.

'I'm Amelia. And this is Lucy,' she said, surprising herself by giving their real names; she'd been enjoying shrugging in and out of other titles. 'Thanks for stopping.'

'No worries,' he said, staring ahead. His arm returned to the windowsill, his sunglasses back on. 'Good to have the company.' He seemed unmoved by her presence, almost as if they knew each other and had planned to meet there, in the middle of nowhere.

A square patch of astroturf rested on the dash. Two plastic cows and three sheep grazed there, and a zombie figurine lurked at the edge of the scene, arms extended.

'Nice farm,' Amelia said.

'Well, thanks a lot. Nice to see a bit of greenery out here, don't you reckon?'

She smiled, and scratched behind Lucy's ear. The long journeys across that territory seemed to demand a kind of nesting in vehicles. She thought of telling Will about the oil tanker driver who had picked her up near Darwin – how he had a scrap of purple crocheted blanket across his lap and a gearstick cover to match – but she couldn't quite force the words out of her mouth.

The rest of Will's dash was dusty; an indecipherable word had been traced along it and then scrawled out with a fingertip. Lucy perched on the middle seat, tongue moving in time with bumps in the road as she looked out the window ahead. Wind blasted through the car and Amelia closed her eyes, feeling it hit her face from different directions; this part was okay, the acceleration after hours of meandering. She put thoughts aside – where to sleep, how to keep moving, whether she had enough food or drink – and surrendered to the thrust of the vehicle.

'Been out there long?' he asked.

She opened her eyes. The question shrank the space in the car so that it pressed in around her; the roof teased her hair and even Lucy's panting was hot and heavy beside her.

'Kind of, yeah. Left early this morning, but nothing till now. Thought it would be a bit easier, to be honest,' she said. Lucy walked across her lap and stuck her head out the window. 'What about you? Been driving long?'

She tried to mirror Will's behaviour. It was a habit she'd developed that made rides as smooth as possible for drivers and for herself, too, providing a guideline for interaction. People wanted something out of picking her up and she tried to be quick in working out what that something was.

'Few hours. Was in Tennant Creek this morning,' he said.

'Right, right . . . What're you doing in Port Augusta?'

'Just started up a business, me and my brother. Moving bits and pieces of construction equipment round. Fiddly things that can be real tricky to get your hands on when you need 'em, especially in these parts. Supposed to be a tiny thing on the side, but it's hard to do small-scale out here, know what I mean?'

'Yeah . . . Must be nice to have a job where you can travel, keep moving.'

'Yep, it's all right. Pays the bills. But sometimes it feels like I live out here on the road, you know,' he said.

She wasn't sure if that was a question, so she was quiet.

'What about you, though –' he said, then sniffed sharply and flicked a finger beneath his nose, '– you look like a desert girl. Looks like you belong out here.'

She stiffened at the thought of his eyes moving up and down her, summing her up, but she worked quickly at rationalising his words. He must have had more opportunity to suss her out than she'd had him. He would have seen her as he got closer and drove past, then he probably could have watched her jogging up to the ute if he looked at the mirrors. That was about thirty seconds more time than she'd had. Anyway, his tone was respectful. Desert girl; she didn't mind the title.

'I'll take that as a compliment. May as well let it get under your skin . . . fighting the desert is a losing battle I reckon,' she said.

'Couldn't agree more,' he said with a nod and a grin that made little folds at the corner of his eye. He reached behind his seat and shifted things around, keeping one hand on the wheel and his eyes on the road.

'Thirsty?' he asked.

Her Mount Franklin was wedged in the door beside her, nearly empty. 'Yeah, a bit,' she said.

'Well, I've got something real special. You gotta try it.' He revealed a three-quarters-full bottle of pub squash; the liquid inside was murky. 'Oh yeah!' he said.

'What's wrong with it? Looks funny,' she said.

'This is the ultimate concoction. This ute runs on diesel, and I run on this.' His smile was so big she couldn't help but return it, and if he were Sid, she might have reached out and pressed the softness of his earlobes between her fingers. He placed the bottle between his legs and unscrewed the cap. He held it to his lips, pausing momentarily before drinking deeply, Adam's apple bobbing as he swallowed. When he was finished, he let out a sharp exhale, then tossed his head from side to side, energised, as if he'd plunged his head into a bucket of cold water.

'Here,' he said, offering her the bottle.

'You gotta tell me what it is,' she said. 'It's a weird colour.'

'Whisky.'

'What?' She looked across at him and he was biting back a grin.

'Just kidding. It's pub squash with orange cordial. The drink of champions,' he said.

She frowned. 'Dunno if I believe you.'

'Righto, your loss. It's bloody delicious. Liquid gold.'

Lucy had sensed the excitement and stood, wondering what the commotion was, looking back and forth between them.

Amelia held out her hand and he passed her the bottle. 'Prepare your tastebuds,' he said.

She took a swig. 'Oh my gosh,' she said, wiping a dribble that escaped down her chin.

He laughed as she took another sip. This time she savoured it, allowing the bubbles to pop around her tongue. It was warm, but the combination of two familiar flavours offered a level of refreshment she hadn't felt in weeks.

'It's good, huh?' he said.

'It's a wizard's drink.' She pressed the bottle to her lips for one last taste. Lucy curled up on the seat between them, and they settled into silence.

Will turned the tuner on the radio, catching a crackly Bon Jovi song. He sang shamelessly; at first she hid her smile by looking out the window, but then she wasn't smiling, she was sitting on Zach's bed with Sid, years ago, and Zach was in his rapper phase, learning songs by heart. He performed for them, using his silver spray can of deodorant as a microphone, his face moving so close to hers that spit landed on her cheeks. She didn't move. She waited for the song to end, for the bulging veins in his neck to sink back into his skin. Then she and Sid clapped, the adoring audience.

The Bon Jovi song cut out but Will continued singing, belting out one last chorus. Amelia plucked the rubber bands around her wrist; there was the snap, then the sting, then the next one. It wasn't enough. Zach was there, standing on the front porch of her mother's house only two months ago, just after the funeral;

until that moment, she hadn't seen him in ten years, not since he'd turned nineteen and skipped town. He had a plastic bag of takeaway food. There was a whiteness at the edge of her vision as he was saying, 'I hope you still like Vietnamese,' and she was letting him hug her, listening to him say nice things about her mother, her ear crushed against his chest.

Will hit a lofty note and demanded a high five; she stuck her hand up, then looked out at the desert with narrowed eyes, tried to fill her mind with the deep red of endless sand.

*

It was difficult to account for the passing hours. At one point Will pulled the ute over to mix another bottle of the drink and she couldn't bring herself to refuse his offer of more, though she was nauseated from the initial swigs of sugar on her empty stomach. She filled her Mount Franklin bottle with water from Will's jerry can and held it close, taking regular drinks or sometimes just resting her mouth on the bottle. They played 'I Spy', and she eventually gave up on his word beginning with a C: cumulus cloud, for double points – a rule she'd never heard before. She wasn't even sure if the clouds above them were of the cumulus variety, but she couldn't bear to argue.

It was getting dark, and in the growing night it was strange to be next to Will; she couldn't quite work out how to be.

'Gonna stop in Glendambo for the night,' he said. When she didn't reply, he added, 'It's not far.'

'Oh, okay.' She hadn't considered what to do next. She thought they might drive through the night to Port Augusta, or at least had expected Will to inform her of his plans in time for her to decide her own. A road sign indicated Glendambo was now only five kilometres away.

'So what do you wanna do?' he said.

'Just drop me in town if you wouldn't mind. I'll work something out.' If she'd had a choice, she would have kept driving, maintained the movement, the bumps of the road, the wind, the road posts flicking past.

'Well,' he said, 'there's this little ... um ...' He seemed uncomfortable for the first time that day. 'There's a little house I stay at here ... It's basic but ... well, anyway, feel free to stay if you want.' His left knee bounced up and down and his fingers tapped the steering wheel. 'You can have your own room and everything.' He looked straight ahead at the road, and she examined the side of his face, wishing she could see the look in his eyes. She turned to the sky instead, watching the first stars that had broken through the blackness, and tossed around yet another decision to be made in no time. 'Sounds great,' she said, and the bluffed assurance sounded too keen. 'Thanks.'

As they approached the town, Will slowed the ute to a crawl. The engine quietened; after the hours spent thundering down the highway with wind beating through the windows, the silence was heavy.

Glendambo was a service station, a motel, a pub, a row of prefab houses and a postbox. Will pulled into the car park, which seemed to facilitate all three of the businesses; the ute's head-lights lit a row of campervans and four-wheel drives, all covered in a layer of red dust.

'You hungry? I'm starvin',' he said.

She had nibbled on a couple of rice cakes throughout the day because she thought it would be strange not to while he downed a bag of chips and two meat pies. The desert had shrivelled her hunger, but now, at the mention of food, her stomach rumbled. She shrugged. 'I've got some stuff in my bag.'

'Come on, my shout,' he said. He got out of the ute and shut his door, then headed across the car park. He didn't look back. Amelia grabbed her yellow envelope of money and flicked through the contents; she had about one hundred dollars left. She shoved the envelope into her back pocket. Digging through her bag, past the bottle of sunscreen at the top, she retrieved Lucy's bowl and a can of food. She turned to go then changed her mind, instead unzipping a hidden pocket of her pack; she gently pulled out the list, touching each of the softened corners with her fingertip before unfolding the pale blue paper. Her mother's scrawl was still there, listing items inside a printed border of brightly coloured vegetables.

Milk

Cornflour

Muesli bars . . .

She folded it and pushed it into her pocket.

As she walked towards the bar she told herself not to accept Will's hospitality, to buy her own side salad for dinner and be done with it. She took bigger strides than usual, stepping into footprints he'd made in sand, where the car park bitumen now showed through.

Amelia walked up the steps to the pub's verandah. In the glass door of the entrance, she could roughly make out her own reflection: her gangly frame, the mess of dreadlocked curls. The dark grey of her favourite Rage Against the Machine T-shirt had faded. It was a men's large size, and she liked the way she could hide within the generous cotton, how it didn't hug any part of her. It used to be soft, too, but she'd been wearing it since she left the white room and a hardness had set in to the material. She washed the shirt by rinsing it under taps, using public bathroom soap to clean the armpits. Then she wore it wet to help cool herself down.

Lucy sat at her feet, looking up, her tail thumping on the wooden decking. A battered old couch overlooked the highway; Amelia flopped down into it and began to work the can open. Lucy stood, then sat, then stood again, sniffing the air for what she knew was coming. Amelia slid beef and liver into the bowl.

'Good girl. Don't go too far, please.' Lucy chased the food around with her tongue; the bowl crept away from her so she pinned it down with a front paw. Amelia scratched the bristly fur on the back of Lucy's neck, then pushed open the door to the pub.

An electric fly killer emitting blue light hung over the bar; it announced a death with a zap as she wiped her feet on the welcome mat. A few heads turned slowly towards her as she walked in. The place was dimly lit. She scanned the faces for Will and thought she saw him, but couldn't be sure. She'd only really looked at him in profile, learned his cheek and the smooth ramp of his nose, how it ended in a pinkened, peeling tip.

Rows of red diamonds on olive-coloured carpet made her dizzy as she crossed the pub. It was him, sitting in a booth in the corner, and he smiled, half got out of his seat then sat back down.

'Hey,' he said. 'Long time no see.'

'Hey,' she said, moving into the booth across from him, her thighs making tacky sounds as they stuck and unstuck to spilt drink on the vinyl. An oblong lampshade hung long and low above the table. She reached up and touched its beige tassels, stirring a soft shower of dust.

'Thought you might have run off,' he said.

'Nah, still here.' A schooner of beer sat on a coaster in front of her, its head diminished so it was now like spit floating on top.

'Thanks for this,' she said, lifting the beer towards him.

'Cheers,' he said, clinking his glass with hers. They drank in unison, holding eye contact for a moment above their beers. His ears stuck out enough to make her wonder if he was ever self-conscious about them.

He slid a maroon menu across the table towards her and opened up the one in front of him.

'Get whatever you want, honestly,' he said.

It had been so long since she'd sat face to face with someone that she couldn't remember how to do it. Her body tensed at the delicate way his lips rested together, at her proximity to them as he read. She opened her menu and turned the laminated pages. A fly was squashed between the starters and mains.

'Right, what'll it be?' he said.

'I'll just get myself a salad, thanks.'

'No way, you gotta eat something proper. Schnitty? With chips? And veggies?'

'I'm fine actually.'

'Schnitty it is, then.'

'Really, I don't need . . .'

'Gravy?'

She paused before returning his smile. 'Sure. Thanks.'

He slapped his menu shut and bopped along the seat until he was out of the booth.

The food arrived too fast for it to be fresh. Will got a burger, which was both wide and high, stacked with the lot. He held it with two hands, and with each big mouthful something slapped to the plate – beetroot, pineapple, tomato – and juice ran down his fingers and wrists. She ate slowly, tasting each component of her meal separately: one chip, a piece of carrot, a squared bite of schnitzel.

'So, what do your folks think about you getting around the country like this?' he said.

Unprepared for the question, she swallowed a half-chewed chip and felt a sharp edge slide painfully down her throat. She drank some beer.

'Well, it was always just Mum and me. And then she – well, she died, so . . .' She trailed off, dabbing her fingertip at a little pool of liquid on the table.

'God, I'm so sorry.'

'It was a couple of months ago. She was sick for a long time.'

'I didn't think . . .' he said, shaking his head. 'Sorry.'

She shrugged and hated the way she smiled, but she had to do something. She couldn't stand watching him struggle as he tried to think of something to say. He made a fist and punched it gently into the palm of his other hand. He gave a slight nod, and his look pinned her back against the seat.

'What about you then?' she said. 'What's your deal?'

For a moment it was like she could see the flicker of something behind his eyes, and though she recognised it, she didn't know its name. Then it was gone.

'Time for another round, don't you reckon?' he said.

He slapped his hands on the table, rattling cutlery. She shifted in her seat to cover her jump at the sudden gesture. He moved sideways out of the booth and she sipped the last of her drink, her confession hovering above the table, unreciprocated.

She watched him make his way through stools and tables. As he walked, the grey waistband of his underwear sat above his shorts. Zach used to wear his jeans slung low like that. He would reach up, the private frame of his pelvis on show – the way it had made her blood throb was private, anyway. She hadn't known what that feeling was. Her blood throbbed now, beginning at the base of her spine, and she was glad when Will finally hitched his shorts up at the bar. Sinking deeper into her seat, she snapped the bands around her wrist one by one, waiting for the sting to dissipate each time before moving on to the next.

Will returned and placed a beer in front of her.

'Thanks,' she said.

'No worries.'

A whirlpool spun in the glass. The froth stuck to her upper lip as she took a sip, and she quickly wiped it away with the back of her hand. He watched her, then took a big gulp from his own glass. She had nothing to say.

'You gonna eat that?' he said, pointing at the leftovers of her meal.

'Nah, I'm full,' she said, resting her hands on her belly. His fork was already poised, and he began stabbing at pieces of carrot, then balanced a forkful of peas all the way across the table to his mouth. She pushed the plate towards him. She was quiet while he ate and tried to look around the bar and not at the cartilage in his neck that went taut and relaxed as he chewed.

His mouth was full with the last of her schnitzel, and he held a fist to his lips while he spoke. 'Game of pool?'

'Sure,' Amelia said.

'You might show me up,' he said, wiping his mouth with a serviette.

'We'll see, I guess.'

'Righto, let's do it.' He winked, then drummed the table.

She peeled the backs of her thighs off the seat, and when she was out of the booth, his hand awaited her. It rested for a moment on the small of her back, guiding her in front of him, then it was gone. The hairs on her arm bristled. She led the way across the pub.

'Wanna break?' he said, chalking the top of a cue.

'Nah, you go ahead.'

There was something extra in the way he looked at her during the game, and she knew she was giving the same look back – they exchanged it each time the cue was passed between them, and neither of them opted to choose a second cue from the rack. His hand touched her back again, lingering. He took fancy shots and she laughed for his benefit. She watched him for longer than before, studied the way his tongue went to the corner of his mouth while lining up a shot. Following several failed attempts, she managed to touch his forearm, the skin there much softer than she had imagined. After that, they traded touches after each shot: his hand on her waist, her fingers brushing his. She surprised herself with her bravery as she placed her hand at the point where muscle rose above his elbow. He looked down at her, pulled her into him.

'I'll get us a round,' she said, pushing back from him, hotness rising in her as she walked away.

She went outside for air. The verandah had a view of the highway and the sky, stars stretched out in a huge dome. Insects tapped at a lone orange light in the car park. Lucy walked over, paws clicking on the deck, and Amelia stooped to give her ears a scratch. Her hands were trembling. She stood and leaned forward onto the verandah railing, holding her hands in front of her. She traced over the pale clusters of scars where Zach had first burned her when she was a kid, heating up the top of a lighter then pressing it onto her skin to make little blisters in the shape of a smiley face. When he showed up uninvited at her mother's house just after the funeral, he seemed unchanged from the teenage boy she had known. He acted as if the ten years that had gone by meant nothing. He talked a lot and when he stopped he pressed into her so hard that the bricks behind her scraped off her skin. It was familiar, the rough way he moved his tongue inside her mouth, the shock that ran cold through her and froze her for a moment before she ducked out of his hold. Then she was leaving, backpack on, Lucy at her side; she was walking beneath the streetlights of the suburb as they flickered on above, through the sounds of her neighbours' dinner dishes clattering, taps running, and to the highway.

The pub door slammed behind her as a couple walked out. A man had his arm slung around a woman's neck, and she laughed as she stumbled, grabbing the railing for balance. They wobbled across the car park to the motel. She could be like those people: unified, intimate, easygoing. They made it look so simple. No harm done. She could do this, with Will; she would prove it. She pushed herself off the railing, ran her hand down Lucy's back, then walked back into the pub.

She ordered two beers and carried them to the pool table, spilling the drinks despite her careful steps. Will leaned against the wall, holding the cue between his legs, resting his hands over the chalky end. She smiled and it felt too big so she bit down hard on her bottom lip.

'Took your bloody time,' he said. 'I'm thirsty.' She handed him the beer and he raised it in the air. 'Well, cheers again, to a fun night and to . . . I dunno . . . how about to chance encounters in the desert?' He was smiling, his eyes all lit up.

'Cheers.' She thought of the couple outside, raised her glass, and held her nerve.

*

Lucy stood up and stretched as they stepped out of the pub. She'd befriended a little tan mongrel, and it lifted its head but didn't get up. They crossed the car park to the ute and Amelia opened the passenger door.

'Whatcha doin'?' he said.

'Um – getting in the car?'

'No need – it's just over there.' He pointed towards the row of houses about a hundred metres away, the moon reflecting off the ridged metal roofs.

'Oh, okay.' In the quiet of the desert, he was a stranger again.

She heaved her bag out of the tray and onto her back, refusing his offer of help.

'All set?' he said. A sports bag swung from his shoulder. He shut the door and took off towards the houses.

'So do you own this place?' she said, jogging to catch up with him.

'Nah, not really.'

'Whose is it then?'

'Me and some of the boys just use it as a kind of halfway house, you know, when we're out on the road,' he said. Then added, 'But none of them are there right now.'

As they got closer, stepping out of the glow of the car park and into darkness, it looked like he was right. The row of identical houses seemed to be unoccupied: no strips of light escaping from behind curtains, no muffled voices, no open windows letting the breeze move through stuffy rooms.

She had questions that she couldn't bring herself to ask. At least she knew where the highway was; her mother had always said it was important to know your exits.

Will dragged his feet across loose stones. Lucy scampered ahead then came back to meet them. Will's place was second from the end of the row; they climbed the concrete steps to the door. Lucy snorted in the dust somewhere beneath the deck. There was a second of stillness before they could hear the sound of piss puddling on the ground.

'Sorry 'bout that,' Amelia said.

He chuckled. 'She's all right.' He rummaged through his bag, producing a set of keys, but when he went to put the key in the lock the door opened from the pressure alone. 'Well, there you go,' he said, mostly to himself it seemed. 'Good one, boys.' Then louder: 'Safe area, you see,' he said. 'Crime rate of zero, population of no one.' She thought it was a joke but wasn't sure, so she just blew air out of her mouth in acknowledgement.

He stepped inside, fumbling against the wall. 'Now remember, I told you it's not much,' he said. The flick of a light switch revealed a bare, beige hallway. As she stamped the dirt off her shoes, Lucy pushed past her and went inside.

'Okay for her to be in here?' Amelia said.

'Yeah, of course,' he said.

Amelia followed him down the hallway. The house held the heat of the day and smelled of old coffee. A light flashed once, went black, then flashed on again, bathing the kitchen in fluorescence. Lucy sniffed around the base of the cupboards, stirring up dust then sneezing. She found something unidentifiable to eat. Will dumped his bag on one of the benchtops that lined the perimeter of the room.

'Right,' he said, rubbing his hands together. 'You can put your stuff in the bedroom off the hallway if you want. To the left.'

'Thanks,' she said.

The room was musty. A chain hung from an overhead fan, and when she gave it a tug, the blades started a slow, laboured rotation, clicking as they spun. She lowered her pack to the floor; the beginnings of a headache tapped at the front of her skull. A single bed centred against the wall of an otherwise empty room, a white sheet pulled tight over the mattress. She slid open a small window, pushing the blinds aside. There was no screen so she stuck her head out, sucking in the night air. The slightest desert breeze touched her skin and she shivered as her sweat cooled. In the near distance, the lights of the pub blinked off. She breathed deeply, gathering energy to return to the bright kitchen, to Will.

The highway slept. It was the kind of blackout quiet that Sid liked. They were different in that way. She liked to hear the carrying on of things: the ocean, cicadas, rain on the roof. She closed her eyes and tried to guess what Sid was doing at that moment. Her mind raced across the red desert, zipping between skyscrapers and into his room. She pictured him lying on his back, limbs spread wide, just beginning his usual battle to fall asleep. She thought of one night they had sneaked out of their houses when they were kids. He'd knocked on her window because he couldn't sleep, and they'd gone down to the stormwater drain. They found a syringe and cautiously handed it back and forth, holding it upright so they could examine its tip. She remembered the shake in Sid's voice, the little stutter he made before saying the f-word: 'F-f-uck,' he said. 'F-f-ucking hell.'

Something crawled down her back. 'Shit!' she said with a jolt, her head bashing against the window frame.

'Jesus, sorry, I – I called out but –'

'It's fine, sorry … just got a fright,' she said. Her head throbbed from the impact but she let it be. Will looked down on her, his body between her and the exit from the room. His face was so close that she had to take his features in one by one, had to breathe in his air, the smell of barbecued meat.

'You okay?' he said, reaching out to touch her head where she had collided with the window frame. His hand rested there, too heavy and for too long, then slid down the back of her neck.

'This room stinks,' she said, dipping out of his grip. He stepped aside and she squeezed past him.

In the kitchen she splashed water on her hot face, then busied herself patting Lucy, scratching the spot beneath her collar that got really itchy. Will stayed in the other room and she listened to creaking floorboards, a thump, him clearing his throat as she waited for an opportunity to go in, grab her stuff and leave, get away from the trap of that room, that bed. She couldn't go through with it, after all.

There was a footstep in the hallway and Lucy scampered to her feet. Then he was there, filling the doorway. He gave a small side smile, showing no teeth, and she guessed he was embarrassed.

'You all right?' he said.

'Yeah, fine.' She looked away from him and concentrated on scratching behind Lucy's ears. 'Sorry.'

'What for?'

She shrugged, tried to make her mouth shape words that would lead to her escape. 'I dunno.'

'How 'bout a cuppa?'

She took a deep, quiet breath; her mind was blank, unable to come up with a plan B. 'Sounds good,' she said, exhaling slowly and gently, so only Lucy noticed.

He filled the kettle. 'Please, take a seat,' he said, gesturing towards the benchtop. She lifted herself onto it so that her legs dangled down in front of some drawers. He picked up a mug from the sink, and his hands made it appear miniature as he rinsed it.

He opened several cupboards, all of them empty, before finding teabags. Task completed, he rocked on his heels, hands in pockets, before dropping into a crouch next to Lucy.

'What type of dog is she?' he said.

'Kelpie cross. Not sure what she's crossed with though.' Lucy flopped her tail up and down against the linoleum as Will gave her belly a scratch.

'How long you had her?' he said.

'Five or six years . . . We found her when she was a pup.'

'At a shelter?'

'Nah. There was a box of them. My friend and I found it, this shoebox stuffed with puppies.'

'Shit, really? What happened to the others?' he said.

'All dead except her. We found them by a creek. She was kind of buried under the rest of them . . . They were these little sacks of cuteness, bodies all floppy, you know. I dunno how, but she was fine.'

He cupped Lucy's head in his hands and spoke in a cutesy voice: ''Cos you're tough, aren't ya,' he said, his nose against hers.

The water boiled. Lucy stood beside him while he filled the mug and bobbed the teabag up and down. 'Hope you like it black,' he said.

'That's fine,' she said. 'Thank you.'

He took a sip, then pushed the mug towards her. He leaned back on the sink, arms crossed over his chest so that his biceps were hardened bulges. She picked up the mug and held it in both hands, touching her wrists to the ceramic to feel its burn.

'Didn't realise we'd have to share,' she said, forcing a half-smile.

'Can't say I didn't warn you about this place,' he said with a shrug, then returned her smile. Steam hit her cheeks as she blew on the tea, and when she took a sip, a fuzziness formed in her belly. *A cup of tea fixes everything*, her mother had always said.

'A cup of tea fixes everything,' Amelia said, sliding the mug towards Will.

'Too right,' he said. 'Ta.'

He didn't take the tea.

He was quickly in front of her, between her legs, his face blurred. He kissed her softly, one hand moving up to cup her face, and this helped her not to pull away. The tip of his tongue entered her mouth, pushing against hers, then retreated.

He traced his fingertips up and down her arms, goosebumps rising beneath his touch. His tongue grew faster, more urgent. It became Zach's tongue, and she was thirteen, by her mother's back fence, frozen, breathless, trying to force air up her stuffy nose.

She opened her eyes. Will's were closed, his face serious, forehead creased in a yearning she wasn't meant to see. She jammed her eyes shut. Concentrating hard on this kiss, not the other one, she dedicated herself to learning the new pace, to accepting the beery taste of his saliva.

The surface of the benchtop was smooth and cool beneath her fingertips. Her shorts slid across it as he tugged her to the edge, into him. He pulled back her hair and left a tingling row of kisses up her throat. She swallowed and hung her head back; he held her waist tight.

If she was going to do this, she would have to do it better. She lifted her hand off the bench and lay it on his. Her finger set out along the rise and fall of his knuckles, then went to the inside of his arm, to the bumps of veins. There was a prominent one that she lingered on, pressing in and letting it go, the feel of it as it popped back into place vaguely soothing.

'Tickles,' he said in a high pitch, pulling his arm from her.

'Sorry.' She bundled her hands in her lap. He sucked on her neck, his hands moving up and down her back beneath her T-shirt. She watched the clock on the microwave flash zeroes and managed two small, secret snaps of the rubber bands; the sting wasn't sharp enough.

'Hey,' Will said, resting his forehead on hers, his eyes seeming to merge into one. 'It's okay. Everything's okay.' He kissed her mouth, gentle again. He lifted her hands and placed them around his neck. She crossed her wrists over casually, her hands dangling carefree as if she'd put them there herself. That easygoing, carpe diem girl was who she needed to be till this was over.

He grabbed her bum and she wrapped her legs around his waist, clung to his neck as he lifted her. Entangled, they crossed the kitchen. Her foot caught on the door and he stopped, reversed, then proceeded, his lips never leaving hers as he bumped the walls of the hallway.

In the room, the overhead fan was still turning. Strips of moonlight fell across the white sheet. A surge of energy had her wiggling in his arms, her body ready to run. She fell from his grip as he bent over the bed, clunking down against the springs.

'Sorry,' he said, serious as he climbed on top of her. He looked down on her, his head angled. He paused like that, eyes narrowed, as if capturing a detail of her he'd not noticed before. She stared back at him and she was sure her eyes were too wide, her body too rigid. Her mouth was dry.

He sucked on her bottom lip, pushed his groin against her, sucked harder. His weight crushed her chest, allowing her only short, sharp breaths. He cupped her breast, still shielded by shirt and bra, and squeezed. Unsatisfied, he moved his hands lower, running a finger around the waistband of her shorts, back and forth. He wrenched her shirt up over her ribs, working one arm out then the other. He pulled upwards and the shirt caught on her chin; it stayed there, resting around her neck.

His frenzied hands found a resting place on her hips. She worked hard to remember that this creature was Will, the same man she'd travelled alongside all day: the person who sang, who told bad jokes. He shuffled down and planted kisses along her belly, moved lower. She squirmed, tried to close her legs.

'Hey,' he said, 'what's all this?'

She scrunched her eyes closed as he pulled her legs apart. He moved his fingers up and down the skin on the inside of her legs, over the scars she'd cut into neat rows. 'It's nothing,' she said.

'Holy shit.' He sat back, allowing moonlight to illuminate the damage. Amelia closed her legs, the feeling of exposure pounding through her body.

'Okay, it's okay,' he said, shuffling back up the bed. He placed delicate kisses across her belly. His hands crept beneath her bra.

He held her breast firmly in his hand and squeezed, gave a slight whimper. A dead cold locked her limbs. The pressure of that hand became the pressure of Zach's hand. Sun was hot on her face, rocks jabbed into her back. The neighbour's wind chimes moved in the afternoon breeze as Zach lifted her limp arm towards him and showed her what to do.

She dug her fingertips into Will's shoulders.

'You right?' he said, his face rising up to hers, lips brushing her forehead, her cheeks, her neck. She looked beyond him, tracking the slow rotation of the fan above.

'My shoes are still on,' she said.

When she was naked, he revealed a condom. The packet glinted in the light coming through the blinds. He knelt above her while he fumbled the thing on; she crossed her arms over her chest, pinched hard on folds of flesh at her sides. He kissed her quickly then pushed into her. He groaned and she bit down on her lip. The fan rotated above her and she tried to count its clicks, tried to stay there, in that room, as Will moved above her, inside her. She lost concentration and when she closed her eyes, Zach's were there, bloodshot and the brightest, brightest blue as he thanked her.

When Will was finished, he was puffed; he lay on top of her catching his breath. Her body was slick with his sweat. An itch spread across her front and she forced her hand beneath him to scratch. He moved off her, and she saw a few of his chest hairs lying across her breasts and collarbones. She scratched hard.

'Shit,' he said.

'What?'

'It's broken.'

She sat up fast and pulled the sheet over her breasts.

'What?'

He held it up to the light, pulling the rubber taut. The contents bubbled out through an invisible tear. He lay on his back, dragging a hand over his face, pushing in on his eyes. 'What do you wanna do?' he asked.

She worked calmness into her voice, practised the sentence in her head before saying it. 'I want to sleep. I'll sort out the pill tomorrow.'

While he disposed of the condom she fumbled for her clothes. She pulled her undies on, but then he returned and she scampered into the bed, curled up with her back to the door. He squeezed in beside her and untangled the bedsheet, pulled it over both of them.

'Goodnight,' he said, patting her on the shoulder.

'Night,' she said, eyes shut tight, holding her breath, waiting for him to lift the heat of his hand off her.

He fidgeted for a few moments, and she lay still until his breathing was deep and heavy. She got up and crawled around the bed until she found her shorts. She reached into the pocket, pulled out the piece of paper, and sat by the window where she could see best. She went through the items one by one: *Milk, Cornflour, Muesli bars, Lentils, Yoghurt, Almonds* . . . She read it over and over, taking deep breaths, imagined standing beside her mother, plucking items off the shelves. She read through the tiredness that clouded her sight. She rubbed her eyes till they burned, as she had done by the back fence after Zach was gone, because the grass had stirred up her hay fever.

*

Lucy barked somewhere outside the room. Amelia sat upright, struggling to see in the morning light. A door slammed; the force of it made the bedroom door shudder in its latch. She scrambled to get under the sheet, then shook Will, his skin clammy beneath her hands.

'Someone's here!' she hissed. Will moved beside her, slopped his tongue around his mouth.

'Hello?' A man's voice.

Lucy barked. 'Who's this then?' the man said. His voice was closer then, right outside the door. Amelia watched the door-handle, waited for the twist of it. 'Yoo-hoo.'

Will covered his head with a pillow, groaning.

The bedroom door burst open.

'Ah, there you are, mate, having yourself a nice sleep-in, eh?' He looked at her, small, deep-set eyes shifting over the line of her body beneath the sheet. 'Didn't know you had company.' He laughed as Lucy ran into the room, and he stepped back, crossed his arms over his chest, burgundy shirt rolled up to the elbows. 'Brought another one to the palace, eh, Will boy?'

'Piss off, Jez,' Will said from under the pillow, his voice croaky and muffled.

'This little one's a real step up for you, mate, by the looks of it.' The man lingered, leaning against the doorway. Amelia gripped the edge of the sheet, pulled it up further to cover more of her chest. Lucy faced the man and let out a soft growl, her mouth twitching slightly over her teeth. The man cracked his knuckles, then stretched. 'Well, I'll leave you to it.' He rapped the doorframe twice with his knuckles before turning into the hallway.

Amelia threw the sheet off. She searched on the floor for her things, throwing Will's discarded clothes across the room. She found her T-shirt and shorts, felt under the bed for her bra.

'Hey, what're you doing?' Will said, one cheek flat on the pillow, an arm dangling from the mattress.

'Leaving,' she said.

Lucy went out of the room. Amelia summoned her, but her paws continued to tap away down the hall towards where the man creaked and rustled in the kitchen.

'Come back to bed ... don't worry about him,' Will said, rubbing his eyes. 'He's my brother – he'll leave us alone.' He put his hand out and grabbed her thigh. She yanked herself out of his hold.

'Come on,' he said, sitting up, stacking the pillows behind him. He held out his arms. 'Give me a cuddle.'

She found her bra tangled in the sheets, half-buried beneath Will. She tugged it from under him and bunched it up in her hand. 'Lucy, come,' she said, pulling her T-shirt on, struggling with the zip of her shorts. This time Lucy listened. She appeared in the doorway, tail raised. Will clicked his fingers at her but she stared at him, unmoving.

Amelia lifted her pack over her shoulder, collected her shoes from the base of the bed.

'What . . . seriously? Just wait,' Will said. He moved his feet to the floor, and she left the room. Down the hallway, Jez had his back to her, his head lowered over something on the benchtop. He turned and she went to the front door, her pack scraping the wall.

'Amelia, wait,' Will called.

She swung the door open and Lucy shot outside. Amelia ran as fast as she could, bra in one hand, shoes in the other.

'Oi!' Jez called from the steps of the house. 'Oi, I'm talkin' to you.' She kept running, the ground already hot beneath her feet. 'What the hell are you doing?' He ended in a high-pitched tone, then he was laughing. 'Run, bitch, run!'

Amelia reached the car park. She turned and Will was outside, bare chest, grey undies, his hands open to the sky. 'Wait up,' he yelled. He whistled and Lucy turned to face him, a low growl in her throat.

Amelia headed around the side of the pub, Lucy at her heels, and ran up onto the verandah. The door moved in its frame, but it was locked. She peered inside, her nose streaking the glass; the lights were off and there was no sign of movement within. She knocked on the door with a fist and waited, but no one came. There was a flash of colour beside her and she whipped around; the mongrel from the night before approached and sniffed at her feet.

She left the shade of the pub. Each step was harder than the last as she ambled towards the servo, grit sharp beneath her feet. Lucy was ahead, her nose to the ground.

There was an alcove at the entrance to the shop and she sat Lucy there. Amelia pushed the door open, setting a bell ringing; a woman sat behind a fan at the counter. She watched as Amelia walked down an aisle, following signs to the bathroom at the back of the shop. She passed through coloured streamers.

The toilet was spattered with piss. She hovered over it, gagged, but whatever was inside her wouldn't leave. She pulled her T-shirt over her head, stepped out of her shorts and undies. Lukewarm water trickled out of the tap when she pushed the button down; she collected it in the cup of her hands and poured it over her head. The tap timed out and she pressed it in again, throwing handfuls of water down her back, over her belly, washing out her mouth and spitting down the sink. She wet a wad of toilet paper and scrubbed at her skin, between her legs. She did it again, rinse and repeat, and again, scrubbing and scratching till skin peeled off her and the paper disintegrated in small bundles.

Brown water pooled at her feet.

She picked up her T-shirt, wiped it over wet shoulders; it released a smell of Will, and she threw it back to the floor. She unbuckled her pack and pulled out items till she found a new shirt, new undies, new shorts. The clothes were too tight, too close against her. She picked up the discarded shorts and, making sure her hands were completely dry, she transferred her mother's list to the special pocket in her pack. She pulled on her shoes.

Her abandoned favourite shirt lay crumpled in the corner. She couldn't bear to leave it; she scooped it up and pushed it down the side of her pack.

A bang on the door. In the slit between floor and wood, there were two shifting dark patches. More banging: three hard, decisive knocks.

'Oi,' said a woman's voice.

Amelia shoved things down in her bag, the items damp now from the wet floor.

'That your dog out there?' the woman said. 'It's going nuts, barkin' at me customers. Get out here and fix it, would ya?'

Amelia swung her pack onto her shoulder. As she opened the door, Lucy's barks became piercing. The woman from the front counter stood with her hands in fists on her hips, an apron with native birds spread across her front. Amelia pressed past her, trapped for a second against the pillows of her breasts. She ran down the aisle and to the door.

Jez squatted at the entrance, holding a crust of bread out to Lucy, speaking to her softly. Lucy was quiet now, though her lips still twitched.

'Well, what are the chances,' he said when Amelia stepped out of the shop.

The door closed behind Amelia, bumping her pack. 'Stop it,' she said. 'She doesn't like you.'

He looked up, touched his thick neck. 'Dunno why, I'm a nice guy. She just doesn't know me.' He adjusted his shirt collar as he stood. Amelia turned her back to him and crouched down to stroke Lucy's side. He loomed over them, and Amelia watched his shadow as he took a step closer.

A truck pulled into the service station; she stood, grappling with her pack.

'Where do ya think you're goin'?' Jez said.

He stepped in her way, smiling, as she tried to pass, and when she changed her course he blocked her path again. He was laughing at her as she managed to dodge around him. The truck stopped beside a bowser. She summoned Lucy to follow and they approached the vehicle as the driver lowered himself from the cab.

'Excuse me,' she said. 'Hi.'

He was an older man, hunched, with golden eyes beneath a faded red cap. He looked at her quickly then walked past her to unhook the petrol pump.

'Can't help ya, love, sorry,' he said.

'Please,' she said, taking a step forward. 'Even if it's just to the next town.'

'I've got a job to do. Sorry.' He wiped a chequered hanky over his face. 'Need something to drink? Food? I can help you with that.' The hanky disappeared into the pocket of his shorts. He dug around and brought out a handful of coins, which glinted in his worn hand.

'No, no,' she said, and stepped backwards. 'We're fine, thank you.'

'Suit yourself.' He returned the money to his pocket, lowered his cap.

'Sorry to bother you,' she said, lingering in case he changed his mind. The man shrugged.

Amelia looked out to the still highway. She hefted her pack higher and walked back between bowsers towards the car park.

'Rejected, huh,' Jez said. He caught up to her, nudging her shoulder as he matched her stride.

'It happens,' she said. She stepped away from him and he quickly filled the space.

'Yeah? Well how 'bout I take ya?'

'No thanks.' She walked faster, and Lucy broke into a trot at her side.

'Why not? Too good for me, eh darlin'?' He stopped and she put her head down, walked as if she had somewhere to go. He jogged to catch up to her. 'Well you weren't too good for young Will boy, were ya. Had a good old ride with him.' He stuck his elbow into her side.

There was no action in the car park, no one packing vehicles, setting off for the day. She turned back to the servo, heat prickling her scalp.

Jez turned too, continued walking beside her. 'C'mon, sweetie,' he said, his tone softening; he sounded like Will had the night before. 'I'm just kidding with you. I'll give you a ride.'

'Hey,' someone called, 'wait up a sec.' She turned and saw Will trotting towards her, fresh shirt, combed, wet hair.

'Oi, what are you doing?' he said, stepping past Amelia and going chest-to-chest with his brother.

'I was offering the lady a lift. No need to be so greedy, Will boy.'

'What's your problem?' Will said.

'You gotta share the love, brother. You can't be keepin' all these needy young things to yourself.' He slapped Will's chest and rested his hand there.

'For christ's sake, stop messing around,' Will said. 'You're upsetting her.'

Amelia turned, tried to adjust her face to stop it from giving her away. She walked towards the servo.

'Harden up, mate,' Jez said. 'You're a fucking pussy.'

Footsteps caught up to her and she felt a hand on her shoulder. She pushed it off and turned around. For a moment she met Will's eyes, saw a flash of whatever it was that had coaxed her into this.

'Leave me alone,' she said.

'I'm sorry, okay,' Will said. 'I'll get you some breakfast. We can get back on the road. I'll take you wherever you need to go.' He looked down at her, long lashes, creased eyes. Jez stood behind him, watching.

'Oi!' The woman from the service station made her way across the car park, plastic sandals squeaking. 'What do ya think you lot are up to?' The woman was out of breath, her cheeks glistening, hair stuck to her sweaty neck.

'Come on, Will boy, let's go. Leave these whiny bitches to their own devices,' Jez called.

'That's right, rack off and stop causin' trouble,' the woman said.

Will took a couple of steps backwards, still looking at Amelia, eyebrows raised. A truck drove by on the highway, its shadow passing across them.

'Clear out, eh?' the woman yelled over the last sounds of the vehicle. 'I got work to do.'

Jez walked away, shoulders back, long arms swinging. He turned. 'Come on, mate,' he said, walking backwards while he spoke. 'You're better than this. She's just some girl, givin' it out by the side of the highway.'

Will hung his head and spun around. He followed his brother, dragging his feet so that dust filled the air behind him.

'Come back inside, darl. I'll get ya a drink,' the woman said.

They crossed the car park. Amelia slowed her pace to keep time with the woman's waddle, while Lucy scampered ahead in pursuit of a fly. A chip packet skittered along the ground near one of the bowsers.

'Get that for me, darl,' the woman said, pointing a stubby finger. 'Me back's shot.' Amelia grabbed the packet and stuffed it into an overflowing rubbish bin.

The bell above the door chimed as they entered the shop, and the woman unleashed: 'Bad idea bein' out here alone,' she said, hobbling down the aisle towards her perch in front of the fan. 'You hear what he said about ya? That what you want people to think?'

Amelia stood at the drinks fridge, its coolness touching her cheeks. The woman spoke loudly from the front of the shop in order to reach her. 'Just bad news. Askin' for trouble, I reckon, a pretty young thing like you . . . You don't want people taking advantage . . . you never know who you can trust. Do ya?'

Amelia looked at her hand, bent her fingers towards her. 'Nope,' she said. Dirt mixed with dried blood in little cuts around her nails.

'You gotta be so careful these days, switched on . . .' the woman said. 'There are some lonely fellas out here is all I'm sayin', you catch my drift?'

Amelia peeled a thread of skin back from the nail of her index finger. She pulled it slowly, as far as it would go until it tapered and broke.

'You just don't know what people are capable of . . . Didn't used to be that way, but now? Well, it's just another kettle of . . . You listening?'

'Yep,' she said, examining the triangle of new, pink flesh before blood welled to cover it.

The woman sniffed. 'Good, 'cos you think that dog of yours is gonna make any difference? Reckon you're invincible with that by your side? Whatever them boys were gonna do to you, they certainly wouldn't have shown it any mercy, believe you me.'

Amelia bit around the nail, tasting earth and blood. She softened the skin with her saliva, then slowly pulled back a new strip. She wiped blood on her shorts and watched more ooze out from the vertical wounds, puzzled at how a colour so vivid could come from within her.

'Have the purple one, darl,' the woman said. 'Hardly anyone buys it, dunno why.'

Amelia picked up one of the bottles of apple and blackcurrant juice, the glass wet and cold against her throbbing fingertip. The lid popped as she twisted it off.

'Ordered that one in from Townsville, would ya believe, but no one bloody wants it,' the woman said.

Amelia walked down the aisle to a rack of postcards, her shoes squeaking on the linoleum floor. As she spun the rack, images of desert and coloured skies swirled in front of her. She stopped the spinning at random and pulled out a card: Uluru in cartoon, a caricature cockatoo perched on top of it. Dust stuck to her fingertips as she took the card to the counter.

The woman was absorbed in a magazine spread of celebrities without make-up, the wet tip of her thumb poised over glossy paper. She flipped the page before turning her attention to Amelia.

'Found something you like, darl? And like I said, the drink's on me.'

'Thanks,' Amelia said, almost at the end of the bottle.

The woman held the postcard close to her face, squinting. 'Sixty cents,' she said. 'Got stamps. You want one?'

Amelia walked behind the building and swung her pack down, shoulders aching. She sat in the shade, back against the wall, legs up to her chest. She turned the postcard over and over, picturing its journey from her grasp to Sid's. His gardener's hands would be rough from hard summer soil, and he would read it as he walked slowly down the path and into his home. Last time she'd seen him he said he was worried, and he'd been all squinty in the sun, rogue red hairs in his dark hair catching the light. He had a gift for her, a pen with a plastic rocket on top, flames running down the side; he held it up between them, smiling. 'Don't crash and burn,' he said, 'but if you do, you know where to find me.' He clicked the pen up and down, up and down as they sat in her backyard, Lucy lying across their toes, the smell of star jasmine lingering on the breeze.

She moved things around in the side pocket of her pack, searching for the feel of plastic. She flipped the card over, wrote Sid's address in boxy letters. For the rest of the message she used the symbols of a code that had been devised by the two of them as they hunched behind a tree overlooking their suburb. It was a simple system, designed as a way to keep their childhood secrets intact while using the adult world of the letterbox. Each letter was represented by a symbol: *M* was a four-leaf clover, *D* a trapezium, *T* a fish. She wrote:

Made it to the middle. Still not enough space . . . maybe you were right. Got red sand between my toes. I'll save you some.

She put three small stars at the bottom, which meant missing, wishing, thinking, then added: *PS. Don't worry.*

She leaned her head back against the brick wall of the shop, clicking the pen up and down. Lucy nudged the postcard out of the way, seeking a pat. Amelia stroked Lucy's hot fur and closed her eyes. Bright specks rushed across her vision. Moments from the night before pricked at her, trapped under her skin. She wondered if her mother had seen Will's hands moving over her body, if she'd seen the images of Zach in her head; wondered if she knew now what Amelia had never told her. And was her mother able to turn her head away in disgust, or did death's all-seeing eyes mean she must endure it?

Gravel popped beneath tyres. She stood, heart pounding. The sun angled in towards her, hitting her shins. The skin there was pink and warm to the touch. She shoved the postcard into the back pocket of her shorts. Lucy stood at her heels as she peered around the edge of the shop.

A white Subaru was stopped at the bowser; a woman sat in the front passenger seat, still and staring ahead while a man filled the car with petrol. He was compact, tucked tightly into pale, acid-washed Levis that fell short above white sneakers. Amelia returned to her pack and lifted it onto her shoulders. She practised a smile, the skin on her cheeks feeling stiff, her lips cracking. When she caught her reflection in the glass of the shop she quickly looked away, but not before a surge of violence; she imagined smashing in her glass face, making shards of her nose, her eyes, her mouth.

She crouched, cupped Lucy's head in her hands. 'We've got this.' Lucy's dark eyes were a balm; she wagged her tail, her rump swinging from side to side. As Amelia left the cover of the building, she composed herself: long, steady strides, lifted chin. *Confidence is key*, her mother would have said. *Shoulders back.*

As she neared the car, the man's aftershave cut into the air, citrusy and strong.

'Excuse me sir – hi.' She raised her hand in a half-wave but it was too desperate, so she tucked both hands behind her back.

'Hello,' he said. After a nod and a curt smile, he returned to watching the numbers on the bowser ascend. His face was immaculately shaven and his hair was gelled into spikes. A cold sore crusted in the corner of his thin lips.

'Hot one today, eh?' Amelia said.

'Yup.' The man turned away from her. Dimples in his pale skin gave away a clenched jaw. Amelia bent to acknowledge the woman through the passenger window, but she continued a flat, straight stare ahead.

Amelia stepped around the man, tried to catch his eye. He moved his stocky figure further so his back was to her.

'You, ah, headed south at all?' she said.

His shoulders rose, his cotton shirt smooth across his back.

'I was just wondering if –'

'Yeah,' he said, giving a sharp sniff. 'We are.'

She nodded slowly, held one arm tightly in her other hand behind her back. The shifting ligaments in her wrist helped her to stay focused, in character. 'I'm headed that way too, actually.'

The man pulsed the petrol pump, the cents creeping up.

'Any chance you might be able to give me a ride?' Amelia said.

The man continued to pump bursts of petrol. Beyond him, crows gathered around a red patch on the highway, fighting each other for strips of leathered skin. She shuffled her feet, wondered if he had heard the question. She spoke louder: 'Even a lift just a bit further down the road or something would be great.'

The cost of the petrol reached a clean fifty-five dollars. He hung the pump then turned to face her.

'And the animal?' He moved his head in the direction of Lucy, who was snuffling at the tyres of his car.

'Yeah, her too.' Amelia tried not to stare at the shine of the man's forehead, the place where his hair receded. 'She's good company, actually.' She clicked her fingers and Lucy returned to her side.

The man moved around the car and Amelia got out of his way. He licked a finger and rubbed at a mark on the bonnet. 'I don't pick up hitchhikers,' he said. 'It's dangerous and I'm with my wife.'

Amelia glanced towards the passenger seat again and the woman looked away. 'Well, I don't want to –'

'Wait,' the man said, lifting his palm to her. 'I'm trying to think.' His tongue flicked out and moistened his cold sore.

Amelia stepped back. Lucy held her ground, looking at the man, her head tilted sideways. He turned away and faced the highway. The passenger window lowered; the woman looked out with wet, red-rimmed eyes that wouldn't settle on Amelia. 'Ron . . . sweetie? You're not forgetting how tired you are, are you?'

Ron turned and rolled his eyes. The woman continued, her long, heat-rashed neck extending from a vibrant floral dress: 'And you wouldn't really want a dog on your nice new leather seats, would you?'

Ron stepped further away, spread his legs into a wider stance. The woman resumed her flat stare. Ron's face was lifted to the sky and Amelia followed his gaze, tried to find whatever had grasped his attention up there. She gave up and looked to the car park; Will's ute was in the same place as the night before. Acid rose in her throat. She focused on the rise and fall of Ron's shoulders, wishing on each of his breaths for a yes.

'Fine,' the man said. 'Fine, fine, fine.' He turned and walked in the direction of the shop, digging in his back pocket and pulling out a wallet. He turned again, pointed a short finger at her. 'Don't get in yet. I'll put a towel down.' The tone of his voice brought a flush to her face, as if she'd already done something wrong. He continued walking and pushed open the door of the servo.

Amelia breathed deeply through her nose. Blood pounded in her ears. She shifted her weight from one leg to the other.

'Sweetheart . . . what's your name?' The woman's voice was soft. Amelia stepped closer, ducked down to the window.

'Amelia.'

'Amelia. Well, what a lovely name.' The woman paused. 'Look, Amelia, I hope you know that we'd love to help. I do wonder though if you'd be better off trying someone else.' She looked up from beneath thick, wiry eyebrows. 'I know my husband, you see, and, well, he's had a big few days.' The woman blinked three distinct times, as if each one held a secret message. 'He really is very, *very* tired.' The woman gave a slight nod, setting her pinned arrangement of curls jiggling. 'I know him better than he knows himself, you see . . .'

'We won't be any trouble,' Amelia said, trying her stiff smile. 'Promise.'

The woman slid the window up. Amelia knocked lightly on the glass. 'I'll be back in a sec,' she said, getting Sid's postcard out of her pocket, pointing to it. The woman blinked, looked away.

Amelia walked over to the postbox at the edge of the car park. As she neared Will's ute, she could see herself sitting in the front seat, feel the coarse material beneath her, smell the car's odour of fried food; she wished she could reach into the car and shake that girl.

She pushed Sid's postcard through the slot, listened to it flutter to the bottom. She stood for a moment, rested her head on the warm red metal, peering into the gap. She could picture him walking down the garden path at his place, his fingers finding a corner of the card in the cobwebbed letterbox; his face lighting up, then sinking in disappointment as he read her effort. At least she didn't have to disappoint him in person.

Lucy barked and Amelia looked up; Ron had returned to the car and was scrabbling through luggage in the boot.

She worked up a fresh layer of sweat as she jogged the few metres back to the car, her skin irritated beneath the scratchy material of her replacement T-shirt. Ron was spreading a dark pink towel over the back seat, pulling the material tight and straight. The name *Brenda* was stitched in purple cursive in the corner.

'I wonder if I should use something of mine . . .' Amelia said. 'That towel looks pretty special.'

'Yes, it's a very nice one – a wedding present from my great-aunt,' the woman, Brenda, said, turning round in her seat.

'It's fine,' Ron said. 'Just make sure your dog enjoys it.'

He threw a lime-green towel at Amelia; she caught it, then held it up by the corners, letting it unroll. 'For you,' he said. It took her a moment to comprehend. She spread it across the other half of the back seat.

Ron settled in behind the wheel, rolling his shoulders back, moving his head from side to side until his neck cracked. As they pulled out of the service station, she caught the eye of the cashier; the woman shook her head.

Amelia leaned back in her seat, let the tick of the indicator wash over her. As they turned onto the highway, she looked out the back window, watching Glendambo as it was swallowed by desert. She patted her pockets, pretending her unease might be lifted simply by assuring herself she hadn't left anything behind.

Ron accelerated hard and blasted the air conditioning; the fan was loud, making conversation difficult. She dropped her persona, sinking into the seat and back into her own skin.

The kilometres racked up as the car bumped over uneven patches of the highway, setting Brenda's curls bouncing. Ron drove fast. Amelia closed her eyes and submitted to the thrust of the vehicle. If they were to crash – if Brenda's head were to be bobbing on an airbag, her legs broken and trapped beneath the dashboard, if Ron's delicate eyelids were to close, blood dripping from his temple, and Amelia was to finally leave her body, watching the scene from above – then at least she was rushing towards something. Amelia reached across the back seat and rubbed Lucy's neck, causing her back leg to twitch when Amelia reached the itchiest places. She took hold of her collar, huddled in closer; Lucy couldn't be part of that scene.

'You're lucky it's me picking you up, you know,' Ron said, his voice raised over the roar of the air conditioning.

'Thank you,' Amelia said.

'It's not safe for a girl like you to be out here alone.'

Amelia nodded, bit down on the gummy ulcer inside her mouth. Red sand scattered on an otherwise spotless mat beneath her shoes. Lucy perched on the plush towel and looked outside, her wet nose leaving streaks on the window. Amelia struggled to keep count of the road posts as the car rushed past.

Brenda held the handle above the door. Her arm was sprinkled with moles, her fair skin glowing pink. That patch of skin could have belonged to Amelia's mother, also prone to heat rash and sunburn. Her heart picked up even as she told herself it couldn't possibly be, that it meant nothing. During her first year of high school, Amelia had come home one day to find her mother sunbathing topless by the pool. Triangle sections on her breasts were a few shades lighter than the surrounding skin. There was a cocktail glass on the ground beside her, one Amelia had never seen before, and flies gathered around the slice of pineapple that adorned the side of the glass. Her skin was already a dangerous red. Amelia rubbed sunscreen into it, making sure to cover the little section of caesarean scar showing above her bikini bottoms, white and ragged on the soft, rounded flesh of her tummy.

The car surged forward, the force pushing Amelia into her seat. She placed a hand on the black leather and it was cool to touch. Through the hole in the headrest, she could see the goosebumps that rose on the skin of Brenda's neck, the muscles beneath locked stiff and straight. Amelia lifted her hand from the seat and examined the greasy print it left behind.

Lucy sat up, her eyes flicking between the view from different windows. Amelia leaned forward, adjusted the tongue of her shoe and sneaked a glimpse at the speedometer. Thirty kilometres over the speed limit. Ron's arms were at full extension, each hand gripping the wheel. His skin was hairless, his fingernails trimmed and the cuticles pushed back to reveal perfect crescent moons. He caught her staring; his eyes met hers in the rear-view mirror. She looked away but his gaze remained, saw beneath her clothes, crept across her skin. He could see the pulsing tracks of Will's fingertips. He followed the map of touch branded across her body, found the hotspots where Will's prints overlapped with those left by others.

She glanced back at the mirror and Ron's eyes were there, waiting. A car approached in the opposite lane and the passing force of it buffeted the Subaru. She willed Ron to go faster.

Sweat cooled and thickened on her skin as they continued through the desert with the air conditioning on full. She began to shiver. She tucked her arms inside her T-shirt and folded them across her belly. A ray of sun angled into the window and she moved over to capture its warmth. Lucy yelped, only once, small and high-pitched. She looked at Amelia, then circled around on the towel, lying down with a sigh, head on her front paws. Amelia cupped her head, massaged her ear.

The car drifted towards the middle of the road as Ron fiddled with buttons on the steering wheel. He clicked one but didn't get the desired result. He pressed again, holding it in this time. There was no apparent reaction from the car. He hit the row of buttons with his fist. Lucy sat up with a start. The car beeped.

'Piece of shit!' he said, then corrected the vehicle with a sharp swerve, sending a fat strawberry air freshener swinging. Avenues of cartilage rose from Brenda's thin wrists as she tightened her grip on the handle above the door. Ron punched a different combination of buttons with his index finger: no result. He mashed several buttons at once with the heel of his hand and finally there was a response; the car shifted gear and lurched forward. Lucy sat up, barked.

'Shut that thing up,' Ron said, still pounding buttons. Lucy scratched at the seat. Amelia tried to grab her paws, to draw the towel back under her, but Lucy continued scratching, leaving long white lines in the leather.

Ron turned, inspecting the damage: one hand on the wheel, the other on Brenda's headrest.

Brenda screamed. There were kangaroos, big reds, two of them. The smaller stood on the side of the road, scratching its belly. The other was just ahead of it: tail flat against the black surface of their lane, nose to the ground. The kangaroo looked up and observed the vehicle's approach. It turned and moved outside of the lane, then took a big hop back into the car's path. Amelia gathered Lucy in her arms as Ron yanked the wheel and they headed sharply towards the wrong side of the road. The car screeched as it gripped the edge of the bitumen and then careened to the left. Lucy was ripped from Amelia's grip and flung across the back seat, slamming against the door. Amelia braced herself for the violence of the flip, imagined the crunch of sand on the roof as they eventually stopped, a boat coming aground in a bay.

Brenda's shouting was shrill: 'Stop! You idiot!'

The car headed off the left-hand side of the road and caught loose gravel; it squiggled back onto the asphalt then headed sharply into the right-hand lane. Ron no longer had any control over the vehicle; the wheel spun and he was unable to get a hold. Brenda threw herself across the car and grabbed the wheel with both hands. She yanked down. The car obeyed but overcorrected; she jerked the wheel the other way and they were back on the road, slower and straight.

Ron sat, frozen, left hand limp and white beside his red seatbelt buckle. The wildflowers of Brenda's dress splayed over the gearstick as she continued to steer the car.

'Take it!' Brenda said. In the rear-view mirror, Ron's eyes were wide open, locked on to something ahead. He slowly took hold of the wheel, flicked the indicator on and rolled to a stop by the side of the road. Brenda shut the air conditioning off. They sat in silence, except for the ticking indicator and Lucy's panting. She was unhurt, her tongue dangling out the side of her mouth.

Amelia looked out the back window; the kangaroos were there, pelting across the desert, a trail of dust behind them. The car had left skid marks, black snakes curving and flicking their way down the highway.

'Continue to follow . . . the road.' The female voice of the GPS delivered a stilted, conglomerate sentence. Amelia lowered her window, shuddered as the wall of warmth collapsed onto her.

'Continue to follow . . . the road.'

Brenda gathered her dress then opened her own window. Ron's manicured hand moved towards the back of her neck.

'Get out,' Brenda said, dodging his fingers. Amelia was out, Lucy behind her, in an instant.

'Not you,' Brenda said, glancing up through the window, a strand of hair out of place across her forehead.

'Ron, move,' Brenda said.

Ron covered his face with his hands, rubbed up and down.

'Get in the back,' Brenda said. 'Now.'

Sun beat down on Amelia; she shielded her eyes from the glare. Ron opened the driver door and stepped out, walking with shoulders hunched to the back seat.

Brenda looked to Amelia again. 'You can get in the front here, sweetheart,' she said, red patches of skin flaring across her cheeks. She got out of the car. 'I'm so sorry about this.'

'It's fine, really –'

'Please. The front seat,' Brenda said, leaving the passenger door open and walking around to the driver's side.

Amelia rearranged the pink towel on the back seat. She clicked her fingers and Lucy jumped in. Ron had discarded the lime-green towel on the floor near Lucy and Amelia picked it up, began spreading it on the front passenger seat.

'Oh, sweetie, don't worry about that,' Brenda said. Amelia looked to Ron, who avoided eye contact. 'Please,' Brenda said, 'you're fine. Just sit down.' Brenda patted the seat beside her, blinked slowly. Amelia climbed in.

Brenda turned the air conditioning to a gentle, comfortable cool then selected some classical music to play, volume lowered. She checked her mirrors, indicated, and pulled onto the highway. The next few kilometres were peaceful and steady, Brenda sitting straight and alert at the wheel. Ron was silent in the back; Amelia put her hand behind her neck, blocking the space in the headrest.

The soft rocking of the car sent Amelia into snatches of sleep, and she woke with a start as her head fell to her chest.

'Amelia, sweetheart . . . why don't you have a little rest,' Brenda said, her voice soft; for a moment Amelia felt her mother's palm resting on her forehead, the pound of a headache subsiding.

'Ron, would you please pass Amelia a pillow?' Brenda said.

There was rustling and muttering at the back. Amelia turned to see Ron out of his seat and reaching over into the boot. Lucy was curled up, her chin resting in the crook of her hind legs. Amelia faced the front as Ron grunted, swore to himself.

A white pillow appeared in the gap between the seats.

'Thanks,' Amelia said, resting the pillow across her lap.

Brenda pulled in at the next service station they reached, saying she needed to get a few supplies. 'Can I get you something?'

'No, I'm good thanks.'

'Are you sure? I can get anything you like.' Brenda's eyes searched Amelia's. 'My shout,' she said, raising her purse in the air.

Amelia unclipped her seatbelt. 'I'm fine, really. Thank you though.'

She and Lucy stretched their legs while Brenda was gone, avoiding Ron, who sat dozing with his frowning face propped up on his fist.

Brenda returned with a bag of groceries, which she unpacked in the boot. They got back into the car; the whole efficient stop was over in less than five minutes. Brenda dabbed at her cheeks and neck with a tissue, then re-pinned strands of hair that had come loose around her face. Before setting off, she opened a packet of chocolate-covered raisins, positioning them carefully in a cup holder in the centre of the car.

'These are really nice,' she said, popping one into her mouth and closing her eyes to savour it.

Brenda guided the car back onto the highway. Keeping her eyes on the road, she reached down and widened the opening of the packet of chocolates. 'Please, help yourself,' she said.

'Thanks,' Amelia said, but didn't take one. She looked out the window and started a new count of road posts.

'These are my favourite but he doesn't like them,' Brenda said, flicking her head towards the back seat. 'It's nice to have someone to share them with.' She held the bag out to Amelia, showing the rash up the inside of her arm. 'It's just the two of us at home, so . . .'

Amelia gave in and took one, rolling it around her mouth as she avoided looking at Brenda.

'What about you?' Brenda said. 'Do you have family around here? Friends?'

Amelia's stomach kicked as she swallowed the sweetness, chocolate slick on her tongue. 'I'm just passing through, really.'

'I see. Well, I'm more than happy to take a detour. I could drop you somewhere if you'd like. We're in no rush.'

'Just further down the highway is good for me. Nowhere in particular. I'm just taking it all in.'

'Maybe a train station, or a bus stop? Anywhere, truly.'

'Wherever is fine – no need to go out of your way. Thank you.' Amelia plumped the pillow up against the window and nuzzled into the crisp material; she fended off further questions by closing her eyes.

*

She woke to the car slowing. They passed street signs and build-ings and she closed her eyes again, lingering in half-sleep as civilisation flickered past in light and shadow.

The indicator was on and the car turned, then stopped. Amelia opened her eyes. They were pulled up next to a park. A family had a picnic spread across browned grass; a woman shooed flies away from a chicken carcass.

'Where are we?' she said.

'Port Augusta,' Brenda said. 'Bathroom stop.' She took the

keys out of the ignition. 'He's still out of it,' she said, then lowered her voice to a whisper: 'Have a look.'

Amelia turned; Ron's head was tipped back, mouth wide open. Lucy yawned and thumped her tail against the leather. Ron stirred and Amelia looked away.

Brenda opened her door and swung her legs out of the car. Amelia let Lucy out then walked behind Brenda towards the toilet block. There were two cubicles inside, each with battered apricot-coloured doors. The smell of dried piss was sharp.

Brenda's feet shuffled in the gap under the wall between the stalls. The toilet seat was on the floor, so Amelia hovered over the silver bowl. She finished quickly. Ants crowded around the sink, scurrying into action when Amelia rinsed her hands under the trickle of lukewarm water. She made a pool with her hands and scrubbed her face. Amelia turned and Brenda was there; they each stepped to the side, trying to get out of the way of the other.

'Sorry,' Brenda said, giggling. She stepped forward to the basin, dodging the squares of toilet paper littering the floor. Amelia wiped her hands on her shorts and turned to head out of the bathroom.

'Amelia . . . wait a second,' Brenda said. 'I wanted to ask you something, if that's okay.'

Amelia paused, then turned to face Brenda. 'Ah, I'll just be out there,' she said, pointing to the exit.

Brenda shook her hands out, reached for a paper towel. 'It'll only take a moment,' she said.

Amelia could barely hear her over the filling of the toilets. She leaned against the brick wall, felt the bite of it against her arms. 'What is it?'

'Well, I was just ... wondering about you. Wondering if you're okay.'

'I'm fine, thanks,' Amelia said. She pushed off the wall.

'Wait,' Brenda said, grabbing her shoulder with a moist hand. Amelia flinched and Brenda let go. 'Sorry, I didn't mean to ... I just wonder if there's something we can do to help.'

'All good, thanks,' Amelia said, unable to hold Brenda's searching, red-rimmed gaze. 'The lift is great. Very helpful.'

'Well, okay, but ... do your parents know where you are?'

Graffiti patterned the tiles behind Brenda, and Amelia read a section of blue scrawl: *Evie P is a slut.* 'Of course.'

Brenda lowered her tone and stepped in closer. Redness spread across her chest. 'It's really not safe, travelling around like this.'

Amelia crossed her arms, looked at the shapes of leaves and branches resting on the corrugated perspex roof above.

'Why don't you come back to Mildura with us? At least we could keep an eye on you ... And you'd have somewhere to go if you needed, even for a night or two. We've just repainted the spare room a really lovely turquoise.'

Amelia moved again towards the exit, fought the urge to punch the wall; she wouldn't add fuel to Brenda's cause.

'Look – will you at least take my number?' Brenda said. 'So if you do need anything, even just to talk, you can give me a call.'

'I really don't need –'

'I would just feel better knowing you had it,' Brenda said. 'Will you take it, for me?'

A woman entered the bathroom holding a young girl's hand. She started to direct the child through the toileting process.

'All right.' Amelia shrugged.

'Great, thank you, thank you,' Brenda said, her hand deep in her bag. 'Gosh, now I've got to find something to write it with.' She dug through her things and eventually pulled out a dark red lipstick. 'This'll have to do,' she said. 'What should I write it on?'

Amelia dipped into her pockets and, on finding nothing of use, tugged down on a sheet of paper towel. Brenda took it, the paper thinning where her damp hands made contact. 'Oh,' she said. She dried her hands, put it in the bin and grabbed a fresh one. 'Now we're in business,' she said, then spoke the number out loud as she wrote ten digits in obtuse curves and dead straight lines. 'Here,' she said, handing the paper to Amelia. 'That's my number. My personal one.' Amelia took the paper. 'Ron's a good man, he is, but he can be a bit funny about these things . . .'

'Right,' Amelia said. 'Thanks.' She folded the paper into a neat square and slipped it into her pocket.

Lucy was playing with two children when Amelia came out of the bathroom, having adopted their ball as her own. Amelia called to her and she left the game.

'Oh, another thing,' Brenda said as they walked back to the car. 'We'll be stopping in an hour or so in Crystal Brook. We have a room booked there for the night.'

'Sounds nice,' Amelia said.

'We can see about having you there too,' Brenda said. 'Thought you might like to take a break.'

'I'm okay, thanks. I'll probably keep moving.'

'Well, we'll just wait and see.'

The journey was quiet, punctuated by Brenda's regular rustling in the bag of chocolate raisins. 'Help yourself,' she reminded Amelia, but Amelia put her head back on the pillow and closed her eyes.

It was almost 2.30 in the afternoon as they rolled into Crystal Brook, and Brenda murmured about needing to eat something proper. The car bumped over a railway crossing at the entrance to the town. A brown creek ran beside the road, reeds arcing over the water's edge. Brenda squinted as she looked from side to side. Amelia took a deep breath, preparing herself for the resurrection of the GPS. The car crept along through streets where weatherboard houses popped up from dry lawns. Nestled among these homes, a white-brick archway rose to meet them, pronouncing their arrival at Wattle Lodge. Amelia lifted her head from the pillow. Her limbs were heavy, her mind a thick fog as she took in the green, cream and maroon colour scheme of the motel's exterior.

The car crunched to a stop on gravel; Amelia unfastened her seatbelt and unlatched her door. Brenda reached across and touched her wrist.

'Why don't you just wait here. I'm going to go inside and discuss our situation with the manager,' Brenda said.

'Thanks, but –' Amelia said, and Brenda silenced her with a squeeze, then got out of the car. Through the dusty windscreen, Amelia watched her open a hole-ravaged screen door beneath the *RECEPTION* sign. Ron moved in the back seat, made the groans and squeaks of waking.

Amelia unfolded herself from the car. She stretched, holding down the edge of her ill-fitting T-shirt to cover the skin of her belly. She opened the back door and Lucy scampered from the car, had a big shake. Wattle Lodge was a drive-in motel with two storeys; the windows of the rooms looked onto the white lines and vehicles of the car park. *Room with a view*, her mother would have said, as she did any time they stayed somewhere crap. Weeds pushed up through paving stones around Amelia's feet.

A curtain in a nearby room moved. A girl with two plaits stepped behind the glass and stared out. They looked at each other, unflinching, like dogs in a frozen battle. Amelia surrendered as Brenda exited from reception, watched her close the screen door with long, gentle fingers.

'Room number seven,' she said with a proud smile. 'We need to allow the staff half an hour to arrange the bedding. You can stay, though, Amelia. It's all sorted.'

There was a huff from Ron, who had got out of the car and now watched Brenda, one hand protecting his eyes from the sun.

'Oh, um, are you sure?' Amelia said.

'Of course. It's our pleasure.'

Amelia hadn't been in a room of her own since the white room at the coast. She pictured herself spread out on a bed, imagined the friction of a fresh towel against her skin. Maybe there'd even be those little round hotel soaps, wrapped in puckered paper.

'Thanks, I really appreciate it,' she said, and, as she did so, she caught the eye of the girl in the window, still staring.

'And don't worry – seven is one of the pet-friendly rooms,' Brenda said, handing her the key.

Lucy's tail wagged as if she knew she was the subject of conversation. Amelia slipped the key into her pocket. She crouched, scratched behind Lucy's ears; Lucy licked the air.

'I'm gonna take her out for a wander,' Amelia said.

It was easy, in the end, to get away; by the time Amelia was ready to go, Brenda had an esky out and was making very organised cheese and chutney sandwiches. Ron stood a few metres away in a patch of shade near reception, crunching on a green apple. As Amelia dragged her pack out of the boot, Brenda said, 'Oh, you can leave that here. We're not going anywhere.'

'Thanks, but I'd rather take it,' Amelia said, hauling the pack on.

Brenda looked hurt, perhaps even panicked. She wiped her forehead with her arm, her hands occupied by crumbs and a butter knife.

The straps of Amelia's pack found the familiar strips of chafed skin on her shoulders; she was unable to leave her loyal friends behind, her mother's shopping list, her rocket pen, her favourite T-shirt, however tainted.

'Well, at least take one of these,' Brenda said. She cut a soft sandwich in two triangles, then placed them in a perfectly sized

Tupperware container. Amelia wanted to decline but Brenda held it out to her, did her three slow blinks.

'Thanks,' Amelia said, unbuckling her pack and pushing the container inside.

She walked down the main street and Lucy trotted ahead, stopping to investigate wads of fossilised gum on the ground. It was quiet and muggy. Colourful lights flashed above the entrance to a Video Ezy, and the lull of the street was broken by the blare of gunfire and helicopters as she passed. She didn't like her chances of finding a pharmacy, and, in there, the morning-after pill; the only way to wipe Glendambo off the map completely.

Automatic doors slid open at the supermarket as she walked past, and she lingered in the flow of air conditioning; Lucy stopped for a moment, her snout lifted. A man in a grey singlet walked out, thongs slapping. One thick arm balanced a case of beer on his shoulder, the other held a phone to his cheek. He spoke loudly as he walked away from her, feet pointing out at angles, milk-bottle calves curved and twitching: 'Yeah mate . . . No worries . . . Yeah . . . Nah . . . Yep, on me way . . . See ya.'

She put her hand to her belly, tried to tell if something was forming, and, if it was, whether it was more alive now than it had been a few hours ago.

'Oi. Where you going?' The voice came from behind her. It was the staring girl from Wattle Lodge; she held on to a post, arm extended, her weight dangling off it.

'Chemist, hopefully,' Amelia said.

'What for?' The girl had a row of freckles across her face, decorating a small, elegant nose. Her skin was summer brown, her eyebrows almost too white-blonde to see. Wisps of wavy hair had escaped her plaits and stuck out at her temples.

'Because I need something,' Amelia said.

The girl's white dress had diamond shapes stamped out across the hem, and it crept up her thighs as she swung from the post. 'Like what?' the girl said. The orange strings of a bikini top were tied around her neck.

'Something to make me feel better,' Amelia said. It was difficult to tell how old the girl was. Perhaps nine, but possibly a skinny, small twelve-year-old.

'Can I pat your dog?'

'Yep.'

'He doesn't bite?'

'Nope. And she's a she.'

The girl let go of her post and stepped off the kerb. Sunlight brightened her eyes; the left one had a patch of copper amid its clear blue. Lucy's tail wagged slightly as she inspected the girl's extended hand. She scratched the dog's head and ears, then ran her hand down her neck. 'What's her name?'

'Lucy.'

'Where'd you get her?'

'My friend and I found her.'

'And you got to keep her? I never get to keep anything.' She crouched down next to Lucy, who sniffed her face, then licked at her chin, setting the girl giggling.

When the girl had had enough, she stood up and said, 'So what are you gonna buy?'

Amelia squinted at a shop up ahead. 'Is that a chemist? I can't tell.'

'Yeah – I've been there before. Got some bandaids. See?' She held up a small, delicate hand, where a bandaid formed a shoddy thimble around her index finger.

'Ouch. How'd you do that?'

'Jammed it in the door. We come here every year, you know.' She looked at Amelia as if making certain that the information was clear and understood; when Amelia nodded, the girl said, 'I'll show you the chemist. It's easy.' She skipped ahead onto the road, not bothering to check for cars.

The chemist was shiny and new, and belonged to a chain that was all over the cities too.

'I'll take care of Lu-Lu,' the girl said. As they walked up the ramp to the entrance, she dragged her hand up the metal railing so that it screeched.

'If you want. Won't be long.' Amelia leaned her pack up against the red brick of the building, found her envelope of money, and ordered Lucy to stay. A doorbell sounded throughout the store as she stepped inside the automatic doors.

A cardboard garden gnome was propped up at the entrance, promising a sneeze-free existence with antihistamines. Amelia remembered the gnome from the chemist at home; he'd had the same smile after her mother's initial diagnosis, after the surgery, and even four years later when it came back. It was her first lesson in the carrying on of things despite the way her mother's sickness had skewed her world. They lopped off both of her mother's breasts. Amelia adored the way her mother continued to cross the hallway from bathroom to bedroom naked, the lumps of flesh and scar tissue on her chest bare, glistening with vitamin E cream in the morning sunlight through the window.

Amelia turned her back on the gnome and tried to chase the image of her mother away. She couldn't be here now, watching each of Amelia's shameful steps past the eczema treatments towards the counter.

'Can I help you?'

A white-haired woman approached, a well-prepared, lipsticked smile beaming down the aisle.

'Hi,' Amelia said. Her knees softened as she imagined melting into this woman's arms, letting herself be held, putting her cheek against the rough material of the woman's pastel pink polo shirt.

The woman's eyes narrowed and she tilted her head. Her name badge said 'Sandra'; brooches and pins flourished around it in proud chaos. 'Can I help you find something?'

The entrance doors slid open; outside, the girl hung upside down from the ramp railing, plaits touching the cement. Her dress hung down, revealing orange swimming bottoms and a lean, straight torso. The doors closed, but the girl swung, her movement sending them open again.

Sandra gave another warm, crinkled smile.

Amelia spoke as quietly as possible without whispering. 'Ah, I need the morning-after pill, please.'

Sandra sucked air in through her teeth, but quickly regathered herself. 'Oh, okay, I see. Come with me.'

The automatic door slid open and closed, open and closed as Amelia walked to the counter. The woman fossicked through shelves behind the prescriptions desk. Amelia sneaked a look outside. Lucy was lying down, her chin resting on her front paws; the girl continued to swing from the railing, her face red from the rush of blood.

Sandra mumbled to herself, shifting boxes, and Amelia drummed her fingers on the counter. She tried to avoid looking at the packets of jelly beans her mother had loved – tried not to think of her popping them into her mouth, the sweet smell that was released as she chewed – but the unmistakable colours blared on the shelf in her peripheral vision.

A man in a white coat pushed open a door behind the counter. He had a dark beard and thin-rimmed glasses; a sheen of sweat on sallow skin made him look ill.

'Everything okay, Sandra?' A waft of curry accompanied the man, and he looked between Amelia and Sandra while he finished a mouthful of food.

'Everything's fine. I was just finding the emergency contraception for this young woman,' Sandra said. She seemed to have shrunk, her warmth doused.

'I see. Do you know that this drug has to be administered by me?'

'Yes, I know, but I didn't want to disturb you if it wasn't in stock.'

'It should absolutely be in stock.' The man leaned over Sandra, plucked a box from a shelf above her head. Sweat patches made the underarm of his white shirt transparent.

Sandra was red-faced and flustered; her crease lines now defined the wince of someone who'd spent a lifetime being put in her place. Amelia smiled at her; Sandra smiled back, kneaded her hands.

'Come with me,' the man said, looking at Amelia over his glasses. He walked out from behind the counter and Amelia followed him to a blue curtain; he yanked it across, revealing a white desk and two chairs squished into a cubicle. They stepped inside, but when he pulled the curtain across a large gap remained so that Amelia could see out to the store beyond. He sat down and Amelia squeezed into the seat across from him.

'Now, there are a few questions we have to go through,' the man said, opening a folder and extracting a piece of paper. A selection of pens with the names of different drugs were lined up on the desk. He selected a green and pink one and filled in the date at the top of the page.

'I'm the pharmacist here.' He gestured to a certificate hanging on the wall above his head, but Amelia couldn't make out the name. She nodded. That information earned a tick in one of the boxes on the page.

'Right, have you taken emergency contraception before?'

'No,' she said. She took a deep breath, and as she did so, the girl passed the gap in the curtain.

'When's the last time you had unprotected sexual intercourse?' The pharmacist sniffed, and Amelia concentrated on the dark tufts of hair creeping out of his nostrils.

'Last night. It was an accident.'

He marked the questionnaire again. 'An accident?'

'Yeah. The condom broke.'

'And you're not on the contraceptive pill?'

'No.'

'Well, the pill is recommended, particularly if you're going to continue to have unprotected intercourse.'

'It wasn't unprotected on purpose. It was an accident.' Amelia's face was hot. She looked through the gap in the curtain but there was no sign of the girl.

The pharmacist stretched his legs out so his feet were on either side of her, hemming her in. His suit pants exposed socks decorated with watermelon slices. 'Are you in a relationship?'

'No.' Amelia moved her chair back a couple of centimetres, until she hit the wall. The pharmacist raised an eyebrow, made no mark on the form. A mole above his lip twitched.

'How long have you been sexually active?'

Coldness gripped her chest. The zigzag pattern of the curtain seemed to move across her vision until she was seeing instead the dark hair that ran downwards from Zach's bellybutton, the bolts of his spine as he moved in the sun.

'I had a boyfriend when I was nineteen,' Amelia lied, forcing herself to meet the pharmacist's dark eyes.

'Right.' He held her eye, tapped the pen. Made no mark on the paper. The girl appeared at the gap in the curtain, then ducked away as Amelia saw her.

The pharmacist spoke for a few minutes, outlining the potential side effects of the drug, the instructions for its use, and stressed again the need for people like her to be on the contraceptive pill.

'Do you have any questions?' he said, turning the box from edge to edge.

'No,' she said, watching his hairy knuckles.

He signed the form with a loopy signature, then slid the box towards her. Amelia grabbed it and stepped out of the cubicle, breathless. She leaned on a display holding pedometers, tried to calm herself.

The girl was right there across the aisle. She knelt in front of a rack, flicking through neon-coloured hair accessories. She looked up, craning her neck to follow Amelia's movements past her.

'Hi,' the girl said.

'Hey,' Amelia said, and her own voice seemed to echo in her ear. The girl scurried along behind her.

Sandra had recovered herself. She held her chin high, and her smile was warm and apologetic. 'All sorted?' she said as she scanned the barcode on the box.

'Yeah, thanks,' Amelia said.

The girl grabbed a packet of jelly beans, stared into the clear plastic window. She took them to Amelia, held them up. 'Can I have these?'

'No,' Amelia said.

The girl was wounded.

'Hey,' Amelia said. 'Why don't you choose a postcard for me off that rack?'

'Really?' The girl said.

'Sure.'

The girl scampered over and spun the rack fast. She stopped it suddenly, plucked a card, and then continued spinning. Once she'd selected two cards, she held them up, drawing them close then holding them at arm's length as she deliberated. 'This one,' she said, shoving the rejected card into the wrong slot before running back to Amelia.

'Good choice,' Amelia said. Four images detailed the changes of Crystal Brook's main street through its history.

Sandra scanned the card. 'That'll be forty-two seventy-five.'

Amelia grabbed her yellow envelope of cash. She handed over three twenties.

The till popped open. 'Have a wonderful afternoon,' Sandra said, placing the change in Amelia's hand. She lingered, closing Amelia's fingers over the money, holding on to her fist.

'Bye,' Amelia said, lowering her hand. The girl nestled into Amelia's hip as she turned around from the till. Amelia lifted her arm and let it hover over the child before resting her hand on her bony shoulder.

'Whatcha get?' The girl said as they walked out the door. Lucy stood in welcome, the wag of her tail slow in the heat. 'What is it, what is it, what is it?' the girl said, tugging at Amelia's T-shirt as she put her money away.

'It's private.' Amelia hoisted her bag onto her knee, twisted it round to her back. The girl made a lunge for the paper package; Amelia held it up in the air, out of reach. The girl jumped, giggling, swiping the air above her head. Lucy spun around and barked, eyes on the package too.

The girl stopped, short of breath. Through her laughter, she said, 'Just show me, pleeeeease . . .' She pointed her chin up, her eyes bright and flitting over Amelia's face as if searching for weakness.

'It's an adult thing, not something for you to worry about,' Amelia said, unable to avoid smiling back at the girl.

'But I know about . . . sex and stuff.' The girl bluffed her way through the word 'sex'.

'Were you listening to my conversation in there?' Amelia said.

The girl crinkled her nose. 'Is it like a tablet that takes it away once you've done it?'

Amelia straightened her shoulders and took hold of her straps to still her trembling hands. 'It's a little bit like that. It doesn't take it away, but it stops you from having a baby.'

'Oh yeah, that's what I meant.'

Amelia turned and took a last look at the gnome inside the glass doors: the red hat, the blushed cheeks. Beyond that, the pharmacist stood behind the counter and she caught his eye by mistake. She turned and walked down the ramp, sweat prickling at her temples. The girl followed, pulling on a loose strap of Amelia's pack; the muscles in Amelia's shoulder twinged with each tug. Amelia paused when she reached the main street. She looked in the direction of Wattle Lodge. A hot breeze pushed down the street, lifting a grey plastic bag into the air.

'What's your name?' said the girl.

'Amelia. What's yours?'

'George. Let's go.' She latched on to Amelia's hand and pulled her ahead. Amelia dragged her feet in big, heavy strides in defiance of the excited tugs. Lucy jumped up and nipped at George's fingertips, setting her giggling again. Amelia wondered where the girl's parents were, why she was out here alone.

She led Amelia behind the supermarket, jumping between wooden pallets. They picked their way up a rocky ridge and met a wall of scrub. 'Come on, I know the way,' George said.

George and Lucy charged ahead through the long grass. Her mother's voice was there – *Watch out for snakes* – but Amelia couldn't bring herself to put fear into the girl.

Amelia didn't have the energy to keep up and soon lost sight of them. She walked, slapping at her sticky, itchy legs, until she reached a clearing; a brown creek ran before her, perhaps twenty metres wide, muddy banks stretching up either side. She closed her eyes and listened to the swelling sound of cicadas.

In the shade of a gum tree, she opened the box from the chemist and pushed the pill out of its blister pack. She placed it on the back of her tongue and swallowed, feeling the journey of the tablet as it wedged at intervals down her dry throat. She chased it with a mouthful of water from her Mount Franklin then held the bottle in her hand, moving her thumb up and down the ridged plastic. Only a few threads of the label remained, faded and scratched.

When she was staying in the white room, she used to set little traps with her things: the Mount Franklin bottle filled to a certain level, a dead teabag sprawled in the sink just so, the sheets on her bed pulled tight so any pressure on them would show in crinkles. The doorway opened onto carpeted stairs that absorbed her footsteps as she crept up them; she hoped to catch whatever happened in the room when she was absent in action. She'd go around the room, checking each item, as if her mother might disturb something by way of conversation. But each time the room was just how she had left it: the items as they were, awaiting her return.

There was a splash to her right, and Lucy's bark carried up from somewhere below. She turned in time to see water recovering around a point of impact; a rope swing skimmed the surface of the creek and swung silently over the bank, its passenger delivered. She watched the murky water, waiting for George to emerge, but the ripples receded into stillness.

'Lucy, come.' Lucy's collar tags clinked in response as she made her way to Amelia's side, stirring a mob of sulphur-crested cockatoos from a bottlebrush tree. There was a flurry and then their urgent, invasive screeches overhead. Shadows of eucalypts played tricks on her and several times she thought she saw the girl's body moving to the water's surface. She stepped right up to the edge of the bank; the rope's passage pointed to George's white dress, discarded on the shore.

Lucy barked once, then again, her front paws in the creek. Too much time had passed. At the moment Amelia readied herself to jump into the muddy water – pack on the ground, muscles tensed, heart beating at the base of her throat – George emerged with a spurt, three-quarters of the way to the opposite bank.

'This is the furthest I ever got!' She was gasping for breath, her voice echoing between the mud banks and walls of trees.

'Pretty far,' Amelia said. She crouched down, spread her fingers on the dirt for balance and allowed her heartbeat to slow. Three mosquitoes landed in quick succession on her arm; she slapped them off, squashing one of them in a spray of blood and dismemberment.

'Can you do it?' George called, head bobbing in the water. Amelia stood and wiped the dead insect on her shorts.

'Doubt it,' she said.

'Jump in!' George said. She dived below the surface of the water, flashing the orange of her swimming bottoms. Amelia wanted to sit down, to lean against a tree and take a break. Lucy snuffled at some tree roots halfway up the bank; George surfaced and rubbed her eyes. 'Come on!'

The kid was so excited; an only child herself, Amelia knew the thrill of finding someone to play with on holiday. At home, Sid was there, an only child too – she remembered how they sneaked into his neighbour's pool at night, the way they moved silently through the water. They submerged themselves and tried to find each other in the darkness; she knew the squirm of his slippery, thin limbs, how when she'd come up for air her nostrils filled with the smell of lavender. Sid would be catching his breath, water falling from their faces and pattering into the pool.

Amelia picked her way along the creek until she reached George's dress, high up on the bank. She slipped off her shoes, unbuttoned her shorts and let them drop to the dirt.

Amelia lifted her T-shirt over her head and George called from the water: 'Woo woo!'

The little bow at the top of Amelia's undies seemed somehow too intimate. Her bra was edged with lace, displaying her breasts in a perky, rounded fashion. She crossed her arms over herself. George had made her way over and stood knee-deep in the water a couple of metres from the bank. Her body was flat and rectangular, though Amelia recognised the hint of a curve at each hip. Her own hips had been a surprise to her, discovered by Zach's hands the day he finished planting her mother's seedlings in neat rows. After he found them, Amelia stood naked and alone in front of the mirror, running her hands over her chest, her hips. She saw the changes for the first time, her body transformed by the way he touched her, by the things it did to him.

She would not have been that different from George, and Zach only a bit younger than Amelia was now. The material of the girl's bikini top was crumpled and empty over the place her breasts would one day grow. No one needed to see the child's body, not yet. Amelia wished she had a towel in which she could wrap the girl up.

'How old are you?' Amelia said.

'Eleven and a half.'

George adjusted the string of her swimming top, stared back at Amelia with blatant inquiry. Amelia dropped her eyes, concentrated on wriggling a bull ant off of her big toe.

'How deep is it?' Amelia said. She peered over the edge of the bank, gauging her potential course on the rope swing.

'Real deep. I can't touch, see.' George swam out again, near to the place where she'd first disappeared beneath the water. She held her hand up straight and sank. She was gone for a few seconds, then reappeared, eyes shut, water falling in a sheet over her face. 'Didn't even make it to the bottom. No rocks or anything, promise.'

The rope hung dormant over the water. Amelia crept down the bank, the mud slimy between her toes. She stretched out at the water's edge, managing to collect the rope in her fingertips, then gripped the coarse, tight weave in her hand. She walked backwards with it up the bank, careful not to slip, not to falter under George's gaze. She pulled down on the rope, testing it with her weight. The branch overhead creaked but was solid. She held her hands as high up the twine as she could reach, then launched off the bank, scrambling in midair to place her feet on the scratchy knot at the rope's end. She swung, squealing despite herself as the rope cut cleanly through thick air, her hair whipping around her face. Her grip slipped and her arms burned from the effort, but the rushing wind, the graze of the rope on her thighs, was so good that she clung on for another flight over the bank.

On the return journey, she let go of the rope at the highest point of the swing, slapping the water with the side of her body.

Her skin tingled from the impact. She relaxed, allowing the momentum of the fall to take her below the surface. The world became quiet and dense; she was aware only of her own body, the clicking of her bones, the release of air from her mouth, the gurgle of her left ear filling up with water.

Sid had been so excited for her to meet his cousin. He'd told her so much about him but Amelia was unprepared for how big Zach was. His lanky frame filled the doorway and she had to take a step back in order to look up at him. He introduced himself, his voice growly and deep, and she took his extended hand, felt the thickness of his knuckles. His blue eyes were pale and piercing in the sun. A nipple poked out the side of his grey singlet; she knew she shouldn't look at it, but she couldn't drag her eyes away.

She opened her eyes beneath the water, heart too fast. Time for air. She kicked hard upwards; the sun shone down on the water's brown surface, making it pale like the dregs of a drink once the ice has melted. She reached oxygen just in time, sucking it deep into her lungs.

Lucy barked from the bank, her tail wagging.

George clapped. 'I'm gonna have another go!' she yelled. She splashed water in two arcs, the droplets sprinkling Amelia's face and shoulders. George swam to the shore and ran up the bank with fearless agility while Amelia lay on her back, gently kicking her arms and legs, chest heaving. A wasp drifted by her vision; it used one wing like an oar as it tried to save itself from drowning. Water seeped into her other ear. She floated between the buzzing world above and the slow, addictive depths.

Sid would have loved it there. Up until he left for Melbourne when he was eighteen, he'd gone with her down to the gully at the edge of their suburb, jumped into the cold water then spread out on the sun-warmed rocks. They walked for hours, Sid with his bird book tucked into his back pocket, stopping to listen for the elusive glossy black cockatoo. When they finally saw a pair of them, Amelia didn't know whether she preferred to look at the red tail feathers of the discovery or to watch the delight on Sid's face, the way he glowed, hardly blinking.

'Waaahoo!' George screamed as she swung from the rope again, dropping into the water in a tight bomb. She swam up to Amelia and draped her arms on her, squeezing her legs around Amelia's waist. 'Piggyback,' she said.

Amelia tried to give her a ride, spluttering in the water as her head kept sinking below the surface. Short of breath, she said, 'It's too hard, I can't touch the bottom.'

'Let's go again,' George said, pushing off Amelia with a knee to the back. Amelia returned to lying in the water, eyes closed, the sun flashing over her eyelids as she drifted between the shade of gum trees.

George's energy was endless and infectious. Amelia climbed up the bank over and over, addicted to the abandon of swinging out over the water, the letting go of the rope, the falling. Blisters worked their way onto her hands. She collected scrapes and bruises from scrabbling up the rocks out of the water. George scored each of Amelia's dismounts out of ten and Amelia did the same for her, her applause at George's creativity travelling down the creek.

'I'm hungry,' George said after a particularly elaborate somersault and twist. As she caught her breath on the shore, her ribs pressed against her skin, the twitch of her heart visible.

'Me too,' Amelia said. 'Wanna share a sandwich?'

Amelia made her way to shore and dug Brenda's Tupperware container out of her pack. George settled on a flat rock, her legs dangling into the water, then beckoned Lucy to follow. Amelia sat next to them, pulled off the plastic lid and handed half the sandwich to George.

'Thanks,' she said. She bit all along an edge of crust, her cheeks bulging. Amelia took a small bite; the chutney was made from red onions and was rich and sweet.

Lucy searched for crumbs in George's lap, and she broke off the other crust and gave it to her.

'So, that pill you took,' George said, displaying the squashed bread in her mouth as she spoke, 'that must mean that you had sex.'

Amelia inched forward to the edge of the rock, dipped her toes in the water. 'Yep.'

'What's it like?'

'What's what like?'

'Sex.' George was fighting off a shy smile. 'What's sex like?'

Amelia took a deep breath, made ripples in the water as she moved her legs in a slow circle. 'It depends. But you have a long time before you need to think about that.'

'But I want to think about it now.'

Amelia took another bite of her sandwich, fed Lucy a piece of cheese. She pulled Lucy in close and rested an arm across her back. Something splashed in the water a few metres away; Lucy scanned the area, lifted a paw in readiness.

'So?' George said. 'What's it like? For you?'

'For me?'

'Yeah.'

The cicadas seemed to grow louder, and as her vision wavered it was as if for a moment the insect vibrations were coming from inside her own head. 'Well, it's complicated, I guess.'

'Complicated how? Like, is it good or bad?'

'I guess that depends. It's best if you feel safe. If you trust the person you're with. Then it might be good.'

'Hmm . . .'

'But really, it's way more fun being a kid. Once you're an adult and maybe doing those things, you'll wish you could go back to being a kid.'

George kicked her legs, made a flurry of white water. 'Wanna swim again?'

'Yeah, sure,' Amelia said.

*

They walked barefoot along the main street towards Wattle Lodge. Amelia's hair released drips down her back and a patch of George's dress darkened as it grew wet. The air was warm but the sun was beginning to set, surrendering its sting; the town was painted golden. The patterned materials of a sewing shop danced behind glass.

The swim had lightened Amelia's steps, loosened something. The tiredness in her body was vivid, in her upper arms and stomach from clenching around the rope; she would sleep well tonight. She imagined a hot shower, then melting onto the mattress at the motel. She'd close the door behind her, just for one night.

George ran her fingers along buildings as she walked, leaving slimy trails along shopfront windows. She sang to herself, lifting her fingers at certain sounds, sometimes adding a twirl before returning to her path. Her feet slapped against the pavement and the remaining sunshine caught the fine hairs on her brown legs. She spun again, and there was a round stain on the white material of her dress; it had the deep red-black of blood.

'Stop for a sec,' Amelia said.

'What?' George said, turning to wait for Amelia to catch up.

'Are you hurt?'

'No, why?'

'There's a mark on your dress.'

George looked down. Lucy sniffed at the girl's ankles.

'Sugar,' George said, holding her dress out to examine the stain. She hitched the material up past her waist, showing the row of blue flowers along the top of her swimmer bottoms. A fat, black leech took its fill, attached to George's not-yet-there hip. Bright, fresh blood was smeared around it. George smacked at it once, but it didn't let go. She hopped up and down. 'What should I do, what should I do?'

'Calm down. Just stop for a sec!'

George managed to slow herself but couldn't help flapping her hands around the leech. Beige stripes ran up its ribbed, pulsing body, both alien ends of it suctioned onto George's skin. Amelia's own skin crawled; there was every chance they were hanging off her too. As if it were aware of having been discovered, the leech dropped off, hitting the ground without a sound in the eerie way of insects. It wriggled, full and stupid from its meal. Lucy sniffed at it but didn't go too close. George jumped away and Amelia stepped back, too.

'You all right?' Amelia said.

'Yeah,' George said. 'Fine. See 'em all the time.'

The leech continued to wriggle between their two sets of bare feet; Amelia considered squashing it with a stick or a rock, but decided to let it be. George had other ideas; she slipped on her thongs and hovered her foot over the creature before stamping down hard. The leech exploded, and George lost her balance for a moment on the slipperiness of it. The murder scene glittered in the afternoon sunlight.

They continued walking. George was silent after the shock. Amelia searched her own body for invasion, running her hands up and down her legs and arms, willing herself to do so even though if she had one or more on her, she'd prefer them to remain a dirty secret, dropping off when they'd taken what they wanted.

'Lift up your shirt,' George said. 'I'll check ya.'

Amelia leaned her pack against a pole then held out the material of her T-shirt. George placed her clammy, small hands on her abdomen, gently spinning her around, her face serious while she inspected Amelia. 'Okay, crouch down.' Amelia's knee cracked as she squatted to George's height. She held Amelia's wrist, ran her finger over the rubber bands.

'What are these for?' George said.

Amelia shrugged. 'I just like them.'

'They're too tight. You should take them off or they'll cut off your circulation.' George held her eye and flicked one of the rubber bands. Amelia didn't flinch.

George continued the search, pulling at the neck of Amelia's T-shirt and feeling the surface of her back with her palms. 'All clear,' she said, her voice full of importance. 'Now check me.' She lifted her arms in the air and turned slowly. Amelia looked down her back, checked her armpits and neck; George lifted her dress and Amelia scanned her tummy.

'I've got an outie,' George said, fingering her bellybutton.

'Mine's an innie,' Amelia said. 'All clear.' She pulled George's dress back down, wished all the protection she could muster over the child and her bright, blind trust.

'Phew. That thing was a jerk,' George said.

Amelia hoisted her pack on and they continued down the street, George checking her reflection in the glass of shopfronts, trying to catch a glimpse of the red blotch on her dress, of the blood splattered up her ankles.

By the time they returned, dusk had settled over Wattle Lodge. A man and a woman leaned over a balcony wearing matching singlets and holding a stubby each. Amelia watched them track George as she crossed the car park.

When she was near her door, George dropped to a crouch and gathered Lucy in her arms; she draped herself around her neck, clutching her fur in melodramatic fists. 'Bye, Lu-Lu,' she said. Lucy wriggled to get free and George stood, squaring up to Amelia. They stared at each other. George's skin was lit orange by an overhead lamppost, her limbs stretched long in her shadow. George turned and leapt over a row of bushes.

'Hey,' Amelia called out.

George turned, the whites of her eyes glistening.

'See ya,' Amelia said. She took a couple of steps towards the girl, lifted her arms in offer of an embrace.

'Bye,' George said. She ran, her feet slapping on the cement. She pushed softly into the room, then closed the door on a wedge of light coming from within.

Amelia dropped her arms, shifted the weight of her pack. She watched the window where she had first caught George staring, searched for one last look at her open, freckled face. The curtains remained drawn.

The hiss then crack of a can opening came from above; she looked up and the same man was there. He sipped his drink, nodded to her. She walked beneath the balcony. Once out of view, she unzipped the section of her pack containing her rocket pen, then dug out the postcard George had chosen. The glossy side held the child's fingerprints, the whorls visible when Amelia held the card up to the light.

Lucy rustled in a nearby garden bed. Amelia sat cross-legged on the ground and wrote Sid's Melbourne address, resting the postcard on her thigh. The rocket pen struggled and she shook it back to life. Having not planned what she would write, she carefully shaped the characters of their code:

Remember that day we tried to get lost in the gully? We both pretended we didn't know the way home and then we started to believe it.

She paused, tapped the postcard with the rocket end of the pen. Lucy approached, then stopped in front of her, ears raised, head cocked. Amelia gave her a soft tap on the end of the nose with the pen and Lucy's tail wagged as she mouthed at Amelia's wrist.

'That's enough,' Amelia said, patting Lucy's back down into a sitting position. 'That's it, good girl. Good girl.'

Amelia wrote:

I'm thinking of coming to see you.

She looked at the symbols – a circle, a pair of glasses, a tree – that had smudged beneath her wrist. She scribbled the last line out, cutting deep lines into the cardboard, then blocked it out with a long, black rectangle. She signed off with their three stars, missing, wishing, thinking, then:

PS. Happy birthday.

She had to squeeze that part in, the symbols slender and small. There was something else she wished she'd written, but she couldn't quite find the words. Each time she drew nearer to them, they moved further away, deeper into the clouds of her mind. She pictured Sid's hands holding the card, his fingerprints mingling with her own, with George's.

Amelia popped open the buckles of her bag, loosened the drawstring. She pulled out a tin of food for Lucy and sifted through things till she found her bowl. Lucy followed Amelia's every move as the items were revealed, her eyebrows twitching. The food was chunks of meat in gravy. While Lucy ate, Amelia nibbled the end of a muesli bar, moved oats around her dry mouth.

The lights went off in George's room across the car park.

The balcony couple had expanded to become some kind of gathering; laughter animated the still night, drifted down to Amelia who lurked below, her back to the wall. She tucked her legs to her chest to make sure she couldn't be seen.

When Lucy was finished, Amelia cleaned the bowl with some toilet paper from her pack and put the mess in the bin. They walked the footpath around the outskirts of the car park, pausing in front of her room. The green paint of the doorframe was splintered and there were punctures around the handle of the screen door. Someone had left a light on for her inside. She scuffed her feet on the welcome mat, dipped into her pocket for the key.

The door wasn't locked. She pushed it open. A double bed filled most of the room. Ron and Brenda sat on top of the covers, propped up by pillows.

'Sorry, I . . .' Amelia backed out the doorway, her cheeks burning.

'No, no, you're fine. Come on in,' Brenda said, smiling. She was in a pale green nightie, buttoned up the front, a round neckline revealing her pink, patchy skin. 'You've been gone quite a while. Everything okay?'

'Yeah, fine thanks.'

Lucy entered the room between the doorframe and Amelia's leg. She went to the bed and sniffed at Ron's bare feet. 'Oi,' Amelia said, 'get out of it.' Lucy's ears flattened, her tail sunk between her legs. Ron's eyes were fixed on the television, light flickering across his face.

Once she saw it, she couldn't look away: a fold-out mattress was tucked into the narrow space between the television cabinet and the foot of the double bed.

'It's certainly not the finest of establishments, but it will do,' Brenda said. 'We're in close quarters tonight. Like camping!'

Amelia stood for too long, her feet pinned to the ground. Ron's ankles were crossed and beige boxers bunched up around his crotch. His knees protruded in white, bony hills, and at those, she looked away.

'There's animal fur everywhere,' he said. His eyes remained on the television.

Brenda rested her hand on Ron's. 'Hopefully you'll be able to get a good night's rest, safe and . . . comfortable,' Brenda said, smiling sweetly at Amelia.

Amelia nodded, shifted her weight. 'Thanks.' The vision of a night to herself evaporated.

She swung her pack to the ground. As she delved in to find her toiletries, she was conscious of each clang and rustle. Ron turned the volume up. She gave in, lifted the whole thing onto her back and edged through the gap between her bed and theirs. Ron craned one way then the other as she blocked the television. Amelia lifted her hand to Lucy, mouthed 'Stay'. She grabbed the white towel from the end of the fold-out bed and pushed open the bathroom door.

Fumbling up the wall, she found the switch; a light blinked on, accompanied by a loud exhaust fan. The tiles were brown, the sink chipped and cream-coloured. The door had no lock. She rested her pack up against it. She undressed, keeping an eye on the doorhandle, anticipating its twist.

With one foot resting on the bath, she prodded at bruises on her legs, the newer ones giving off small flares of pain, the older ones numb. A bite on the side of her thigh oozed as she squeezed it. There was a scar on her knee, the new skin still sensitive; a chunk of gravel was trapped in it, knobbly beneath her fingertips.

Leaning in close to the mirror, she found new lines on her forehead, around her eyes. Her collarbones were more prominent than she remembered and her shoulders were browned, the skin tight over curved bones. She tried to examine her belly, but the angle was all wrong. She stepped up and balanced on the bath's slippery edge. She crouched so she could see her stomach and the tops of her thighs in the mirror. Her belly was curved and hard. She pinched with her thumb and index finger and collected a small fold of skin. She tried to turn around to see the cellulite that dimpled the area at the back of her thighs but lost her balance, stepped down onto the warm tiles.

She scratched at the point between her breasts where lace and sweat had made a raised, red rash. Her nipple hardened as her hand brushed it, and she cupped her breast, holding her own eye in the mirror. She pushed her breasts together as she had when she was a child, before there was much to hold, trying to understand what Zach felt beneath his hand when he touched her, how it differed from his girlfriend who was the same age as him. Now, her own touch was hard to bear as she held the weight of each breast in her palms. Her heart was there beneath the barrier of flesh, quickening. She released her grasp, closed her eyes. *Stupid girl.* It sounded like her mother's voice. *Stupid, stupid girl.* She opened her eyes, but could look at the mirror no longer.

In the shower, she scrubbed herself with vigour, softening her skin with water so hot it made her catch her breath. A pink razor rested in the soap dish. She could pop the blade out and make simple, straight lines of pain in her skin. Pain of her own design, with a beginning, and an end; pain that she could see. But George's little hand was holding her wrist, turning the skin white, and she was saying the bands were too tight. The child was shaking her head, eyes widening in disapproval.

Amelia flicked the bands at her wrist, turned her face away from the razor and into the scalding jet of water.

When she was finished, she stepped out of the shower and wrapped herself in a towel. She longed to put on her favourite Rage Against the Machine T-shirt, to feel the soft material hanging loose around her body. She yanked it out of the side of her pack. She held it out in front of her, her old friend, curled the seam of it around her finger and pulled it. The material remembered Will, brought him into the bathroom: the smell of his sweat, his ute, his mouth. The betrayal was swift; she bundled the shirt up and shoved it down the side of her bag.

When she stepped out of the bathroom, the room was dark, the television off. A small desk fan creaked from side to side. Light from the car park entered the room and showed the shapes of Ron and Brenda beneath a sheet. Lucy stood from her position by the entrance, her collar tags chiming. Amelia rested her bag against the wall. She crawled over her bed and lay on her stomach, pressed the side of Lucy's face into her own, then slid between cool, crisp sheets.

There was stirring from the double bed and Brenda sat up. The numbers on the alarm clock gave her face a red glow.

'Night-night,' she said.

'Night,' Amelia said, pulling the sheet high up to her chin.

Her body twitched, her skin prickling with sweat as she waited for the private sounds of the couple's sleep to fill the room. Ron's breaths were long and deep, with a whistle through his nose on the exhale. Brenda's were quick and shallow, as if she was poised on the verge of being awake, ready for action. Amelia forced herself to breathe in time with the movement of the curtain; inhaling as it pushed out, exhaling as it was sucked back into the open window, dragging its ends along the sill.

Amelia and her mother had slept in close quarters like this when they hiked the Overland Track. They slept in cabins along the way, the two of them amid rows of tired bushwalking bodies laid out on wooden platforms beside, above and across from them. It was just after they found out the cancer had come back, and her mother said the trek would be the last thing she'd tick off her bucket list. Amelia could pick out her mother's breathing in the rustle and thump and the breathing of strangers. If her mother was too quiet, Amelia reached out and touched her sleeping bag to feel the movement of her chest, to make sure the breaths were still coming.

Ron mumbled something, turned over with a squeak of springs. He sighed back into slumber. Amelia was hot and sticky beneath the sheet. She lifted a leg out, an arm, but her limbs were too close to the double bed, only a few inches between her body and theirs.

*

Amelia woke during the night and didn't know where she was. Hours, days and weeks seeped into each other, spinning and slipping around her head. Lucy huffed as she rearranged herself; these shared moments of wakefulness were so common now. Amelia reached out to her, awaited the press of Lucy's nose into her palm.

She listened for Ron and Brenda, tracked their breathing, but it wasn't enough. Her sheets were damp and when she kicked them off, Lucy was there, sniffing at her legs. Amelia lifted her pack, tensing her muscles to hold the thing close to her. She stood and walked on the pads of her feet to the side of the double bed, near the door. They lay still, the sheet discarded in a tangle at the bottom of the mattress; Brenda was on her back with her head towards the door, legs open and feet pointing upwards. The fan stirred wisps of hair around her face. The top buttons of her nightgown were open and Ron's arm was across her, his hand inside the material, resting on the bare skin of her breast.

A train hammered somewhere down the road, setting the walls shaking. Amelia stepped back from the bed and crouched in darkness by the door.

'What the fuck,' Ron said, turning over in the bed, still asleep. Amelia thought she saw Brenda's eyes flutter open and then close again. Their breathing settled. Amelia stepped closer, saw how Ron put a hand behind him, maintaining a point of connectedness with Brenda's thigh. A musty smell rose from them, their foreheads each carrying a sheen of sweat. Amelia stood, watching, while the seconds flashed by on the alarm clock: 1.13 am. She leaned over them, her eyes following the shapes of their bodies, the impossible peace and stillness of them.

Ron jerked and Amelia stepped away. She patted her leg, and Lucy was at her side. She lifted her pack over one shoulder and pulled open the front door. She thought she heard a whimper from Brenda, perhaps a question, but she pulled on her shoes and walked into the night.

She passed through Crystal Brook, retracing the steps she'd taken with George. Lucy was beside her, looking up for a direction every time Amelia stepped off a kerb, as if unsure of the plan. Amelia reassured her with an occasional touch to the head. A red postbox stood sentry on the main street; Amelia stopped to slip Sid's postcard through its mouth.

They turned right at a roundabout, following green road signs that indicated the highway. A footpath travelled in front of houses facing off across a wide road. A lull of sleep filled the air. Passing darkened windows, she imagined bodies sprawled across beds, murmurings of dreams, the breath of families mingling in hallways. The street became too small, the homes and dying lawns and potted plants leering at her. She forged ahead, breaking into a run, her chest becoming tight with the effort.

After a rail crossing, houses became more sparse, gardens spreading out into farmland. Amelia stopped, hands on her knees as she caught her breath. Grass rustled nearby, then a thump. The moon was bright, reflecting in the eyes of a group of cows gathered behind a barbed-wire fence. Lucy watched them, raised a front paw.

'Leave it,' Amelia said. Lucy held her ground for a moment before approaching Amelia, tail between her legs. 'That's it, good girl,' she said, holding Lucy's face in her hands; she scratched her ears. 'That's a good girl.' Her voice was foreign; the night was better without it.

A road sign promised a rest stop five kilometres ahead. The white line along the edge of the road faded as she walked, then suddenly grew bold again, as if the line machine had refilled its paint cartridge. Lucy's wet nose touched her calf. She dragged her hand along the curved cement of the road barrier, feeling the private divot where one section joined another; these secrets of the highway confirmed she wasn't meant to be there, but the secrets were safe with her.

When she hiked the Overland Track with her mother, they walked past bundles of wood and wire left in the scrub; they were dropped from helicopters so that rangers could mend parts of the duckboard trail. She had found comfort in this unspoken, inexact process, how the remoteness of the area caused people to adapt. As they walked, she had wanted to tell her mother about Zach. The confession was acid burning at the base of her throat. Though there was lots of time as they walked the track, it seemed to fill with small practicalities: adding layers of clothing or taking them off, sharing out handfuls of trail mix, trying to absorb mountain vistas. She couldn't make the words come out, couldn't poison the experience for her mother.

A truck approached behind them. She pressed herself against the cement barrier and tucked Lucy in behind her legs. An image of her body striking the windscreen flashed through her mind too quickly for her to eliminate it. She saw herself lying by the side of the road, her body at odds with the life leaving it.

The power of the vehicle pinned her against the barrier. Once the truck was gone, Lucy whimpered, her ears tucked back on her head.

'Won't be long, Luce,' she said. 'Sorry, girl. Not long now.'

They continued walking along the highway. Amelia thought of all the steps she'd taken with her mother on their hike, how she'd slowed her pace so she didn't get too far ahead. Of bathing her mother's blisters while her mother drank a hot chocolate to sweeten the pain.

Amelia's footsteps crunched over gravel and she wanted to speak to her mother, wondered if she would be able to hear Amelia's thoughts or whether she'd have to say it out loud. She opened her mouth; her throat was dry. She reached for her Mount Franklin and took a sip. The plastic crackled as she shoved it back into the side pocket of her pack. She walked further, washing saliva around her mouth in an effort to keep it moist.

'Mum,' she said. Her voice was a surprise. It hung heavy in the air, unanswered. Amelia left it there, rejected and alone amid the clicking and stirring of the night.

She stepped slowly out onto the asphalt; felt the slick, hard surface of it beneath her feet. The road was quiet, and at the centre of it, where the white line was broken into large dashes, she stopped. With one foot in each lane she stared down any traffic that might be heading away from Crystal Brook. Lucy was obeying her order to stay at the side of the road, though she looked on with her head cocked to the side. Amelia closed her eyes, forced herself to turn; her shoes scuffed as she rotated, facing the other lane of potential vehicles. She held her arms out at her sides as if crucified, dared herself to block her ears. Her scalp bristled; she was suddenly cold. A fresh breeze lifted her hair off her face, and she wondered if that might be it, her mother's answer.

Lucy barked, piercing and sure, and Amelia scuttled back to the side of the highway.

When they reached the rest stop, the night sky was starting to fade into deep grey. A light flickered over the entrance to a public toilet. Poles held up shelters over picnic benches, and they were like her, faceless figures in a sleepless night.

A set of metal stairs provided a bridge over a fence; she crossed it and Lucy followed behind, her nails scraping on the metal. One of the fence posts was surrounded by thicker tufts of grass than the others and she set herself up against it. She took her pack off and opened it, digging around for her jumper. The rocket pen waited in its usual pocket; she fished it out and held it in her hand, clicking it up and down with her thumb. She bundled some clothes into a pillow and lay down, tucking into her pack, its contours pressed to hers. Lucy returned and snuggled against Amelia's stomach; she draped her arm around her and closed her eyes.

*

Liquid pattered the earth near her head. She sat upright, insides lurching as she tried to work out where she was. The liquid slowed and there was a cough, a shuffle of feet, before a second innings. She sat very still. Lucy looked beyond Amelia towards the activity. The smell of piss grew sweet and crisp.

The dawn wasn't deep enough to cover them; Amelia could identify the apricot colour of the T-shirt the nearby figure wore. A joint cracked, a fly zipped up. Lucy stood, her collar tags chiming like a cathedral bell. The intruder whistled and Lucy let out a low growl. 'Here, pup,' the man said.

'Can I help you?' Amelia said. She stood up, shook pins and needles out of her arm.

'Shit!' The man scampered off, checking over his shoulder before disappearing into a car. Amelia reached out to the fence to balance herself; her hand closed around a barb, and she tightened her grip into a fist. The sting of it awakened her, sliced through the mist in her still-waking mind.

The sky was grey, still on the cusp of night, though a thin layer of gold was unfolding along the horizon. The car with the pissing man in it backed out of the rest stop and made its way onto the highway, indicator flashing. She checked her pack for dark patches of piss but it was dry. Lucy sniffed at the wet patch one pole down, then marked her own place there. Amelia followed suit, walking a few steps into the dry paddock. She tugged her shorts down and squatted behind a lone shrub.

Some birds were beginning their day; two kookaburras gargled from overhead powerlines. Amelia pulled out a dog treat for Lucy, then crossed over the bridge into the rest stop. She walked on tiptoe over the crunchy ground, not wanting to disturb the inhabitants of a campervan who were yet to emerge.

The top semicircle of the sun peeked out over the land. The branch of a gum tree framed the pastels in the sky, the curve of the surrounding hills. The light burned white flares into her vision. It was beautiful, that was clear, but it was hard to know what to do with the view. Sitting still to watch it wasn't an option, wasn't the relaxing experience it was meant to be. There was a limit to how much she could appreciate the sky when it was her constant companion.

In the white room, she had dangled her legs out the window and watched the sunrise most mornings. It was easier to appreciate it when she looked out that window, her own private view of the whole big thing rather than it watching her as she travelled for hours beneath it. She had to wrestle the flyscreen off, then sit on the window frame with metal ridges digging in to her thighs, but it was worth the effort. Watching the sunrise from the white room, right on the east coast, she could guess at how many people had seen the sun already that day, and she wondered where she would have to go to be the first. Each morning was a slightly different palette, different shades and strengths of colour, and she liked the structure it gave to her days. That small view of the morning made the following hours simpler, somehow; if she achieved nothing else, at least she'd seen the day begin.

Since leaving the white room, she couldn't get the same feeling when she looked at her surroundings. Instead she found herself standing, staring, as she was then, at an apple-juice box that had tumbled out of a rubbish bin, while the spectacle of the sun or the desert or the rainforest continued all around her.

She crouched in front of Lucy, who wagged her tail and licked at Amelia's face. Amelia pulled her close, laid her face against the fur of Lucy's back. There was a whiff of Brenda's floral perfume there.

She walked to the highway. The traffic came in little bursts, as if a bunch of vehicles had been set loose all at the same time, like racing greyhounds. After dumping her pack on the ground, she stood where an extra lane peeled off, leading to the rest stop entrance. Fighting the reluctant muscles in her arm, she stuck her thumb out and waited.

*

The sun rose and heated the day quickly as the hours passed. Amelia rolled up her T-shirt sleeves so they sat in rings around her shoulders. She guessed it was about ten in the morning. Cars rolled past her, indifferent. Lucy explored the scrub by the side of the road; something stirred and scuttled away. Lucy bounced after it then came to a sudden standstill and sneezed. She caught Amelia watching and her ears flattened, her tail wagging then sinking between her legs as she approached for a pat.

'This is no good, Luce, is it,' Amelia said. She scratched beneath Lucy's collar, then moved round to behind her ears. 'This is no good at all.'

Amelia rummaged in her pack for the remainder of last night's muesli bar, then stepped off the road for a break. They headed to find shade at the rest stop. A few cars passed as her back was turned, and she wondered what opportunities she'd missed. Perhaps she'd be stuck here. She could find a place a bit further from the cars and people, make a little den, and no one in the world would know where she was. Maybe she'd tell Sid, though; walk back into Crystal Brook and send him another postcard to let him know where he could find her. It wouldn't be fair on him if she was to disappear completely.

Three sets of benches and tables were in a line, spaced along the length of the rest stop, each with a metal roof angled over it for shade. The first two were occupied so she walked on to the last in the row. As she stepped up to it she saw a small red knapsack on the ground, leaning against the table. The name D-A-R-R-Y-L was printed on it in clumsy letters with thick black texta. A worn sticker of the Teenage Mutant Ninja Turtles graced the front pocket. Lucy sniffed at the bag. Amelia turned to leave but, as she did so, a man in a beige T-shirt and shorts emerged from the scrub. He wore gaiters, and a set of binoculars hung around his neck.

'No need to go,' he said, walking in big, bouncy strides towards the picnic bench. 'Plenty of room.'

'Oh, it's fine, thanks,' Amelia said.

'Please, be my guest.' He took off his wide-brimmed brown hat. Sweat ran in lines down the side of his face. He sat down. His hair was white and thinning, and patches of bare scalp were speckled with red marks.

'Yes?' he said, looking up at her.

'Sorry?' she said.

'What would you like? You've got questions written all over your face.'

'I was just going to sit here in the shade and cool off.'

'Well, by all means.' He eyed Lucy, who stood at attention, watching him.

Amelia slid in to the very edge of the bench, diagonally opposite from the man, and unhooked her bag from her shoulders. He pulled out a pocket book of birds, scanned the index, drawing a long-nailed finger down the page.

'You travelling alone?' he said, keeping his eyes on the book.

'I could ask you the same thing,' she said, pulling her Mount Franklin bottle out of her backpack and cradling it in her lap.

'You could,' he said. He smiled, his eyes still down, licked his thin lips. Lucy snuffled at his feet, found something of particular interest on his knee.

Amelia lifted the front of her shirt, used it to wipe her face. She unscrewed the cap of her bottle and gulped the warm water. A small island of dry skin had dislodged from the man's scalp and worked its way to the end of a hair.

'I've been looking for birds, you see,' he said.

'Oh yeah,' she said. 'Found any good ones?'

'Lots of *Corvus orru*.'

'Crows?' Amelia said.

'That's right. Eye-eaters.'

She waited for him to go on but he didn't. 'Surely you've seen something more exciting than a crow.'

He smiled up at her, his small eyes flashing with something despite their blackness. 'Well, I found you,' he said.

Something folded over inside her gut; heat rose in her cheeks. 'What bird am I?'

'A Gouldian finch. Rare, fast, colourful.'

She smiled though she didn't want to. He drummed his fingers on the table, then scratched his head. The flake of dried skin fluttered to the bench.

'Will you please get your dog away from me?' Lucy was still investigating something on his leg.

'Oh, yeah, sorry. Lucy, come.' She obeyed. Amelia moved out from the bench, swung her legs around and to the ground.

'I do love dogs. They are an exceptional species.' He held her eye. 'I didn't mean to snap. They're just so changeable. And they usually don't like me.' He laughed and it was reedy and nasal, over as soon as it started. He clicked his fingers, trying to regain Lucy's attention, but she ignored him.

'Well, see ya,' Amelia said.

'Where are you going?'

'East.' She hefted her pack over one shoulder. Lucy followed closely as she walked away.

'But –' he said, his voice breaking. She was already a few paces away as he cleared his throat. 'You can come with me. Gouldian finch. I'll take you!'

Amelia pretended she didn't hear. She raised a hand to her brow as a shield from the sun. In need of a mission, she walked towards the toilet. There was a queue. A child hopped from foot to foot, clutching herself while her father looked frantically for other options. A teenage couple were kissing, and Amelia caught flashes of tongue; the boy's hands were on the girl's bottom, pinching where her shorts revealed the beginning of her bum cheek. Amelia changed her trajectory, turning abruptly away from the couple and walking up beside the toilet cubicle. *Stupid girl.*

A bin overflowed, flies suckling at melted chocolate around the rim. Lucy found half a bread roll; she extracted a slice of ham with her teeth, swallowed it, then ripped into the bread, holding it in place with a paw. Amelia dug in her pockets, wanting to rid herself of junk she'd collected along the trip.

She reached deep into them and thought of the keys Zach always wore hanging from a belt loop near his front pocket. They jangled as he worked in the garden, and the weight of them pulled down on his shorts. At the beginning he gave her some jobs to do to help him, and she'd been bursting to tell her mother how she'd used her foot and the force of her body to break through dry soil. How at first it was too hard, but Zach showed her how to angle and wiggle the fork so that cracks appeared in the ground and it eventually broke through. When he looked at her, her insides turned to powder. He pressed on her lower back to correct her posture as she dug, and as they worked, the smell of his sweat grew stronger.

She plucked the bands at her wrist. *Stupid girl.*

She pulled handfuls of rubbish out of her pocket and threw them away: tissues in dry, hard balls, the foil of the empty pill packet. A two-dollar coin fell out and she picked it up, kept it. The paper towel with Brenda's red digits on it fluttered towards the ground and Amelia snatched it from the air. The numbers were smudged; one of them was either a seven or a one, another a four or a nine. She tore the paper towel in two, then into squares, and smaller still, reaching her hand over the bin and sifting the pieces through her fingers. There was a chance they would drive past her, or perhaps they already had. If she had to see them again, she would pretend she didn't know them, was already working hard to forget their faces.

Next to the bin, a tap was attached to the side of the toilet block. She pulled her Rage Against the Machine T-shirt from the side of her bag, releasing the smell of Will soaked into its weave. She shuddered, holding it between her thumb and index finger. Moving quickly, she put the shirt under the tap and turned it on. Only a dribble escaped but she held the material up to it, kept turning the tap with her other hand, searching for more pressure. It was no good. She scrubbed the material of the shirt together but parts of it were still dry, others hardly even damp.

'Shit.' She shoved the shirt back into the pocket of her bag. Lucy watched, blinking slowly, on the edge of dozing. Amelia took a deep breath, tried to let Lucy's calmness enter her. She crouched and Lucy stepped forward, allowed Amelia to rest her forehead against the soft fur of her own. The sun found a new angle down her neck, heating the skin on the top of her back.

'What are we doing, Luce,' she said. 'What are we doing.'

Lucy pulled away and licked at a wet patch on the ground. Amelia stood up, held her unsteady hands out in front of her, turned them over, palms up. She wet her face, then breathed. Counted to ten. Breathed again.

A group of four middle-aged people sat ten or so metres away on another picnic bench. A curly-haired woman wore a long purple dress, and her feet tangled under the table with those of a squat man wearing a straw hat. The woman threw her head back and laughed. Another man in board shorts and no shirt drank from a large bottle of Fanta, wiped his mouth with the back of his hand, watching the slim woman across from him as she smoked with an averted gaze. Amelia forced herself to walk over to them, each step a battle.

The man in the hat saw her coming, whispered something to the others. They stopped talking and turned towards her.

'Hello there,' the man said when Amelia was still several metres away. 'What can we do ya for?' His voice was low and muffled, his eyes unreadable behind Ray-Ban sunnies.

'Well, looks like you might have a full car, but thought I'd try my luck anyway,' she said.

'Go on then,' the man said, looking around at the others, as if making sure they were tuned in to his performance. Only the purple-dress woman paid attention; she leaned forward, showing the creased, sun-damaged skin of her cleavage.

'I'm looking for a ride out of here, for Lucy and me,' Amelia said, indicating Lucy with a tilt of her head.

'Why?' he said. 'You on the run or something?' It was a joke; he appealed to the others for support. The woman in the purple dress laughed enough to make an opal pendant jiggle on her breasts.

'You have any space for the two of us?'

110

'Well, there's the boot,' he said, and now he had won the whole table over. 'Or the front seat, but that's only if you put out more than this one,' he said, nodding at the purple-dress woman. She pretended to slap him. The smoking woman flashed dark eyes up at Amelia, quickly looked away.

'Great. Thanks for that,' Amelia said, turning her back.

'I'm just joshin' ya, jeez. Try a sense of humour on for size,' the man said. She continued walking, didn't quite catch the man's newest witticism, but heard the round of laughter that rewarded it.

She exhaled and tapped the side of her shorts. *Disgusting. You are disgusting.*

Her skin prickled as she felt the eyes at the rest stop on her, some of them sizing her up, others hoping she wouldn't approach them, pitying her, perhaps even envying her. She'd been told by people that they wished they could be free like her. She tried to be this idea of being free, then, but she was stuck in the small world of herself, unable to grasp any of the liberty on offer.

She and Sid used to catch insects when they were kids. They'd trap moths and other creatures and watch them bump up against the plastic of the bug catcher. They caught a caterpillar once; it was fluorescent green with a yellow underbelly and a series of stumpy, clumsy-looking legs. They decided to mark it in the hope they could release it and find it again later. Amelia had drawn a black line on it with a felt-tip pen, and the ink seeped into the soft green flesh, spreading so that the line grew thicker, blurred around the edges. She still remembered how squishy the caterpillar was beneath the pressure of her hand, how she could have stabbed the pen all the way through it. And how it had already been moving slowly, but when they released it into the veggie patch it was even more slow and dopey, resting on a leaf. Sid thought they'd hurt it but Amelia argued that it was just tired, that its leaf was like a couch and the creature was having a rest. The caterpillar died and the murder meant their bug-catching club became top secret, and though it lost almost any link to bugs, it remained a place where secrets lived and breathed, with the knowledge that they could and would always do so.

A group of three sat at the last table in the row. They looked about her age. A woman with black hair in a high, messy bun sat with two men, both in cut-off jeans and thongs. One of them wore a cap, the other had shaggy bleached hair. The three of them leaned into each other, taking photos, a picnic of white bread rolls and deli meats spread out before them. Amelia couldn't make herself move towards them. She stood, her feet immobile, staring at them till the woman looked up. The woman waved. Lucy trotted over, accepted a pat and a piece of meat.

'Nice dog,' the woman called.

'Ta,' Amelia said. She looked to her feet, the familiar fray of her shoelaces. She punched the side of her legs with each fist, tried to spark life into them. Her thighs were tight, holding their own. She called to Lucy and they returned to the highway.

She retraced her steps, walking back towards the entrance to the rest stop. There was a patch of gravel where potential rides could pull over. The shade from a tree was a narrow bar on the dirt, and she stood sideways in it, thumb out.

Traffic buffeted her as it passed, the bigger cars forcing her to step back or rebalance before reclaiming her strip of shade. The pain in her shoulders made her guts churn. She counted the cars, negotiating with herself; at fifty, she stepped back from the road. She swung her pack off her shoulders and rested it against a tree. As she stepped back up to the white line of the highway, a battered brown Kingswood flicked its indicator on. The car drove past but the driver caught her eye in the rear-vision mirror and pulled dramatically off the road, skidding for a metre or so on the gravel, lifting a haze of dust. Before Amelia could approach, a woman was out of the car and leaning over the open driver door, her hand a brim over squinted eyes.

'You okay?' The woman spoke much too loud for the distance between them.

'Yep,' Amelia said.

'Well, shit,' the woman said, lifting a hand to her chest. 'Thought you'd had an accident or something.'

'No, I'm fine. Sorry,' Amelia said. She took a few steps closer, stopped.

The woman seemed shaken, angling her head towards the ground as if to gather some strength before continuing. 'What are you up to then? And don't you dare tell me you're out here hitching . . .'

Amelia shrugged, scuffed her foot in the dirt.

'Oh god, the nerve of ya . . . do you have any idea the nutjobs that are out here? There's a reason people don't hitchhike anymore, sweetheart, and it's a bloody good one.' The woman crouched to look into the car and said: 'You better not be gettin' any ideas, missy.'

Lucy emerged from scrub and trotted to Amelia. 'Ah,' the woman said, 'well at least you're not completely alone. Fi, have a look at this.' The passenger window lowered and a teenage girl in oversized sunglasses pulled herself out of it, perched on the ledge.

'Hi,' the girl said with a nod, and Amelia lifted her hand in a wave. Lucy walked over, her snout pointed upwards. The girl dangled from the car and held a hand out. Lucy sniffed, licked, then accepted a pat.

'Jump in then.' The woman pointed to the car with a twitch of her head. 'We're not going far, but at least you won't be out in the middle of nowhere.' Her face wrinkled into well-used smile lines.

'Thanks a lot,' Amelia said. 'I'd really appreciate that.'

'Go and get that mountain of a backpack. I'll open the boot for ya 'cos it's a bloody nuisance – there's a knack to it.'

Amelia waited in the back seat, sitting on the driver's side, while the woman and the girl went to use the toilet. The seat covers were scratchy, a brown and red tartan that was worn thin where it had rubbed against sitting bodies. Old parking tickets sat up on the dashboard and a plastic bag hanging from the gearstick overflowed with food wrappers. There was a sense of closeness in the car. She looked up. A collage of photographs was tacked to the vinyl ceiling. Mostly teenage faces stared down at her wearing suspended smiles, the girl from the car one of many young bodies pressed in lined-up embraces, arms dangling over shoulders. The woman was up there, too, with the girl and a man, all pulling cross-eyed faces, dressed in neon green and pink.

A buzzing came from the centre of the car. Lucy stepped forward and investigated the well between the two front seats. A phone sat face up. It vibrated again, setting coins underneath it rattling. Amelia's own phone had been mostly still and silent. Even so, she'd destroyed it weeks ago, ground it up against bricks till the screen splintered and went black.

Messages stacked up on the phone, punctuated with x's and emojis, vegetables to vomiting faces. Life was brimming over from this car, bursting at the seams; Amelia felt she was the white styrofoam takeaway container in the footwell, holding a few stale crumbs.

The phone buzzed again and Lucy sniffed at it, left wet streaks from her nose on the screen.

'Out of it, Luce.'

The eyes of the photos overhead seared into her. She considered removing herself, retreating to the surrounding bushes. Sweat gathered on her top lip and she licked at it, held the saltiness on her tongue. There was a sourness to the air in the car and it might have been coming from her. She lowered her window; the handle was stiff and it jammed three-quarters of the way down.

The woman and the girl walked back to the car together, laughing at something, and the girl allowed herself to be brought under the woman's arm and squeezed. The girl's grey singlet was short, leaving a band of skin visible above her green shorts. A pendant dangled on a long chain between her breasts. Amelia was sure these two could tell each other *everything*, that they knew every last detail of each other's busy lives; that in some ways, they were the same person. Amelia's own mother had encouraged this telling of *everything* but neither of them quite managed it; they couldn't access the shelves where this endless and rich information about themselves was stored. Not like this pair. They were tapped into a rich source.

The girl screeched, then nuzzled her face into the woman's chest. Lucy let out a low bark; Amelia quietened her with a hand on the back. 'Shhh, girl. We're okay,' she said. 'We're okay.'

The woman's keys were laden with key rings, which rattled as she approached the door. 'Right, let's get this show on the road,' she said, plonking into her seat, causing the car to sink. A dog figurine on the dashboard became animated, wobbling its head. The girl slipped into the passenger seat, the door cracking as she pulled it shut. She unscrewed the cap of a drink and it gave way with a fizz. As she held the drink to her mouth, thin scars, crossways along her wrist, glimmered in the sun. The action was over quickly, and when Amelia searched for the scars again she couldn't see any blemish on the girl's skin.

'Let's start with your name then,' the woman said.

Amelia cleared her throat, gave her name. 'And this is Lucy.'

'Well, I'm Leanne, and this is my daughter, Fi.'

Fi turned in her seat, gave a curved, left-to-right wave. 'Hey,' she said. She stuck a fist out and Lucy licked her knuckles. From the corner of her eye, Amelia searched the girl's arms for signs of damage.

The girl lifted her oversized sunglasses onto the top of her head, pinning long strands of hair with dyed red streaks behind her ears. She had yesterday's make-up on. The skin beneath her large hazel eyes was speckled with glitter, and black chunks of mascara dotted her cheeks and the inside of her nose.

'Oh, sorry,' she said, licking a finger and wiping it beneath each of her eyes. 'I'm a mess.'

'You're fine,' Amelia said. She'd been staring again.

Fi moved her sunglasses back to her face, pushing them up on the bridge of her nose with an index finger. Her shiny hair was set free again, along with a waft of watermelon shampoo.

'I literally look terrible,' Fi said.

Leanne slapped at the air near her daughter, shook her head. 'I dunno where she gets this rubbish from,' Leanne said, appealing to Amelia in the mirror.

Leanne drove out of the rest stop, the car lurching as she mishandled the clutch. There was a car fast approaching on the highway but she eased out in front of it. Amelia looked out the back window. The car caught up to them, the driver flashing their lights in anger.

'Thanks, darl!' Leanne yelled into the rear-vision mirror, raising a meaty arm, then using it to shift through the gears.

'So, where you from then?' Leanne said. 'I'm assuming you're not local . . .'

'From a little town on the east coast,' Amelia said. 'No one's heard of it.' It was nice to imagine for a moment that everything had begun in the white room by the ocean.

'I know what it's like to come from one of *those* towns,' Fi said. She arched her plucked eyebrows and turned around with a thump, facing forward. She kicked her thongs off and put her feet on the dash. The sunshine highlighted fine hairs on the joints of her big toes, and a few around her ankle that had escaped the razor.

'We're going home, to Tailem Bend,' Leanne said. 'I'm happy to drop you anywhere along the way.'

'Okay, thanks,' Amelia said, trying to place Tailem Bend on the map in her mind.

'You two headed anywhere in particular?' Leanne said.

Amelia closed her eyes as they accelerated, feeling the wind on her cheeks. 'Melbourne,' she said.

'What's there for you, sweetheart?' Leanne said.

'A friend. My best friend.'

'Oh, good. Great,' Leanne said, and there was relief in the way her shoulders rose as she took in a deep breath, sank as she let it go.

'Where's Tailem Bend?' Amelia said.

'Three hours south,' Leanne said. 'It's one of them places no one's ever heard of.' She smiled, half-turning her head.

The car settled into silence. Occasional signs showed distances decreasing as they drew closer to the towns and cities beyond.

Leanne squirted hand cream from a bottle wedged beside her seat, steered with her thighs as she rubbed it in to her skin. Fi was soon asleep, her head crashing forward and waking her up with a start. Amelia took in the photographs above her, spotting Fi amid the different crowds, learning the composition of her posed faces: slight pout; widened eyes, so that she looked at the edge of fear.

'Been at work,' Leanne offered, breaking the quiet and jolting Fi awake. 'This one's been at her friend's place, getting up to mischief, no doubt.'

'As if,' Fi said, stretching her arms. There was still no sign of the marks Amelia had seen. 'There's nothin' to do in Crystal Brook.'

'I reckon you'd find something, little miss,' Leanne said. She leaned back in her seat, flattened a hand near her mouth as if telling Amelia a secret. 'She's got a new boyfriend, you see,' she said.

'Mum!' Fi said, pushing Leanne's arm.

The car was quiet again. Fi gathered her knees to her chest, making a dark crease where thigh met calf. She was long and lean, no hint of an adult's extra folds of flesh. There was a pinkish patch above Fi's shoulderblade; around it, a few threads of sunburned skin that had not yet peeled. Amelia wondered if her boyfriend kissed that new patch of skin; if he held her naked, took her breasts into his mouth; whether he sucked his fingers and put them far up inside her. Whether Fi liked it or whether she didn't know what to feel.

Amelia snapped the rubber bands, felt each sting burn then fade. The tightness of the elastic had left bluish imprints in her skin.

'What you doin' out here then?' Leanne said, shouting over the noise of the wind buffeting through the open windows, and an overtaking motorbike.

Amelia leaned forward in her seat. She spoke loudly, too: 'Just travellin'.'

'Huh,' Leanne said. 'And how's that working out for ya?'

Amelia watched the road rushing towards her, disappearing beneath the car, and she missed the intimacy with it in that moment, wished the rising heat of it against the soles of her shoes, her calves. 'So far so good.'

'Living the dream,' Fi said.

'Living the dream,' Amelia said, settling back into her seat. She placed her chin in her hand, let the wind draw tears from her eyes. Lucy circled on the seat and then curled up, blinked slowly.

'You in some kind of trouble?' Leanne said.

Fi turned in her seat and lifted her glasses. She rolled her eyes, mouthed 'Sorry'.

'No,' Amelia said. 'No trouble.'

'You sure? I'm a nurse, and the mother of a teenage daughter,' Leanne said. 'I can smell trouble.' She lifted a hand off the wheel and waggled a ringed finger, the skin clogged up around the metal. 'Don't think you can get off the hook so easily.'

Amelia's cheeks flared. She ran her index finger between Lucy's eyes, down to her nose and back up.

'You on the run?' Leanne said.

'I'm just seeing the country, taking it in.'

'What's that?' Leanne said.

Amelia repeated herself, leaning forward again between the seats.

'Well, you're on the run from something, that's clear as day,' Leanne said. She adjusted her grip on the steering wheel, puffed hair out of her face. 'I get the message though. I'll stop being nosy,' she said. 'But just know: wherever you go, you gotta take yourself with you.'

Amelia sank back into her seat, clenched her fist hard so she could feel the neat line of her fingernails in her palm.

'You've heard that before, huh?' Leanne said.

'Yeah,' Amelia said.

Leanne unwrapped her hands from the steering wheel, changed her grip, and there was a sense she was preparing another barrage.

'What's Tailem Bend like, anyway?' Amelia said.

Leanne cleared her throat. 'Well, it's quiet ... there's the railway, the river,' she said. 'And it's not far from the coast.' Leanne shrugged, and there was something newly deflated in her.

'There's really not much happening,' Fi said.

There was an appeal in that for Amelia; perhaps there was a place like the white room there. Maybe the river lapped at the shores. Maybe she could sleep. There might be another of the white room's little whirring fridges that spoke to her through the night. Or the same shelves where she could unpack and set out her belongings in neat rows. And maybe out here she wouldn't see Zach holding the door open for someone at the bakery, or the line of his shoulders disappearing beneath a wave.

'Sounds good,' Amelia said. 'Sounds really good.'

'I'll drop you in town if you wanna check it out,' Leanne said. She paused, then continued: 'I've just finished my fifth night shift in a row so I'm a bit out of it. You'll have to forgive me if I got a bit pushy back there. Just can't help myself.' Leanne winked at Amelia in the rear-view mirror.

'No worries,' Amelia said.

She leaned her head against the warmed interior of the car. The vibration of the vehicle travelled through her skin, into her eyes, around her skull. A sense of lightness overcame her, and she sat with it; her dry mouth stretched over dry teeth, forcing fissures in her lips to open. The smile tasted of metal.

'What is it, darl?' Leanne said.

Amelia was caught. 'I've just got a good feeling about this place, I think.'

Leanne nodded slowly, tapped her fingers on the wheel.

Lucy stood up as if sensing a change. She licked at Amelia's chin, then pawed at her thighs in play.

They continued to notch up kilometres. Fi became engrossed in her phone. Crows took flight from the corpses of roadkill as they approached, and Leanne straddled the carcasses that were small enough, swerved around animals too big. Amelia closed her eyes as hot wind dried the sweat on her face and made whips from the knotted clumps in her hair. At lunchtime they stopped for a toilet break and Leanne and Fi shared a sausage roll and hot chips from a servo. Leanne got a black coffee in a paper cup, insisted on buying one for Amelia too. The coffee burned down her throat, made her stomach churn and grumble.

'Yes!' Fi said when the car started up again. She turned the radio up. Leanne broke into song, releasing an impressive voice that managed to match the yodels of the pop singer. Mother and daughter danced, bouncing their shoulders up and down, synchronised. Fi's voice was gentler than her mother's, unable to hit all the notes, but it had an appealing crystal effect, as if it were a vase that would shatter into pieces if dropped. Neither displayed any shyness as they sang, their voices meshing in a way Amelia thought would only be possible for a mother and daughter. She watched their elbows swaying from side to side and was mesmerised. The skin, the point of bone at the joint, the veins visible when Fi straightened her arms to click, all of it had started in Leanne. Amelia had a bodily craving for her mother then, a hollow deep in her gut. She wanted to press against her – she'd even bear the way her mother would twitch and pull away, just slightly, quick to bristle and overheat underneath affection – in order to get up close to her wit and naivety, her gentleness and irritability, all contained in that breathing, beating body. But the closest she could get was her own disappointing, nauseated, lead-weight body; she was all she had left of her mother.

Leanne and Fi were smiling widely and knew the dance routine well. It was like they knew they were lucky to be there, bouncing their shoulders, pointing into the air, going for all of the notes.

It was mid-afternoon when a sign pointed them off the highway towards Tailem Bend. Amelia longed to stay in the car with Leanne and Fi, feeling her mother draw closer there, as if she might arrive only when Amelia was gone.

'You gonna come into town and have a look then?' Leanne said. Fi stuck her hand out the window, curved it up and down over the waves of air.

'Yeah, I'll check it out,' Amelia said.

They took the exit off the highway and Lucy stood, bending her back in a stretch.

'How 'bout I drop you at the tourist office?' Leanne said. 'Seems like as good a place to start as any, don't you think?'

'Sure, that'd be great,' Amelia said.

Fi whispered something to her mother.

'No,' Leanne said, refusing to lower her voice to the same conspiring level. 'Fi wants me to invite you over for tea,' Leanne said, and the back of Fi's neck flushed red.

'Mum!' Fi said, and she crossed her arms over her chest with a thump, then shifted as far to the window side of her seat as possible.

'I'm exhausted . . . just can't do it tonight, ya know?' Leanne said.

Amelia nodded through the rejection. Leanne pulled up in a circular driveway. When Amelia got out of the car, Fi had wound her window up and wouldn't make eye contact. Amelia rapped her knuckles on the window and Fi gave in, holding her hand against the glass. The scars up her wrists were there again;

they had the same silver shine as the tracks of snails. Fi's hand squeaked as she let it slide down the window, and Amelia lost the scars.

Leanne got out of the car and slammed the door. Amelia gently fought her off as she tried to heft her pack out of the boot.

'I've got it,' Amelia said. 'Thanks.'

When it was time to go, Leanne insisted on wrapping her arms around Amelia, grasping her in a sticky hold. She pressed Amelia's head into a nook below her chin, just above her breast, and attempted to stroke her hair. Her fingers got caught up in the knots, so she held her hand over the clumps for a moment before pushing Amelia back out to arm's length.

'I'm a hugger, you see.' Leanne let her arms drop to her sides. 'Hugs can do all sorts of healing, and that's coming from a nurse.'

Amelia adjusted her pack, tucked her hair behind her ears. She met Leanne's eyes. There was something exact in there that she recognised; the sense of the familiar was warm, a trickle down her spine. She realised that it was Fi's eyes she was seeing in Leanne. They were piercing, fixed on something in Amelia that she could only guess at. Leanne took hold of Amelia. She gripped each of her wrists, rubber bands catching on the hairs of Amelia's forearm as she did so. Lucy raised her head, looked between the two of them.

'I can see you in there, girly,' Leanne said, moving Amelia's arms up and down as if they were the reins of a horse. 'I know what pain looks like. Maybe your parents disowned you, maybe your heart's broken . . . maybe you've been assaulted, violated, and you're piecing yourself back together . . .'

Amelia flinched, only slightly, and lost eye contact but quickly regained it.

'That's it, isn't it,' Leanne said. Her voice was soft, old coffee heavy on her breath. 'You're a survivor.'

Leanne squeezed Amelia's wrists, scooped her head down to meet Amelia's eyeline, which had dropped again. Amelia let herself be found.

'Is that it?' Leanne said.

Amelia was shaking but her hands were stilled as Leanne tightened her grasp. 'I don't know,' she said.

'You know what I mean, right? That you've survived an attack, a sexual assault. That you're a survivor.'

Amelia looked just above Leanne's eyebrows, at the lines there that were now deeper. The blood in her wrists pulsed beneath Leanne's grip.

'Okay, hun, okay. Whatever your story is, I wish you all the best,' Leanne said. 'Be a survivor. Things can get better, but you gotta fight. Don't let him decide what you're worth. You'll waste years doing that, believe you me. You hear?'

Amelia nodded, but Leanne did not remove her hot hands until Amelia looked directly at her. Leanne nodded in return and released her.

'Bye then,' Leanne said. 'Hope the town treats you well. If not, we'll be headin' back the same way tomorrow. If you need to get back where you came from.'

'Thank you,' Amelia said, but Leanne continued to stand there, head to the side, lips pursed, so it was Amelia who left, clicking Lucy to her heels.

The car rolled away, spitting chunks of gravel. Leanne gave a double-hoot of the horn and when Amelia turned, Leanne had her arm out the window. Amelia lifted a hand. Her knees were wobbly and she didn't trust them, tried to lock them into place; she concentrated on her feet, on the part of her that met the ground. The car seemed unreal, driving impossibly away in a scene that was spinning faster and faster.

She needed to sit down. She had a strong desire then to close a door on herself, to be surrounded by four close, still walls. Lucy pursued a scent through squat, round bushes that lined a pathway to glass doors. Amelia followed the footpath, her hand clammy as she gripped a chrome railing for support.

The tourist office was closed. Rows of brochures were unlit along a wall inside. She lowered to a squat then fell onto her tailbone, her pack scraping against the bricks behind her. It was cool and shady in the entrance and she placed her hands flat on terracotta tiles beside her, leaned against the wall.

Survivor.

She slipped the straps of her pack off, pulled the thing around to her front. Her mother's shopping list was in its special pocket and she closed her eyes, dipped her hand in and felt the imprint of the penned words on the back of the notepaper. She licked her lips, breathed deeply, swallowed the rising acid in her throat.

Survivor.

Lucy sniffed at her face, then nudged her snout under Amelia's hand.

'You lost or somethin'?'

Amelia opened her eyes, jumped to her feet.

Two girls were stopped on the path a few metres away. One peeled off and walked towards Amelia while the other pulled a trucker cap lower on her head, kept watch through thin hair. Amelia inspected her own fingernails, snatching glances at the approaching girl. The girl's tank top dipped low at the underarm, showing off a red bra and sections of dark skin over her rib cage. 'You lost?'

'No,' Amelia said. Lucy watched the girl, still except for her twitching nose.

The girl in the cap sniggered. 'You're so weird, Cassie,' she said. She turned and walked the opposite way down the path.

Cassie rolled her eyes and stepped up to Amelia. 'Sorry 'bout her,' Cassie said. 'Just wanted to check you were all right.' Cassie pointed at the doors to the tourist office. 'That place is closed.' She blinked, dark eyes shrouded in long, fake eyelashes.

'Yeah, I know,' Amelia said.

'Cass, c'mon. Let's go,' the other girl said, turning towards them. She pulled a phone out of her pocket and held it up as if it were a mirror, narrowed her eyes, adjusted her cap.

'You all right?' Cassie said.

'Yeah, I'm fine,' Amelia said. 'Thanks.' She lifted her pack to her knee then swung it round onto her shoulders, her lower back burning.

'Hey,' Cassie said. 'Do you want a banana?'

'What?' Amelia said.

'I have a banana . . . I'm not gonna eat it.' The girl slung a purple bag off her shoulders, dumped it at her feet.

'I'm okay, thanks,' Amelia said, but the girl searched the bag, pulling out a change of clothes and a notebook covered in scribbles and pictures from magazines.

Lucy had her snout in the bag and it made the girl chuckle, a raspy thing. She continued to sift around, lifting Lucy's face out of the way, and Lucy's tail wagged as she turned it into a game, burying her nose as quickly as possible into the canvas.

'Here it is,' Cassie said, revealing the banana. She stepped forward, holding the blackened fruit in front of her. One end was turned to mush, the skin split and oozing.

'Thanks,' Amelia said, taking the offering.

Cassie shoved her things back in her bag as if in a hurry. 'See ya,' she said, scampering off towards her friend, her bag bouncing where it dangled off her shoulder. The friend exclaimed something at her then grabbed her hand and pulled her down the path.

A chemical vanilla sweetness lingered once they'd walked out of view, their laughter echoing back to where Amelia stood. Slowly, she returned to herself: the creak of her pack as she shifted her feet, the weight of her arms hanging at her hips, the hot breeze drying her lips even as she licked them. The kindness of the banana was heavy, somehow hard to take. She blinked back wetness in her eyes, fought the urge to melt into the ground again.

A poster with a photograph was taped to the door of the tourist office. The green eyes of a lost cat stared at the camera, a child's face squashed into its white fur. Amelia stepped up to it, traced the crinkled paper with her fingertips. She'd printed hundreds of things like these with her mother's picture on the front: the order of service for her funeral. On the day, she'd found a typo on the second page, though she'd read the draft over and over. She sat beside Sid and he linked his arm with hers so tight it was a tourniquet. At the end she stepped outside the crematorium, bewildered by sunlight; she let people shake her hand, pins and needles in her fingertips.

She took her hand away from the poster, from the child's desperate little arms, clutching the indifferent creature.

Survivor.

Just inside the door, a postcard was tacked among advertisements; it pictured a map that gave directions to a 'must-see sculpture': The Big Olive. She set out on her mission, and even though the air didn't have the sticky kiss of the ocean, Tailem Bend welcomed her with purpose: find an olive, find a cat, find a room.

Amelia walked, holding the squishy top of the banana between her thumb and index finger. The sun was a white light behind the clouds. The wind picked up, pushing her forward; sharp debris whipped past her legs. She followed the pavement, avoiding the cracks, and was led beyond houses and into an industrial area of superstores and warehouses. A lighting-shop window was packed with lamps, all of them switched on, alive, trapped in their glass cage.

Amelia unwrapped the banana; she wasn't hungry but was unable to put it to waste. The top of it was beyond saving and she threw it near an anthill for the ants to enjoy. She ate the rest of the banana in three bites, holding the sludge of it in her mouth. She forced herself to swallow, tried not to chew.

A wheelie bin perched on the kerb ahead. She lifted the lid, disturbing flies that sucked at brown juice around the opening; the air inside was hot and smelled of sun-baked rubbish. Her mother was there, then, wearing the pair of yellow washing-up gloves she used for the job of disinfecting the bin at home. Amelia was laughing at her, teasing her for the detailed and regular cleaning of the thing, a perfect waste of time. Her mother wiped hair off her face with her upper arm, tried to conceal her smile.

Amelia tossed the banana skin into the bin and let go of the lid. Her mother was gone.

Across the road, children's screams carried across the sprawl of a car park. A home-improvement store was playing host to a jumping castle. Lucy raised her nose and sniffed as the smell of a sausage sizzle caught on the wind. Amelia stepped away from the bin, crossed the road towards the buzz of people. She stopped as she got nearer, took in the colours of summer clothes, the slamming of car doors, a muffled message from a loudspeaker. Her feet itched to walk the other way, but she forced herself towards the people, her new community. As she walked among parked cars, negotiating her pack through gaps between side mirrors, she saw a brown station wagon identical to Leanne's.

Survivor.

She got up closer, a few rows of cars away, but the Kingswood was empty. People lined up at a marquee for their serve of the barbecue; blood pounded at her temples as she approached. She commanded Lucy close to her and worked her way through the crowd, head down. They reached the side of the store, a huge grey-bricked wall. Amelia took her pack off very slowly, staying with the task well beyond necessity. Once it was off, she fiddled with straps that didn't need altering. Lucy's head flicked around, following the paths of people holding sausages in white napkins. Amelia looked up, scanned the crowd for Leanne, listened for the sureness of her voice. She caught a few people's eyes and quickly averted her gaze. People moved past her, so close she could smell them, hear their thongs flipping up against their heels. She lowered herself to a crouch but it was worse there, the people blocking out most of the sky. An announcement blared out of the megaphone and she flinched, stood up.

The sausage queue had dwindled and she dug out her donation, left Lucy with her pack.

'Hello there, traveller, onions for you?'

'No, thanks.'

'Sauce?'

'No, thanks.'

'Too easy.'

A sweaty man handed her a sausage in white bread, held out a greasy hand and took her money. Lucy stood as Amelia approached, tail wagging. She jumped up, rested her paws on Amelia's waist, sniffing at the sausage.

'Down girl,' Amelia said. 'Down.'

She put the sausage sandwich on the ground and Lucy got to work on it, starting with the meat. Groups of people mingled nearby and Amelia racked her brain for something to say, a reason to approach, but found nothing. She left Lucy to eat, did a round of the crowd, forcing herself to meet people's eyes, to stretch the tight skin of her cheeks into a smile. A few people returned the smile, and though others seemed to look away, she grew more brave.

'Hi,' she managed to say to an older couple. They were eating sausages in front of a trolley full of potted plants. 'Doing some gardening?'

The man looked at her, then looked away; the woman investigated a splatter of tomato sauce she'd dripped on her sneaker. Amelia's face flushed and she put her head down, made her way back to Lucy, mumbling 'Sorry' as she stepped in people's paths.

She let minutes pass, tried to relax into the crowd, fidgeted again with her pack. She stood on tiptoe, looked to the car park. The station wagon was gone.

'Oh well, Luce,' she said. 'We tried.' She put her pack on and walked fast, walked against the sinking feeling in her stomach.

She worked her way out of the last of the people and cars. There was relief in finding her step on the pavement, in the wind at her back. Lucy walked beside Amelia, her nose low to the ground, tail swinging from side to side with her gait.

Amelia assumed the must-see olive would take her into town, but the road stretched long, wide and bare before her. She heaved her pack higher. Reaching round to her shoulderblade, she pressed hard into the knots that were nestled near the bone. She kicked a rock, caught up to it, kicked it again.

Once the jumping-castle screeches had died down, it was strangely quiet: the fall of Amelia's own footsteps on the path, the rock rattling along the pavement, the buzz of each individual fly that moved around her head and the bites on her arms, the swish of Lucy's legs through the grass. These separate sounds became a rhythm: her footsteps the beat; the rattling rock, the buzzing flies and the swish of grass the melody. There were lyrics to go with the tune, looping in her head: *It has come to this, it has come to this, it has come . . . to . . . this.*

The footpath stopped abruptly, ending the song. Amelia walked on the road, steering the stone along with her; she concentrated on the collision of it against her toes, the rattle of it against the bitumen. Lucy's nails scratched along the ground; she was uninterested in sniffing or marking her territory as they passed through the outskirts of town. Amelia reached for her bottle of Mount Franklin, felt the familiar collapse of the plastic. She drank. Lucy refused Amelia's palm of water, stared ahead.

When Amelia next kicked the stone she caught it at an angle; it skittered off course and fell down a drain. She approached the point of its disappearance, knelt down on all fours and peered into the darkness. The weight of her mistake, her betrayal, was instant. *Take more care*, her mother would have said. *Take more care.* Amelia heard the mew of a cat, squinted her eyes to try to see down the drain, to find the white fluff belonging to the lost animal.

'Meow,' Amelia said. She waited, meowed again, but there was no response.

As they approached, The Big Olive didn't look very big. It was an advertisement at the entrance to a business, a device intended to attract people to the shop behind it. She stood in front of it for a few minutes, then circled the olive, checking it out from every angle. It had the same blackish purple shine all around, though an assortment of chips were visible in the paint. Someone had scrawled angular words on its base: *I HATE OLIVES*. Lucy sat a few feet away, her eyes half-shut, tongue hanging out the side of her mouth. Amelia sat on a short wall that surrounded the olive, stared at the sculpture as the sun broke through clouds and created a glare on the shiny surface.

A couple approached from the car park, didn't look at the sculpture, asked her to take a photo of them. They posed in front of the olive, his hand wrapped around the back of her neck, her making a peace sign. Through their smiles, they continued to bicker about who would drive next. They left, happy with their snapshot.

'Let's just go, Luce,' Amelia said. One of Lucy's ears faced forward, the other twitching towards the car park. 'Let's just go.'

Amelia veered down another wide street. A ditch ran beside the road; she stepped down into it and walked in the dirt and tufts of grass, looking for the shock of domestic white-and-grey-striped fluff of a dead pet cat. Lucy didn't follow, stayed instead on higher ground, looking at Amelia as she called to the cat with kissing sounds.

It was mostly tyre scraps down there, the odd corpse of wild roadkill. Rubbish blew along the ditch, too, fast-food bags and chip packets; Amelia scooped up the litter, held it bundled to her chest. Lucy lay her ears flat against the wind. The sky was bright white; dark clouds converged over hills to her left. An old ute pottered past but otherwise the road was quiet. The ditch ended at the mouth of a large pipe. Amelia called once, twice, for the cat but heard only the echo of her own voice in reply.

Ahead, there was a building with a mural painted on a wall facing a car park; a river scene framed by eucalypts merged into a racing-car circuit. An A-frame blackboard perched at the car park entrance, stating:

Breakfast, lunch and dinner

Best oysters in town

Staff needed

Amelia shoved her armful of collected rubbish into a bin at the edge of the car park. She walked up wooden steps, past climbing plants working their way up the latticed walls beside her. She arrived on a deck, Lucy's feet clicking on the boards, and there was a scrap of a river view between trees. Tables were set with wineglasses, and white serviettes rolled into holders, the edges of tablecloths flapping in the wind. There were no diners outside. Through the floor-to-ceiling glass panels she could see more tables laid out. She walked up and down the deck in search of a door, and, finding nothing, pushed on one of the glass panels. She tried again, leaving a handprint on the glass. Inside, a young man in tie and white shirt pointed her around the side of the building, where she'd come from, and other diners came into focus then, their eyes tracking her failure.

She found another entrance, told Lucy to wait, and pushed through the heavy door, sending a Christmas wreath swinging. A sign stating *Please wait to be seated* stood at the top of a red-carpeted staircase. There was a general hush in the restaurant, a few late-lunch diners leaning in to speak to each other, the occasional clang of cutlery on plates. Fluorescent lights shone in a display fridge that showed different ways the restaurant could do oysters. A long, dark hair was trapped under a silver platter.

The man behind the bar saw her and continued to polish a wineglass with vigour. He took his time, moving a cloth around the inside of the glass, pulling it out, holding the glass up to the light from the windows. Pans sizzled within the kitchen and there was a smell of onion and garlic; beneath that was the sticky, pissy smell of a bar. The jingle of poker machines came from behind frosted glass doors to her right, polluting the jazz that played in the restaurant.

The server finished working on the glass. He added it to the rack of wineglasses that dangled from their stems above him, which caused them all to wobble, setting off a soft series of chimes. As he approached, he picked up a bottle of something and tossed it over his fingers and wrists, as if he were some kind of cocktail master.

Her heart was fast, hands moistening. She scratched at the corners of her mouth, collecting gunk, and tried to capture her hair behind her ears.

'Ma'am, how can I help you?' he said. He wore a black nametag, 'Roger' written in golden script.

'Yes, hi,' she said, adjusting the weight of her pack on her shoulders. 'I saw the sign out there, about the job.'

'Right, okay,' he said, and raised a dark, manicured eyebrow.

Always shake hands, her mother had told her before her first job interview at a local cafe. *And be firm; no one likes a floppy fish.*

Amelia stuck out her hand and Roger looked down at it. She firmed it up, moved it towards him. 'I'm Amelia.'

Slowly, he reached for her hand, gave her just his fingers. 'Hi Amelia.'

His fingers were soft, like something secret; the inside of a seashell, an earlobe. 'That's a soft hand,' she said.

'Thanks?' he said, retracting his hand and wiping it on his trousers.

Amelia put her shoulders back, lifted her chin. 'The sign outside . . . it said you need staff,' she said.

Roger stepped back, widened his eyes in some kind of realisation. 'Right, yes, I see. We're looking for experienced applicants. As I'm sure you can understand, we can get very busy so we need someone who is trained in . . .' his eyebrow rose again, '. . . high service. We have a three point nine average on TripAdvisor and we can't have that slipping.'

'I've worked in a cafe, and I've done other stuff too. I'm a fast learner.'

'Right . . .' His eyes flashed to her pack. 'Do you live locally? We need someone who lives nearby, who can come in at short notice,' he said. He turned his head to check on the diners behind him; a customer raised their hand, beckoned to him. Roger went without a word and she cringed on his behalf when she saw the lint gathered on the back of his waistcoat.

His attentiveness was extreme; he placed his hand on the diner, near her shoulder. He swanned behind the bar, removed a wineglass with a flick, then poured wine into it from a great height. He placed the singular drink on a tray and strutted back to the table, one hand resting behind his back.

Roger was serious about this job, and Amelia remembered trying to get things just right when she worked at the cafe. She liked receiving her shifts because they punctuated her week. And there were procedures for everything: how to clean the coffee machine, how to move the oldest stock from the back to the front of the drinks fridge, how to greet people and ask what kind of bread they wanted. She yearned for these systems now, for someone to be expecting her, someone telling her what to do.

Roger had delivered the drink, bowed and reversed. He made his quiet, carpeted way back to Amelia.

'So,' Roger said, 'is there something else?'

'I just wanted to let you know that I'll be getting a place to live, a room or something here,' she said.

'Right, good luck with that,' he said.

'Because you said you needed someone local . . .'

Roger looked again to the restaurant floor; angry, red pimples climbed up his neck. 'You'll need a CV in order to be considered.'

'Yep, I think I have one of those.' She swung her pack off her shoulder, and as it landed there was a draught of dog food and damp clothes. She unclipped it, aware of Roger fidgeting, peering down at her, and buried her hand deep inside. There were some CVs in there at some stage; she'd printed them off at the library in the town with the white room. She was going to apply for a job there, at the art shop below her room.

Her hand touched on something that could have been it, the right size, the right texture; she grabbed hold of it and yanked. A pair of undies was flung out of the pack too and landed on the floor. They were dirty ones; she'd worn them on both sides. Her face was hot as she snatched up the underwear and shoved it back down in her pack, deep down, telling herself he'd only have seen the damage if he was really looking for it.

The CV was crumpled – she kept it in a plastic sleeve she'd found blowing around outside the library, but even that was crushed. Something brown had got to the corner of the document and had seeped in, making it as far as the *To whom it may concern* on the covering letter.

'You can get an idea from this,' she said. She held it out, and when he didn't move to take it she let it hang down beside her leg. 'I could always write up another one and bring it back.'

'Look, to be honest, my manager is . . . quite particular,' Roger said. 'We've had a lot of interest, you see, for the position.'

'Oh, okay,' she said.

'Thanks for coming in,' Roger said. He caught the eye of a customer over in a window seat. As he turned, she saw the transformation of his face, the transition into *At your service,* reserved for paying customers.

Amelia stood, stared at the rows of hanging wineglasses until they blurred. She longed to return to them every day, to grasp each one, to turn them delicately in her hands as she polished, clearing them of each smudge and dust particle. Her feet sank into the soft carpet.

A chef broke her trance, pushing out of double swing doors. He crouched at a fridge, revealing the divot at the beginning of his bum.

People at the tables were watching her while trying to appear as if they weren't: forks hovered over plates, as if the sight of her was putting them off their meals. Some of those faces, the closest woman in particular, biting a purplish lip, had pity in them.

She shoved the CV back into her bag, buckled the thing up and swung it to her knee, then to her back. The straps settled into the ridges they'd dug out on her shoulders. There was a gnawing deep in her stomach, the same gnawing she'd had when she failed her driving test. It was just after her mother's first diagnosis, and they realised Amelia would need to drive her to and from appointments. But at first they had to manage on the bus even though the bouncing of it made her mother ill, all because Amelia forgot a head check, failed, then didn't slow down in a school zone, and failed again.

And now, again.

She walked down the stairs, stopped for a moment to grip the banister, polished golden. Her face was there in distorted reflection: red skin, wild hair. *Stupid girl.*

An unattended desk sat at the exit, displaying a holder full of brochures for local businesses: boat hire, fishing, the not-so-big olive. A row in front of these held postcards that advertised the restaurant. They looked free enough, so she picked one up before pulling open the heavy glass door.

Lucy was stretched out on her side along the wall of the building, her legs straight. The air was filled with the smell of rain on hot cement; the sky spat wet smudges onto the ground. A gust of wind picked up dirt from the car park and swirled it around. Amelia bent down to Lucy and put a hand on her side. Lucy lifted her head, then returned it to the ground with sleepy blinks. Her fur was warm, her heart pulsing beneath her ribs.

'Gotta keep moving,' Amelia said. She rubbed Lucy's tummy, then gave her a couple of firm pats. 'Gotta go, girl.' Lucy's tags clinked as she got to her feet, and her steps fell into rhythm at Amelia's heels.

The sky darkened, the rain growing thicker as they approached town. The water made grey rivulets down Amelia's arm, the trickling down of it like affection. It made her hairs stand on end.

The main street was suffering from the downpour, water overflowing from roof gutters and pooling in the kerb beside the road. An elderly man drove a mobility scooter covered in clear plastic; he reached a puddle that blocked the pavement. She watched to see what he would do now that his plan had proven too difficult. He turned in an eight-point manoeuvre back in the direction he had come, and she admired his ability to surrender, to find another way. On the opposite side of the street, a woman tried to light a cigarette. She leaned against the glass of a hair-dresser, rollers in her hair; a cascade of rain fell in front of her, arcing off the shop's shutter.

A real-estate office dominated a corner block; descriptions of properties for sale and for rent hung from thin metal cables in the window. The office was warmly lit and had purple carpet, purple couches and purple desks inside. There was a purple mat at the entrance to the shop, and Amelia was vigilant in wiping the soles of her shoes, though mud had got up the sides of them and onto her calves. The door was suctioned into its frame, so she pushed all her weight against it. It gave way suddenly and she stumbled the first couple of steps into the office.

People in purple suit jackets and white shirts tapped away at their keyboards, did not look up from their computer screens. A woman clacked out of a side door in heels, her purple skirt rustling against her stockings.

'We're closing, I'm afraid,' she said, reaching past Amelia to flip the sign on the door.

'Oh, really?' Amelia said. There was a purple clock on the wall, the silver hands indicating 4.55 pm. 'I didn't realise . . . the door was open, people are working . . . Do you think I could have a really quick word with someone?'

'You've just missed us for today, sorry madam, but pop in tomorrow and we'll be happy to help.'

The woman gave a tight, deep-red smile, and it said that she knew Amelia wouldn't just pop in tomorrow. It said that their

143

clients were people who spent their days popping in and out of places, weighing up their options, making informed and well-financed decisions.

'Here,' the woman said, 'why don't you take a card?' She reached over to a circular table, pulled a business card from a holder.

'Ah, no thanks,' Amelia said. 'Do you rent rooms at all?'

The woman breathed in sharply through her nose, rested a hand on her hip. 'We have some rooms, yes,' she said. 'But all our properties are pet-free.' Her eyes flashed to the window, where Lucy's back was against the glass, her fur pressed out in a whorl.

'She wouldn't need to go inside,' Amelia said.

'No pets unfortunately. It's an agency policy. Okay?' The woman made her way to the door, giving Amelia and the puddle she'd made on the floor a wide berth. 'Thank you,' she said, holding the door open.

Amelia briefly tried to appeal to the other workers tapping away under spotlit desks, but none of them would save her.

The woman closed the door behind her and slid across a set of bolts. She leaned back against the glass like people did in films when they'd just been through something traumatic, or romantic. The other workers were suddenly animated, gave her a round of applause.

Amelia stepped around the corner, watched them from where she hoped they couldn't see her. She adjusted her pack and walked away, following signs to the river foreshore. The ocean had helped, when she was in the white room, and perhaps the river would now. But the ocean hadn't been enough to make her stay. She'd left the white room on a whim, mid-afternoon; it had seemed, suddenly, that she was too close to home. She locked the door, delivered the keys downstairs to the woman in the art shop. The woman had the same intricate eyeliner as always, curving out from her top lid, and she gave a look that said she thought Amelia was doing the wrong thing. Amelia almost asked her about it, but instead she just said 'Thanks' and walked out of the door, knocking over some blank canvasses in her hurry.

Stupid girl.

A patch of the landscape ahead shifted and glinted: water. After a few minutes, she was there, standing high over the broad, brown river. The wind was stronger at the river's edge, hot and thick, as if it had spent days crossing the desert. Whitecaps turned their backs on her, pushed away by the wind.

She scanned the riverbank for the lost cat, trying to keep some semblance of a hold on that mission, though in leaving the road and coming to the water she felt she was giving up on it. There was no sign of the animal.

She rebalanced her pack, lifting it higher on her shoulders, tightening the strap around her waist. A houseboat drifted along near the opposite bank, spreading the beat of dance music. Someone waved in a big arc from the deck. Their persistence eventually made her lift her arm in the air, signalling back.

The rain had stopped but clouds made the evening prematurely grey. People were dotted along the bank, fishing, but she aimed for a secluded spot near the remnants of a pier. She moved down the steep, grassy slope towards the water. Her knees ached, the ligaments struggling to work as brakes; if they failed, her momentum might carry her into the river. Her backpack was heavy enough to drag her beneath the water to the riverbed and keep her there. Then her eyes would glisten like the scales of fish.

Her knees and muscles continued working, and she stood beside the pier, at the edge of the river. The water was clear enough to see the sand and weeds below. Something breached the surface nearby, catching the sun in a silver flash, and then was gone. Lucy stood, ears pricked, staring at the place the creature had jumped. She let out a low, private '*ruff*', as if starting a conversation with the other animal. Amelia bent down and picked up a light grey stone, warm and smooth, any rough edges licked away by the water, healed as if they were wounds.

During her stay in the white room, she could watch a patch of beach for hours. She and Lucy walked down to the sand and looked for pipis. The creatures were silent, their suckers busy filtering sand. On calmer days, there was a quiet to the ocean that promised future rage; the waves came in then pulled away, making a triangle in the receding water, with a pipi at its apex. She had wanted to reach her finger out to its suckers, to feel how hard the soft flesh worked, the strength of them against her skin, but she didn't dare disturb it.

She returned the stone to the ground. There was movement on the opposite side of the riverbank and she caught a glimpse of a heron as it disappeared around the river bend. She missed her chance at an exact identification, and she imagined it standing poised and still, taking her measure. She wanted the moment back so she could notice, instead of going elsewhere as she stared downwards, her vision blurring the lapping river near her feet. Sid would elbow her, be ashamed of her for missing the opportunity, for not paying attention. Watching any heron was a majestic experience, he would have said, and it would have been, especially if he was there. His absence was thick and it grew as she stood there, taking over a part of her.

Amelia swung her pack off and to the ground. She pulled out her faithful Rage Against the Machine shirt, imagined pulling it over her head, losing herself in its excess of cotton. It held tight to the smell of Will. She unlaced her shoes, took them off using the toe of the opposite foot, then pulled off her damp socks. She stepped forward into soft water, mud worming up between her toes. She submerged the shirt then stepped onto it, stomped the material into the mud. She picked it up and rubbed it roughly against itself, but the smell remained. She repeated the process twice more, then gave up, walked out of the water.

The cotton did not rip; she pulled as hard as she could at the chest, the shoulders, with no result. Lucy wouldn't help. Amelia had trained her out of clothing tug-of-war, out of running off with undies and pillowcases dropped from the washing basket and shredding them to bits. She stood with wrinkled forehead and pointed ears as Amelia held the material in front of her. She had been swimming and Amelia patted her wet head, the bone of her skull hard and close beneath the flattened fur.

Amelia approached the dilapidated pier, hooked her shirt onto a rusted nail. She pulled, hard, and the material gave, accompanied by the sound of tearing. She hooked it again, pulled, repeated the process, getting faster and faster. Her arms burned till she could hardly feel them, till they were lost to lightness. When she was finished, she held the shirt up. The material flapped open in angled, straight lines, her chest and back sliced through. She returned to her pack and threw the destroyed shirt on the ground, tried not to look at it.

Amelia pulled on her shoes and socks. She removed her rocket pen from its compartment in her pack and dug out the postcard from the restaurant by the river. She stepped onto the pier, facing a gauntlet of rusted nails. Many of the planks had rotted away to leave gaping holes with only narrow beams to balance on. She began picking her way across; Lucy stayed behind, sniffing instead at the base of the pier's foundations. The first gap came a few steps in where two planks were missing. Amelia hopped across it easily. The next gap was a big one. There were at least a dozen planks missing, requiring a five-metre or so balancing act on the outside beam of the pier. The wood creaked as she stepped onto it, her arms stretched out on either side of her for balance. The breeze pushed her and she wobbled, leaning slowly over to the left then quickly to the right as she overcorrected. With pen and postcard in one hand, she skittered along the last few steps, made it to the safety of four planks in a row. *Andrew loves Nicole 4 eva* was scratched into the wood. Andrew was committed; as Amelia worked her way to the edge of the pier, his declaration of love was on every remaining plank.

She was at the last challenge before the end of the pier when she fell. She was balanced, just a few steps away from the end, and then there was only air beneath her foot. She went down heavily, and cried out as her inner thigh took the hit. She clenched her legs and managed to straddle a beam, her feet dangling above the water. She scrambled to solid footing at the end of the pier.

She examined her grazed knuckles, checked her legs for cuts from nails. She had kept hold of her belongings, though the postcard now sported a smear of fresh blood. Her leg was already stiffening up around the injury. She rested on her stomach and caught her breath, writing with a shaking hand.

I've had enough, she scrawled onto the postcard in big letters, not bothering with the code. *Can I come over?*

Can I come over, the same line they had used over and over as children, calling each other up from just a few streets away.

She licked a finger and scrubbed at the blood and mess on the postcard. The injury on her thigh pulsed, as if it had its own heartbeat. Amelia closed her eyes, focused on the pain. She lay with it, still, and let it bloom inside her, let it surround her; she thought of Sid's place, the end of the road, and when her mind wandered elsewhere, she brought herself, again and again, back to her body, to the pain; she touched the skin, hot and already swelling.

It started to rain again. She watched the drops hit the river, breaking the water's surface. Each landing was a silent bomb, an explosion of ripples. The spots increased until there were too many to distinguish, the river stirred up into a warzone. The postcard suffered some heavy drops, making the ink run in places, and she tucked it under her arm for protection.

She closed her eyes, the rain growing sharper against her back, against the exposed skin of her neck, her scalp. She lay there, unable to move. When she opened her eyes it was much darker and she was shivering.

She rolled onto her back and looked sideways, where her body had left a patch. The space where she'd been was drier and lighter than the rest of the pier. She watched that pale version of herself as it was sprinkled with raindrops. She stayed, staring at the wood, the place the outline had been, till it was a dark, slippery brown. Her eyelashes caught raindrops, and when she blinked they loosened and slid down her cheeks. Streaks of dirt ran down her arms like mudslides, and perhaps if she stayed there long enough, she would erode completely.

Lucy was back on the shore, the neat triangle of her sitting beside the upright backpack. She seemed to be staring straight at Amelia, as if by watching her she could stop her disappearing.

The rain grew softer, more sparse, then stopped. Amelia lay sprawled on wooden planks, her body numbing; she wriggled her toes and fingers in order to find them.

The sky cleared in time for sunset; her arm was splayed out beside her and she watched it as the sky turned the skin different hues of pink. The sun had done this same thing at her mother's funeral; she had sat beneath a stained-glass window, and her arm turned green, red and blue. She had watched the colours creeping up to her elbow as the service progressed and knew her mother would have appreciated the bright, changing shapes.

Amelia lay on the pier, still, heavy, until the colours of the sky faded. She forced herself up, and there was a hollowness within her as she picked her way back to the shore.

On the fifth day of the Overland Track, Amelia and her mother had sat on the deck at Pelion Hut. It was late afternoon and the clouds drifted, sometimes framed the peak of a mountain, sometimes concealed it. Her mother said her hands were cold. Amelia's were warm, her confession pulsing at her fingertips. She held her mother's hands in her own, thinking that maybe through that touch, her mother would just know about Zach, know all the things Amelia wanted to say. One ear poked out of the green beanie her mother wore, and she preferred the quiet, Amelia knew, so she said nothing.

Lucy was pleased when Amelia made it back; she jumped up to press her front paws into Amelia's thighs. Amelia dropped to her knees and wrapped her arms around the damp fur, hard body. Lucy endured the hold for a second before wriggling down and out of it. Amelia wanted to press her face into the wet-dog smell, but Lucy was done, restless and ready to go.

As she left the river, Amelia threw her Rage Against the Machine T-shirt into a metal bin. She turned her back on it, walked a few steps away, then hesitated. She retraced her steps and looked down into the rubbish. The torn material lay on top of discarded bags of bait; the fishy, gutsy smell rose to her nostrils and drove her away, pushed her onwards.

Her shoes squelched, and the impact of each step made the inside of her hurt leg throb. As they passed through town, she stopped regularly to place her cool palm over the heat of the injury, felt the hard lump at the sorest point.

An op shop displayed a ragged Santa costume on a model too thin for the role. Further down, she reached a red postbox; she searched for the extra stamp she'd stashed somewhere among her things. Lucy sat beside a puddle and watched as Amelia checked all the zipped pockets, then dug through her pack. She tugged clothing, pots and odd bits of food out, making a pile on the wet cement, only to remember a safe compartment down the side of the bag. The stamp was there. She shoved her things into her pack, the muscles in her arms burning with the effort. Still, she wanted to bash her fists against something but refrained, let the urge boil up then settle.

Sid's postcard was wet, and bent at one corner. She stuck on the stamp and let the card fall through the slot. As soon as it was gone, she wished she hadn't let it go, wanted to get it back and compose something stronger, less desperate. The postbox looked at her with yellow information stickers for eyes, its slit for a mouth, regarding her as if it had something to say. She looked back at it. It said nothing. She got to her knees, placed her open palms on its sides, put her forehead against the wet metal, and begged, pleaded for the creature to spit the postcard back out. It did nothing. The town shut her out, curling in on itself the way she used to do when shielding a winning hand from Sid with her body, holding the cards close to her chest.

They walked, following signs to the highway. New blisters formed on her wet feet. Lucy trotted half a length ahead, her tongue bouncing; she pressed on as if she, too, was committed to putting Tailem Bend far behind them.

The headlights of the highway stretched Amelia's shadow long and thin in front of her. Wind moved through eucalypts beside the road, until she reached a place where the trees were burned, the blackened bones of branches still, reaching into the sky. A gravel shoulder widened beside the road and she dumped her pack there. She dug out a can of Lucy's food: beef and marrow. Lucy sat facing her, whimpering as Amelia scrambled around for the can opener.

'Just a sec, girl. You're okay,' Amelia said. 'You're okay.'

While Lucy devoured her meal, Amelia dragged her pack onto its side then sat down and leaned against it. Prickles and sharp rocks pinched her thighs. She fought to keep her eyes open.

Lucy snorted as she licked the remains of her food. A car went past, sounding its horn. It braked up ahead and she stood. The car pulled over, indicator flashing. She scooped up Lucy's bowl, threw her pack over one shoulder. It was hard to keep her balance as she ran; her pack tugged on her arm, pulling it at painful angles, threatening it out of its socket.

Breathless, Amelia arrived at the passenger-side window, Lucy at her heel. She bent down to the person in there, a figure with dark curls, but as she did so the car screeched and took off, the back tyres passing only centimetres from Amelia's toes. There was laughter and something flew out the window, landed softly at her feet. The top of a burger bun sat in the gravel, the bread puffy, a little smear of mayonnaise where it had skidded on the ground.

The driver of the car held down the horn as they sped away, and then the engine faded out of earshot. The smell of exhaust lingered. Lucy sniffed at the bun, pawed it over so it was wet side up, pasted with mayonnaise and strips of lettuce. She stood over it, panting. Amelia picked up the bun, nursed the soft, dry side of it in her palm; the sesame seeds pressed gently into her skin, shifted, came loose and lodged between her fingers.

A car passed and Amelia was too close to the road, the rush of air powerful against her cheeks, pushing her back a step. She wanted to hold the bun close to her, to keep it. Lucy disappeared into the scrub. Amelia crouched to lay the bun to rest, nudged it back into the place of its abandonment.

She followed Lucy away from the road, scrambling down a rough trail that weaved through long grass.

'Lucy!' she called.

Branches scratched past her and the stirred leaves released captured raindrops. Cool water found the back of her neck, drummed against the canvas of her pack.

The noise of passing cars lowered as they walked, softening until it could no longer be heard. The path gave way to a high wire fence. Amelia stood right up close to Lucy so her hot, damp side moved in and out against her calf.

Behind the fence, a single floodlight was sentry to a large, square paddock. It took a second for Amelia to realise what she was looking at: a train graveyard. Several abandoned carriages sat with no tracks on which to come or go. A well-used hole was dug out beneath the fence and Lucy lowered herself, pushed her way under. It was only then that Amelia saw the yellow warning sign, a stick figure demonstrating the shock of an electric fence. Lucy was unscathed; she waited on the other side, panting, her eyes and the white patches of her fur reflecting the moonlight.

Thunder rumbled in the distance. Amelia slung her pack into the hole and followed it down. A strap caught on a stray wire and she untangled it in the half-light. With both feet beneath her bag, she pushed it under the fence and, legs trembling, up the other side of the hole. Water soaked through her shirt, got to the skin on her back. Once the pack was up the other side, she flipped onto her belly and crawled beneath the fence.

Thistles grew between slabs of concrete, nipping at the exposed skin on her legs. Scorched patches marked the location of old bonfires on the ground, with empty bottles of liquor and cigarette butts scattered at their blackened edges. Her feet crunched over broken glass as she moved towards the carriages. She stopped, then touched Lucy's back so she stopped, too. Amelia listened for signs of life, of others; there was a rustle and grunt somewhere near the perimeter fence, but after a few moments she determined it to be an animal.

Graffiti screamed down the sides of the trains, rendered a dull orange by the light. She moved towards the carriage with the fewest broken windows, stepping over huge, rusted train parts to get there. Lucy sniffed, zigzagging ahead as she followed a trail. Amelia climbed on top of a giant tree stump and peered into a broken window, careful not to touch the sill's jagged teeth. There were seats with ripped upholstery and the glint of brass surrounding tables: a first-class carriage.

The door was loose, hanging from the top hinge. She walked up rickety steps and entered the carriage. Lucy pushed past her, made her way up the aisle. Curtains hung from the smashed window, but on the opposite side the window was still intact. The table there was smooth underneath Amelia's fingertips. She laid her pack out on it then walked down the carriage, running her hand over the tops of seats, wondering how many bodies had been there before her, how many people could fit in this space that was now all hers.

Sections of the train wall were missing, revealing the padding within. There was an edge of piss and rot in the air. Lucy scratched under one of the seats and sent something scurrying. Amelia dug her fingers deep into a headrest, listened; the scrabble of claws, a creature retreating. She breathed again, turned around and went back to her pack.

A gust of wind blew through the carriage, sending a plastic bag skittering up the aisle. It suckered onto her leg. She sat on her seat and was suddenly hungry. Delving into her pack, she found a can of tomato soup. She wiped the crust of dog food off her opener before using it, then drank from the can's metal edge. The soup was rich and her empty stomach kicked from the acidity; she managed four mouthfuls.

She closed the door as best as she could then drew the curtains across her window; the light from outside fell across her in slits where the material was torn. She pulled articles of clothing from her pack to drape across her. With a pair of socks for a pillow she lay across two chairs, tucking her legs up. Lucy jumped up on the seat opposite and circled, lay down, stood, then circled again before settling.

'Good girl,' Amelia said. 'That's a good girl.' She stuck her hand out beneath the table and Lucy licked it.

Amelia's guts fizzed and her stomach pushed out, bloated. She lay back and pulled a shirt up to her chin, nestled deeper into the seats. Her hands rested on her hipbones and they jutted out more than they had before, most of the lumpy, squishy stuff gone; she was glad to be minimal, to carry nothing extra.

Rain started again, lightly at first, before setting in in earnest. Drops from tree branches overhanging the carriage fell the loudest and without a pattern. She closed her eyes. When she'd walked the Overland Track with her mother, she had a proper raincoat. The third and fourth days were wet and when her mother spoke, the rain falling on Amelia's hood made it difficult to hear. 'What?' Amelia said, turning to her mother, whose face was darkened by her own hood.

'I said, isn't it amazing I haven't hurt myself on all this rough terrain.' A few steps later her mother lost her footing, slid down the path for a while before being caught by tree roots, laughing the whole way down.

*

She woke to something moving inside the carriage. She could feel the change, the presence of a stranger. Her neck was stiff and her eyes were slow to adjust; she blinked through an orange fuzz. Lucy was there, her silhouette sitting alert, facing the door of the train. Listening through the drumming of rain on the roof, Amelia waited to hear the sound again, the noise that had woken her.

A footstep and a movement of air, shifting wisps of hair at her cheeks; body odour, smoke. She could make out the shape of human legs by the door. The figure moved closer.

Amelia sat upright, knocked something to the ground.

'Oh shit, sorry bud.' It was a man's voice, hoarse and slow. 'Didn't realise this space was occupied.'

'What do you want?' Amelia said as she gathered her things. Lucy stood on her seat, sniffed at the intruder.

'Whoa, you're a lady!' The man shouted out a broken window: 'Oi, Ricky, come and check this out. There's a chick in here!'

He returned to her, stood at the table. He reached out and she backed herself against the wall. She froze as the man touched her head, firm but gentle, moving his hand across her forehead, her matted hair.

'Wow,' the man said. His breath smelled of marijuana.

Lucy let out a low bark.

'Don't touch me,' Amelia said, her heartbeat violent, filling her ears.

The figure retrieved his hand. 'Just showing my appreciation, angel girl.'

Someone new entered the carriage, colourful glow-in-the-dark bracelets all up the figure's wrists. 'You all tuckered out, eh?' the new man said, leaning over her. He picked up the remaining soup off the table. 'You from the doof doof?' he said, then slurped from the can.

'What do you want?' Amelia said again.

'Hey, easy now,' the first figure said, pressing the air down with his hands. 'You don't own this place.'

The second figure had found her pack, began sifting through its contents. 'Got any more food?' he said. There was a rustle of something as he opened it.

'Get out of my things,' Amelia said.

'Whoa, angel girl, where's the love?' the closest figure said. 'We've got stuff to share, don't worry. Sharing's caring.'

He blocked her way as she tried to get out of the booth. She climbed across the table, bumped her head on the ceiling. On the opposite seat, Amelia landed on some part of Lucy, making her yelp.

'Out,' Amelia hissed, and Lucy scrambled down from the seat.

The first intruder stepped in front of her again, so she couldn't get past without pressing against him. He was shirtless, his skin hot and wet, taut over a round, hard stomach; she pushed him to the side, her fingers brushing his chest hair.

'No need to rush off, angel girl,' the man said, soft and sweet, grabbing her wrist. She yanked it away. 'Peace, little lady, peace.'

The man with the bracelets had disembowelled her bag. She grabbed handfuls of stuff, shoved them back inside. He sat down and watched her, crunching on her rice crackers.

Amelia swung her pack over her shoulder, moved towards the door.

'Why don't you stay and have a smoke, chill out a bit,' the first man said, tugging at a pocket on her pack. 'You don't know what you're missing, angel girl.'

She leapt out the door and swore as she lost her footing, landing in a heap outside.

'You right?' the man said from inside the carriage, laughing.

A bang sent her running, Lucy beside her, charging across the field back the way they'd come. She could feel clammy hands beneath her T-shirt, how the hard flesh of that man would feel pinning her down, the burn as the other one held her wrists; the sound of flies unzipping, the tearing of her clothes, the screech of her skin against the table. And the whole time the man's soft voice, trying to make her calm as if she were a beast and he knew what was good for her.

She plunged under the fence, ripping something on her bag, got to her feet and kept running. The men hooted somewhere behind her. The way back seemed much longer, impossibly long; her breath was jagged as it entered her chest, rain running down her forehead and into her eyes.

She burst out of the scrub and onto the side of the highway. Lucy panted beside her. They ran down the white line of the road, didn't stop until there were headlights, the hum of an engine. Amelia stuck her thumb out.

The driver of an old Land Cruiser kept their foot steady on the accelerator. As the vehicle drew closer she stepped out onto the road, waved her arms. The car veered around her. The thrum of the engine died down. Brake lights. She ran to the vehicle, some of her things still bundled in her arms, wet, heavy. She asked no questions, didn't look into the dimness of the car for a face. She leapt up into the front seat, Lucy at her feet.

'Well, whadda we have here,' the man said.

'Hi,' Amelia said. Then, between short breaths: 'Sorry.'

'You will be,' the man said, chuckling. Lucy was squashed in the footwell next to the backpack, and Amelia couldn't get the door closed over dangling straps and buckles.

'Let's get ya sorted out, eh,' the man said. 'Gee whiz.' He lowered himself out of the vehicle, squinting in the headlights as he walked around the front of the car. He had a dark beard, thick and rounded off. Long, thin arms swung out of a navy blue singlet. He walked too slowly; Amelia scanned the scrub for signs of pursuit. She jumped as he opened her door.

'Give this beast to me,' he said. The back of his arm slid along her calves as he wrestled her pack out of the footwell. Lucy got out of the truck as the pack shifted beside her, then scampered back up in a hurry, as if afraid she'd be left behind.

'Good girl,' Amelia said, running her hands down Lucy's sides. 'We're okay. We're okay now.' Lucy was panting, her chest moving as she caught her breath, heart fast beneath her fur.

The car smelled of petrol and wet wool; the seat was greasy beneath Amelia's thighs. The man threw her pack in the boot, the suspension giving beneath its weight. She twisted around to see her bag but the seats and a caged divider blocked her view. He returned and took the bundle of things from her lap. She was suddenly bare. She pulled the legs of her shorts down as far as they would go, rearranged the stretched collar of her T-shirt so it didn't dip at her chest.

The boot banged shut, confirming she was here, now; it sent a shudder through the vehicle. She gripped her knees, tried to settle. She scanned the dark car for weapons. A small container of toothpicks was tacked to the dashboard.

The man hefted himself up into the car in one movement. Springs clanked beneath him as he adjusted himself on his sheepskin-covered seat.

'Thanks for stopping,' Amelia said, struggling to pull her seatbelt across.

'Didn't see much choice . . . you looked pretty stuck out there.' He reached across her, his rough knuckles scraping her arm as he gave the seatbelt a tug, buckled it in. His armpits released an acrid smell. It lingered in the stuffy air, surrounded her, as if she'd been marked by his animal scent.

The headlights cut through mist as they accelerated onto the road. She checked the side mirror for bare chests, for glow-in-the-dark bracelets, but there were only the posts lining the highway flickering by into darkness. The man let the car roar in each gear before shifting, the gearstick trembling near her legs.

A clock read 11.07 pm. The numbers gave the car's interior a green glow.

'It's a few minutes off,' the man said. She hadn't seen him look at her.

'Right,' she said.

A drip splashed onto her head, slithered down her scalp. She shivered.

'Cold, eh?' the man said.

'Just a shiver. There was a drip or something, I dunno.' She spoke loudly over the sound of the engine.

'Oh yeah, I got a leak. Keep forgetting about it and then it rains and the seat gets wet. Then it dries, and I forget again.'

She was quiet, but he grunted as if expecting something. 'Yep, yep, know the feeling,' she said. Her mouth was dry, her Mount Franklin tucked away in the boot.

'They call me Pops.' He reached across the console with his right hand, keeping his eyes on the road.

She accepted his hand, took hold of it firmly. 'I'm Amelia. This is Lucy.' His handshake was soft; she loosened her grip for fear of him thinking her too eager.

'G'day to the two 'er ya, and welcome aboard,' he said, his voice changing into some kind of tour-guide character.

He released her hand and an oily residue remained; she tried to rub it off on her shorts without him noticing.

'And where might I be taking you on this lovely evenin'?'

'Just as far as you can get us,' she said. It was the wrong thing to say; she should have had an answer planned. 'Melbourne,' she corrected. 'We're aiming for Melbourne. But anywhere that way would be great. Where are you headed?'

'You're lucky it was me who picked you up, darl,' he said. 'This time of night, god knows who's out and about, looking for trouble.' He leaned forward and fiddled with something beneath his seat; the glow of the dashboard showed deep frown lines in his forehead. 'You want my advice, you shoulda waited till daybreak before hitching a ride. Not your first time, but, is it?'

'No,' she said. Lucy squirmed at her feet.

'Well, you know better than me then,' he said, raising his hands off the wheel in surrender. The vehicle headed into the opposite lane, and he corrected it with a soft wobble.

'I wouldn't usually look for a ride at night – I mean, I don't. I just . . . well, I've got somewhere to be.'

'Right, right.' He sucked at something in his teeth. 'Whatever floats ya boat, darl.' The thing dislodged, and he chewed on it. He looked at her, caught her watching; he flashed the white of a smile. He turned his head slowly, looked back at the road. She was grateful for the darkness; her face pounded with heat.

'Everything okay?' he said. 'Do I need to be worried about you? That wild face of yours all lit up in me headlights . . .'

'I'm fine, thanks,' she said. She thought about the men in the train, about telling him, but instead she poked at the bruise on her thigh, tried to relax into the ripples of pain.

'Have it your way then, darl, suits me. Ask me nothing and I'll do the same for you . . . deal?' His hand snaked across the car again, searching for hers. She left it hanging there, pretended for a moment that she had a choice, then shook it.

Lucy struggled to get comfortable in the cramped footwell; Amelia tucked her knees up to her chest to make more space, her feet on the seat.

'Uh-uh,' Pops said. He swiped her feet off the chair. 'Not in my baby,' he said.

'Sorry,' she said. Her shoe had caught Lucy on the chin, and she cried out. 'Sorry,' Amelia whispered, and she cupped Lucy's face in her hands.

Nausea stirred in Amelia's stomach. She leaned back against the headrest, pressed into her temples, moving her fingers in small circles.

'Doesn't mean we can't chit-chat,' Pops said. Amelia stiffened, lowered her hands to her lap. 'The no-asking-questions thing. I didn't mean, you know, that we gotta sit here in silence.' He slapped a hand down onto his thigh; the movement made its own little wind.

'Yep, okay.'

'Maybe you're just a quiet one,' he said. 'I get that. I'm a bit of a shy guy myself.' He moved his hand across the car, let it kick and vibrate on the gearstick.

She flicked the rubber bands at her wrist, tried to spark life into herself, to make herself do better. 'Thanks again for picking us up,' she said.

'Well, now, you're very welcome. Your type is rare out here these days . . . Very rare. Wouldn't want to miss the chance to pick up a real-life hitchhiker. And a chicky, at that!' He clapped loudly. 'You're a bloody endangered species!' He laughed, punctuated by a whistle through his teeth, a bobbing of his shoulders. The movement released the smell of beast from his underarms.

'I'll kick off then, how's that?' he said. 'Where ya from? That's a nice easy one for ya, eh?'

'Sydney.' It was right for her to choose a big, anonymous city, but it got stuck in her throat, a slight shake at the end of it.

'Right, right, which part?'

'Bondi,' she said, surer and stronger this time.

'Oh yeah, the beach and that,' Pops said.

'Yeah, the beach is good. Love the water.'

Lucy stood up in the footwell. She lifted her paws onto Amelia's seat, her eyes a soft glow.

'Uh-uh,' Pops said in reprimand.

'Off please,' Amelia said. Lucy held her position, defiant for a moment, before scraping her paws to the floor.

'Topless, isn't it?' Pops said.

'What's that?'

'The beach. Bondi. You can go topless if you want. You know, take off the bikini, even out the tan. Not that those little triangles cover much.' He looked over at her.

'Right,' Amelia said. 'There's a pretty relaxed vibe there, I guess.'

He pulled out a toothpick from his container on the dash and held it in the side of his mouth as he spoke. 'That's just what I remember about the place. All these tits pokin' out at ya. Hard to know where to look, if you ask me. All shapes and sizes, too. All sorts, honestly. Even fatties, they didn't care.' His voice grew louder as he continued: 'Half-naked women runnin' after their kids, hot chicks all lean and long, blonde, most of them, then the tourists . . . Some of 'em so dark of skin they definitely didn't need a tan. And others still who won't get their kit off. They're trying to swim in tracksuits! The lifeguards are dragging them out of the surf fully clothed!' He turned to her, his teeth bright within his beard. 'You know?' He shook his head, whistled through his teeth.

'Right.'

'Yeah, and some of them get that lobster colour and you just wanna tell them they'll spend the rest of their holiday locked away in their fancy hotel, sheddin' skin like a brown snake.' His voice was high as he reached the punchline.

'Sounds about right,' Amelia said, nodding along. She clenched her jaw and kept nodding, nodding.

'Yeah, I liked that place, actually, come to think of it. Bondi Beach. Got a good ring to it,' he said.

A car approached in the opposite lane, headlights catching the grey in Pops's sideburns. His forearms were sinewy and smudged with black. The approaching car's high beams were on and Pops flashed his lights at them, clucked his tongue.

He cleared his throat regularly as they drove. Amelia braced herself each time, the sound a threat that he would say something new. The inside of her elbow itched but she didn't dare scratch it; she sat as still as possible, shrank into the seat, made sure that even her breathing was undetectable. She got away with this for ten minutes, fifteen, half an hour.

He rounded a bend in the road. Her shoulder pushed into the door and Lucy tensed at her feet as she slid across the floor.

'You're not really from Bondi, though, are you darl,' he said, accelerating out of the curve. He turned his head towards her. 'I call bullshit.'

She wriggled in her seat, moved closer to the door. 'Yeah, I am,' she said, straightening her shoulders. 'We weren't right on the beach though . . . we had to walk to get to the water.'

'Suit yourself,' he said, and there was a tone of resignation, of injury. 'You just don't seem like that type.' He rubbed the side of his nose, sniffed. He looked towards the driver's window, muttered 'Bullshit' and a string of other, indecipherable things. She held her breath until the onslaught ended.

The white trunks of gum trees lined the road ahead, skirts of bark discarded at their bases. The trees were her only witnesses; they'd watch if she jumped from the car, observe her injuries as she hit the ground and rolled to a stop at their feet. Perhaps her blood would spatter far enough to paint them.

Pops didn't speak and neither did she. Another drip fell and she was still, let it trickle down into her shirt. She was cold and sticky.

Approaching an uphill, Pops's hand knocked her leg as he changed into third gear.

'Sorry,' she said, snapping her leg away from the gearstick.

'You're all right, darlin', you're all right,' Pops said, revving the engine to get to the hilltop, then finally sliding into fourth, then fifth. The surface of the silence was broken, and it was easier, then, to speak.

'So, where are you from?' she said, putting her energy into the words, designing them to be sweet and sincere.

'What's that, darl?'

She tried to match his volume: 'Where are you from?'

'Ah, well. Now, that's a question. Don't you remember the rules?' He laughed, shoulders bobbing again. 'I did ask you, though, didn't I . . .'

He said nothing more so Amelia offered, 'Yeah, I guess.'

'All right, fair's fair. I've moved round a lot, here, there and everywhere. I've lived all over, except Tassie, would you believe,' he said. 'Born in Broken Hill, though, so I guess that's me answer.'

Amelia nodded with feigned enthusiasm.

'Been to Tassie, though. Bloody beautiful,' he said. 'Now there's a place you should be hitchin' around. Can't go wrong over there.'

'Huh,' Amelia said.

'Bloody beautiful,' he said. 'A special old place, that.'

He seemed happy to leave things there; she didn't have to talk about Tasmania, about doing the Overland with her mother. He sank deeper into his seat and sighed; his breath reached her at a delay, stale and sour. His nose was runny and he sniffled every few seconds. When it became too much, he collected snot on his arm in a firm, fast wipe, keeping the toothpick lodged in his mouth.

'There's some errands I gotta do,' Pops said, breaking the quiet.

'No worries,' Amelia said. Something in her chest loosened, let go. 'Just drop me off wherever works for you . . . Anywhere here will do.' The last part was too much, too obvious.

'Calm ya farm, sweetheart, I don't mean right now,' he said. 'Down the road a bit, I gotta drop in on a mate's place there – told her I'd keep an eye on the joint while she's away. Water the plants and that, you know.'

'Right,' Amelia said. 'Well, just let me know when and I'll leave you to –'

'She's off in Bali or Thailand, one of them places,' he went on, speaking over her. 'You might like them places, being from Bondi.'

'Oh, yeah, guess I would.'

He left her alone again then, returning to his pattern of sniff, sniff, sniff, wipe and repeat. Occasionally he lifted his singlet to blow into the material, exposing skin on his stomach.

Never trust a bad driver, her mother often said, but Pops was a good driver, smooth and steady, as if the car was an extension of his own body.

He's a good driver . . . he's a really good driver.

Lucy was restless. She stood, pushing against Amelia's legs. Amelia rested a hand on her, tried to push her bum down, but Lucy mouthed at her wrist, refused to settle.

'How's your temperature, darl?' he said, holding a hand out to the air vents.

'Yeah, fine thanks,' Amelia said.

'No air con in here,' Pops said. 'Just a blower . . . I'm a windows kinda man myself, so I don't miss it. Know what I mean? Insects

170

get in at this hour, though, with the window down,' he said. 'They smash against your face, on your lips, they don't care. Bloody kills if one gets in your eye,' he said.

Amelia managed a laugh to match his, and he looked over at her with a big smile, then laughed harder, thumping the wheel a couple of times in appreciation of his own comment.

'Well, it sure is nice to have the company,' Pops said. He said it with a new gentleness and Amelia straightened up in her chair, took a deep breath.

'Yeah, you can say that again . . . So, where are you headed?'

Pops shook his head. 'Remember that deal we made?' he said. 'No questions?'

She waited for the bounce of his shoulders, for permission to laugh. He turned to her, serious, beard revealing no teeth. He looked back at the road, and then he was laughing; the whistle, the shoulders. 'If I told ya, I'd have to kill ya!' he said, then quickly: 'Nah, nah, nah, I shouldn't make those jokes around you, you poor thing.' He continued to chuckle to himself. 'I've got you all scared now, haven't I?'

'No,' was all she could manage. She tried again: 'Guess I just don't get it.'

'No questions, remember? Simple. You got a memory like a sieve, darlin' . . . Unless you want to start answering some?'

'You said that we could still talk, so I just thought . . .' Amelia paused. Her throat dried and she tried to swallow, her saliva thick. 'I wasn't sure about the rules.'

'That's fair enough, sweetheart, fair enough,' Pops said. 'Gosh, I'm a bastard, aren't I? Making your life difficult, huh, when you've obviously got enough on your plate.'

The vehicle shuddered along. Lucy calmed down, accepted Amelia's insistent massage around her ears.

Pops proved to be good at the no-questions thing. He ran a commentary, with interludes, and all she needed to do was demonstrate that she was listening. 'Never much traffic along this stretch, for some reason,' Pops said, or 'Bloody rich farmin' out here, I tell ya,' and, after a long stint of nothing, 'Had this car for its whole life. She just goes and goes and goes.' To these Amelia responded with affirmative sounds and words: 'Huh', 'Right', and 'Wow'.

They'd been travelling for just over three hours when he said, 'Me mate Linda's house isn't far now. I'll just pop in, won't be a minute.'

'Right, okay. No rush. I'll leave you to it. I'm pretty tired so . . .'

'You're not thinking about leaving me, are ya?' Pops said. 'Don't go breakin' my heart.'

Amelia said nothing.

'It wouldn't sit right with me, leaving you out here . . . God only knows what trouble you might find. I just couldn't do it. Anyway, there's a bloody big pot she wants moved and I need your help. You scratch my back, I'll scratch yours . . . You don't mind helping me out, do ya?'

Pops flicked on the indicator for a turn-off Amelia couldn't see. No street signs, no driveways, no pots to water. Paddock fencing along the road promised farmhouses somewhere in the distance.

Pops pulled in and stopped at a gate, wrenched the hand-brake up. The engine puttered, threatening to stall.

'Well, out ya get,' Pops said.

'Sorry?' Amelia said.

'The gate, darl. Driver never gets the gate, didn't you know?' His shoulders were bouncing, teeth whistling.

'Right, got it.'

'No gates in Bondi, eh?' he went on, still laughing at her. She slipped down and out of the car.

Lucy followed her, pissed by the side of the driveway, where wheel prints were pressed into the dirt. Amelia narrowed her eyes in the headlights. Her vision was blotched with white as she walked to the gate, took in the opening mechanism; her every move was exposed and she was determined to get it right first time. A padlock was attached to a chain, though, on closer inspection, she saw it was unlocked.

The gate opened and she pulled it away from the car. Pops moved slowly through the small gap. She held the fence against her like a shield, gripping and releasing the rounded metal. Grip and release, grip and release. She could run, now. Her body tingled, the bottoms of her feet already feeling the pound of the road as she sprinted down it, her arms pumping back and forth, her legs absorbing her weight, pushing it up again, the pull of barbed wire in her hair as she ducked under a fence and hid. The throbbing heartbeat of being followed, of being found.

Red lights came on, the brakes squeaking. She closed the gate and climbed into the car.

Stupid girl.

'Ta, darl,' Pops said. Lucy jumped into the footwell and Pops pushed the handbrake down. The dirt road was rough, with potholes so large Pops almost reached a standstill, negotiating them in first gear. Amelia held on tight to the handle above her door with one hand, Lucy's collar with the other. Fallen branches were lit by the headlights and Pops snapped over them, the bigger limbs scraping the undercarriage of the car as they passed beneath.

'This road's shithouse,' Pops said. 'You're holdin' on for dear life, aren't ya darlin'?'

'Yeah,' she said.

They drove for a long time; it was clear she had made the wrong choice. Three more bends, and she promised to ask how much further. Then she didn't, and she didn't, and she didn't.

But then the road had flowers in pots, and white pebbles running alongside it, and a weatherboard house grew out of the shadows ahead.

'Here we are,' she said. Lucy stood, sensing the change, her hot breath on Amelia's leg.

'Here we are,' Pops said, crunching to a stop beside a Hills hoist with bare, misshapen arms. The car rolled backwards slightly as his foot left the brake. He swung down to the ground, slammed his door. As she sat there, still, everything seemed to dip and roll.

A knock on her window and she jumped. Pops's face was right up beside hers, the tip of his nose pressed against the glass.

'See ya in a sec,' he said. He gave the window a farewell knuckle-tap, ducked under the clothesline and disappeared around the side of the house. The windows were all dark, and she waited for the house to light up as he moved through it.

The car hissed and ticked as it cooled. Minutes passed, and no light shone from inside the house.

She wound down her window, sucked in fresh air, then listened. The angry-insect sound of a small engine started up, revving high. It drove out from behind the house and away from her; a red tail-light gave away the motorbike's movement, then a headlight flashed on, illuminating clumps of dry grass before it. The bike travelled up and over mounds and then was swallowed by bushland.

Moments later, the lights reappeared higher and much further away. The bike had made rapid progress. The journey of it gave Amelia a sense of the surrounding landscape: the house was in a valley, hills and bush looming over her. Then the bike was gone.

She listened, tried to block out the cicadas and the call of a bird she didn't recognise, and tune her ear to the vehicle. If it was there, somewhere in the distance, it was beyond her perception.

The wind shifted a set of chimes hanging at the corner of the house. She wound up her window. Lucy nuzzled her leg and Amelia rubbed the soft fur beneath her chin while scanning the terrain out the front window for a flicker of light. It was darker out there than it had been before, now that she'd had the light and lost it.

She pressed the lock down on her door, reached across to the other doors and did the same. She waited. Her jaw was clenched and she opened it wide; the click of it reverberated in the car. Her eyes adjusted and she listed items as they materialised from the grey fuzz: watering can, window shutter, lattice. No human figures waiting in ambush.

Resting her hand on the door, she closed her eyes, counted three breaths, and unlocked it. She jumped to the ground, landed light and ready, but there was no attack. At the back of the car, she ran her hands down the boot, searched for a handle. Dust collected on her fingers as she traced over the keyhole, went lower and under to find the latch. Locked. She tried it again, harder, then with a jiggle. Still locked. She pulled hard enough that something gave way near her shoulderblade. The boot didn't open.

A twig cracked. Amelia tensed, pressed flat onto the car, waited for an ensuing footstep. Nothing. Lucy sneezed, snuffled at the car's back tyre.

Amelia climbed up to the passenger seat and reached across the console, felt around Pops's seat for the sharp metal of keys. She climbed across the gearstick and sank into the mould of his body; the sheepskin remembered the shape and smell of him. The keys weren't in the ignition, either. Slapping at the roof for the interior light, she scanned knobs and buttons in the yellow glow for one that would pop the boot.

'No, no, no,' she whispered, pulling and twisting things, pressing on panels, popping the bonnet by mistake. She stopped, filled her lungs, then started again, moving methodically across the dashboard from left to right.

She sat back in Pops's seat, rested her cheek on the wool. The passenger seat was there, the place she'd been, and she was him, watching on. He would have seen the whiteness in her hands as she tensed them, her chest moving in and out with controlled breathing, the way she tugged at her clothes, hiding skin. She shivered, looked away.

She clicked off the interior light, slid down and out of the car. The smell of Pops was strong. She held her breath. Blinded by the fresh darkness, she reached out her hands to feel for him, thought of touching him in the wrong places by mistake: her fingers dipping in to soft skin folds, scruffs of beard, warmth and wetness. But she touched only air.

A shadow passed over white curtains inside the house. She watched the same window, the exact spot she'd seen movement, until a shadow crossed over it again, and then again. At the edge of the house, beside the window, the silhouette of a tree moved in time with the shadow, bending in the wind. She bowed her head, raised it again at the next noise, a snap, and the next. The night was moving in around her.

She followed a pebbled path around the house, walking between garden beds lined with rocks. She tripped on a metal bucket and it clanged along the ground; she froze, straining to hear waking scrapes and groans from the house, someone rising

177

from bed, walking down a hallway to the front door. But there was only Lucy snorting in dust somewhere near the car.

As she walked around the corner of the house, a light came on with an innocent click: she was caught. She blinked against the sudden flare of brightness. She waited there, listening and still. The light switched off; she moved her arm, and it came on again.

A birdcage sat on a porch, a ragged cockatiel clutching its white rung. Yellow thongs sat weathered and loyal by the top step.

Amelia pushed down on the front screen door's metal handle; it opened with a shiver. Lucy appeared at Amelia's calf as she reached out and touched her fingers to the rounded doorknob; it was greasy and warm, and it twisted easily. Amelia recoiled as the door creaked open a crack. Lucy opened it further with her nose, setting the whine of its hinges echoing into the house.

'Get back,' Amelia hissed. She pulled the door to. Despite her attempts to be gentle, the screen shook in its frame as it closed, the sound continuing even as she turned her back.

Crunching a few steps away on the pebbles, Amelia turned and watched the entrance. Insects mobbed the sensor light, the larger ones hammering against its plastic.

On the way back to the car, a tension gripped her low down in her belly. She walked with her hand on the skin there, looking out around her.

It has come to this. It has come . . . to this.

She gathered spit in her mouth then swallowed it down, pretended it was water. Lucy hesitated at the car door, lowered onto her haunches as if about to jump into the passenger seat, but didn't.

'Come on, girl,' Amelia said, clicking her fingers, and Lucy obeyed. Amelia pulled her in close, wrapped her arms around her and buried her face in Lucy's fur. She held her there, tightly, until Lucy wriggled and pulled away.

Amelia reached through and unlocked the back door. She crawled onto the back seat, pushing aside newspapers and empty drink cans. She stretched out as best she could across the prickly back seat, trying to find a position where seatbelt plugs did not dig in to her back. A rag dangled out of the seat pocket near her head; she gave it a tug. It smelled of petrol but she pulled it over her for the comfort of its weight, the flannel soft on her thigh.

Lucy stirred in the front of the car, panted. Amelia bent her arm behind her head. Exhaustion ached through her body but her mind darted towards each scrabble and rustle outside. She rolled over to her side, pressed her back into the curve of the seats, and closed her eyes.

*

She sat up with a start. Morning light filled the car. Outside, the house was still, the path of pebbles blaring white in the sun. The land dipped away behind it then rose again into bushland. She placed a hand low on her belly, beneath her shorts, and felt the tensing and shifting inside. She flinched at a sudden internal tug, leaned back against the inside of the door. She closed her eyes against nausea.

There were new bites down her arms and legs, on her neck, but she let the itches tingle, pressed instead into the ache, into the hardness in her abdomen.

Lucy stirred and appeared between the front seats, two paws on the centre console, releasing hot breaths. Amelia lolled her head towards her, gave her a half-formed smile. Lucy licked her hand with a dry tongue.

'Okay, girl, okay,' Amelia said.

Amelia worked in stages: she dragged herself to vertical, moved her legs to the floor, then rested her pounding head against the back of Pops's chair, gathering herself; she opened the car door, sat at the edge of the seat, hung her legs outside. Lucy scrambled across the console, left white scratches on Amelia's thigh as she pushed out of the car.

The air smelled of eucalyptus leaves drying. It was hot, but the sky held the deeper blue of morning; she guessed it was about seven o'clock. Her throat was dry. She lifted her T-shirt to let the heat of the sun soothe her belly. A pair of crimson rosellas flew above her, chirping, flaunting their energy.

She slid down from the car, kept a hand on the warm metal of it while she checked the boot. It was still locked. Wetness spread into her underpants.

She reached through the back and unlocked Pops's door, climbed up behind the wheel. In the new light, she went over every button and switch, but nothing opened the boot. She tried to get comfortable in Pops's seat, to fill the shape of his back and bottom. Outside, Lucy lapped at a muddy puddle in a rut.

It has come to this.

Amelia lifted the top of her shorts, the seam of them constricting over the tender area. She sat in a moment of relief, before the cramping took hold again. She willed herself to her feet, slipped down from the car. A small patch of blood spread where she'd sat, the edges creeping out then darkening as she watched.

She buried her hands in her pockets but there was only lint and crumbs. Pops's glove box, the sides of the doors, the pockets of the seats held nothing of use. She bundled the oily rag she'd used as a bedcover into her fist.

An orb spider had built a web strung between two branches; the creature waited in the perfect centre of it. Amelia ducked beneath it and crouched behind a tree. The deep red in her undies had gone through to the crotch of her shorts. She peed, dark and pungent, then gathered bark and gum leaves from the ground, choosing a handful that were relatively intact. With these she tried to wipe out what mess she could; her blood was violent against the green of the leaves.

She laid a handful of foliage on her undies and wrapped Pops's cloth around these, tucked it into itself. She cleaned her hands as best she could on the cloth then dragged her fingers up her calves to get the remaining blood off, leaving faint, fading red stripes. She pulled up her shorts.

The bulk of the pad changed the way she walked. At the edge of the scrub, she reached up to a branch and pulled down on it, stretching out the tightness in her pelvis. Her back cracked and she stretched deeper. Beyond the house, she could now see a rusted tin shed and another structure of green plastic, partially obstructed from view at the far corner of the house. She released the branch, improved her angle of vision: a water tank.

She sprinted towards it, leapt over garden beds, the pad loosening in her crotch. Lucy bounded along beside her. A hose was attached to the tank and she reeled the orange nozzle in, turned the tap on. There was a delay before a choked spurt. Water streamed out, sharp, and she filled her mouth, let it bubble over. It was warm at first and tasted of plastic, but this gave way to cooler, fresher rainwater, spiced with the flavour of sticks and leaves. She sprayed it on her face, the jet burning up her nose so she spluttered and struggled for breath. She shook her head, sending drops flying.

Lucy barked, her back arched, bum in the air and front legs spread in play. Water soaked the front of Amelia's shirt, ran down in streams that filled her shoes. She held the nozzle over her head, soaking her hair, savouring the shock of coolness down her back. She closed her eyes, let her ears fill with water, scrubbed the raw skin on her face.

'What the hell do you think you're doin'?'

Amelia opened her eyes; a woman crunched around the side of the house holding a pair of old gardening scissors. Amelia directed the hose to the garden, fumbled the tap off.

'Sorry, I –' Amelia said, gasping, wiping snot from beneath her nose.

'This is my property,' the woman said, stopping a couple of metres up the path. She put her hands on her hips, the scissors at an angle, sharp ends out.

'Sorry, I was waiting here –'

'You're trespassing.' The woman was in a faded blue nightie. A jagged fringe sat on her eyebrows, a long, thin ponytail hanging over her shoulder.

'I'm waiting, a guy called Pops brought me here, he said he –'

'Why would I care? You're not s'posed to be here. This is private property.'

Drops tinkled from Amelia's body, hitting the cement. 'But your friend, Pops. He left me here, said he was looking after your place while you were away . . . are you Linda?'

'What were ya gonna do? Take my water then snip me hose, make a happy little bong for yourself?' She wiped her mouth with the back of her hand. 'Scared the shit outta me.'

'I've been out here all night, in the car, I didn't know –'

'Ya can't just camp out in someone's yard, girly,' she said. The woman stood on one leg while she scratched the inside of her calf with a big toe.

'I know, I'm sorry . . . my stuff's locked in the car.' Amelia was hunched over with cramps; she tried to straighten up.

'Not my problem. Get.' The woman stomped a foot towards Amelia, brandished the scissors. Lucy skittered back a few metres. 'Go on, get,' she said, swooping her arms forward, then bluffing another charge. 'You're bloody lucky the old man's passed out or you'd be in some real trouble,' she said. 'I'd be clearing out in a hurry if I were you.'

'I'll go, I'll go,' Amelia said, taking a step backwards, her hands raised in surrender. 'But please – do you mean Pops?'

'What would I know about your little friend? Shove off, girly, I'm serious. Go and do your wandering somewhere else. And don't you dream of wasting a drop more of my water, you greedy bitch.'

'But my stuff is locked in the car, and I need –'

'You've got no idea, do ya? Go, *G-O*,' the woman said.

Amelia lowered her hands, turned around slowly.

'No use huffin' and puffin', girl,' the woman said. 'You're getting off lightly. This is private property . . . Giving me the spooks first thing in the morning . . .'

Amelia turned. 'I just want to know –'

'See ya,' the woman said, fluttering her fingers in a wave.

Amelia scuffed her feet as she walked away, holding shaking hands across her belly. The rag between her legs smelled of oil as she walked. A piece of bark worked its way free of her undies and sliced at the inside of her thigh. Lucy walked ahead, unable to keep the slow pace. She stopped and turned, waited for Amelia to catch up, but was soon ahead again.

Sweat gathered at Amelia's hairline though she was suddenly very cold. She walked downhill, her feet slipping on the steep dirt road. Her insides flipped, pulsing beneath her fingers. The pulling pain multiplied and spread, punctuated by isolated wrenches that made her gasp.

She stopped to endure one of these attacks, turned to see if she was a peaceful distance from the house. The woman had followed her over the ridge, stood facing her in the middle of the driveway; she widened her stance, crossed her arms over her chest.

Amelia straightened her shoulders, turned around, and kept walking. She was registering all the items in her pack, everything she had left behind. She gripped her mother's shopping list in her mind but she was already forgetting the angle of each letter, the amount of blank space between the edge of the page and the words, the exact place of the scribble her mother had made to bring the ailing pen back to life.

The track dipped and curved between dry paddocks afflicted with weeds. The sun bore into her scalp, finding strips of exposed skin where her hair parted. Her headache was sharp and insistent. At intervals along the way, she held her head in her hands and pushed hard, the pressure offering momentary relief. Beads of sweat dripped down her face and dried in stiff, salty lines on her cheeks. A haze on the horizon promised more heat.

Barbed wire fences stretched out on either side of the path and it was as if she were skewered on that metal, the spikes catching then ripping through her insides as she forged onwards. She curved over the pain, her arms crossed low and clutching at her sides.

The feeling of being watched persisted. The gum trees became Pops, their long branches his arms, his face pressing out from inside trunks. She stopped and turned suddenly, trying to catch him or any assailant off guard. The house looked down on her from a distance. From its windows, she could easily be tracked: a flare of colour and a small puff of dust as she dragged her feet beneath her.

She picked up a fallen branch in case she needed to defend herself, and used it to take some of her weight. Lucy pushed her dry muzzle into Amelia's hand; her fur was hot, the darkness of it absorbing heat.

They walked, and the sun got higher, centring itself in the sky. Fence posts became both the passing of time and a measure of progress. She committed to a post in the distance, promised to make it there before resting. Each challenge she set for herself grew shorter and shorter till she only made it from one post to the next. Once there, she would bend over the post, head on her arms, with the roughness of the wood beneath her fingertips. A currawong followed her every move; it chose low branches from which to watch her pass, then flapped ahead to reach a vantage point further along the trail.

'I've got nothing,' she told it, her voice hoarse. The bird didn't listen.

Flies formed a halo around her head. At first she swiped the air and blew them off her lips but as she weakened, she surrendered, carried them on her skin, imagined that maggots would hatch from her pores. Hives rose in clusters on the inside of her forearm and she spat on them, rubbed the saliva in. She tried not to scratch but the effort became too much. She attacked them with abandon; scabs dislodged and pus smeared with blood across her raised skin. The flies found new energy.

Her legs gave way before she reached the next post. She collapsed onto all fours, loose rocks cutting into her knees. She retched. The channel of her throat was narrow and dry.

She heaved again, released a bitter string of pinkish bile. Each breath carried a moan she couldn't control. Lucy approached and sniffed at the wetness around Amelia's mouth.

Amelia crawled into the feeble shade of a tree. The ground sent heat up through her as she lay on it; a thistle leered over her, plucking at her T-shirt. She closed her eyes.

*

Amelia roused from a feverish vision of her mother. Her hands were lifted, palms open before her eyes; in her confusion, she had been trying to wash her face. She put her hands to her cheeks in case they were actually wet, in case there was water, in case her mother was really there, breathing in the next room. But her hands were dry, her cheeks hot and sweaty beneath them.

The scene began to taper away, so she closed her eyes and went back to the memory of the final moments, when she was beside her mother's bed, keeping vigil; her mother was too small beneath the covers. Amelia hadn't slept in days. Cushions from the couch were stacked up beneath her. Amelia stood, walked the few steps to the bathroom. Used the toilet, washed her face. Her hands were cool and damp against her cheeks as she crossed the hallway, which was dim with dawn light, and returned to her mother's bedside.

It was in those moments of absence that her mother had died.

'Mum?' Her voice was a husk and yet it was too loud, clarifying her aloneness on the dirt. The sky was too lively a blue above her, the pressure from stones and twigs too sharp beneath her.

She didn't want this world; she closed her eyes, and in the red-tinged darkness her mother was a possibility again. She reached out as her mother swirled away, tugged her back, demanded her attention: there was something Amelia needed to tell her. Amelia brought forth a series of scenes and populated them with remembered detail, each of them holding solid after a decade. She lifted each one up for examination, as if she were a child holding out a drawing for her mother's approval.

The first showed Zach unhooking her fingers from a drink of water, slowly, showed him watching her while he put his mouth on the glass. He handed it back to her, the ice clinking, and pointed to the place where his lips had been. 'Drink,' he said.

The next began with the bolts of his spine as he shovelled, the moment he caught her watching. The perfect stun of his closeness: a trap of skin, sweat, breath, hair.

Then, his hands removing seedlings from pots, planting roots in the holes she dug. The softness in his voice as he told her what she liked, the soil beneath her fingernails as he moved her hands around his body, teaching her.

Finally, by the back fence, behind the fig tree: the grass that she let grow long and wild after he was gone, weeds choking the climbers he planted, pulling down fence palings, letting light through.

She asked her mother: *Do you see? This happened to me.*

She cycled through again, slower this time, much slower.

*

188

It was early afternoon when she heard the rumble of a truck in the distance. She lay with her eyes closed, listened, unsure if the noise was real. There it was. Lucy lay on her side, legs straight, her tail thumping in scattered tree bark as Amelia sat up.

The highway became louder as she ran, legs unsteady, down the track. There was a new lightness to her movement, though her head pounded with each step, and white flecks skated across her sight. Lucy ran ahead, whipping around in excited circles.

The gate was there and she opened it, her hands remembering the movements from the night before.

'Easy, Luce, easy,' she said. Lucy went through the gate, then waited, panting, as Amelia closed it.

They stood where the highway met the dirt path. There was a tenderness to her abdomen, a memory of the earlier pain. A plastic bottle was tucked into grass beside the road. She went to it, unscrewed the lid and pressed the opening to her mouth. It was empty but she held it there hoping to coax out any lingering moisture.

She raised her thumb to the passing vehicles. A red car with bicycles balanced on its roof didn't stop. A sunglasses-wearing man in a Corolla made no acknowledgement of her. A Commodore approached with pillows pressing against the windows, and the eyes of children stared at her out the back window as the car sped away. A sleek silver bullet of a car, a wobbly ute stacked with chairs and a desk, a livestock truck pushing the smell of shit-soaked animals against her: none of them stopped.

She counted the red cars, Sid's colour. Each one became significant, likely to stop for her and take her to Sid's door. She conjured him, then, his calm, the way she could meet his eye and hold it. The consistency of him in the days after her mother died, lying on his camping mat beside her bed, watching over her.

An orange kombi flashed its lights at her. Its engine altered and there was the crunch and rev of lowering gears as the van went past. Gravel popped beneath its wheels. The driver gave a quick toot of the horn, stopped with a skid. He bounced out of the door: a man in a leather waistcoat, chest bare.

'Hey there,' he yelled. He walked towards her, doing a big side-to-side wave, arm in the air. He let out a hoot, happy to be alive. She was rigid as he approached, taking in the plaited goatee, his billowing pants.

'Hey,' he said again. She raised her hand then let it fall. Lucy stepped forward, sniffed.

'That dog friendly?' the man said, pausing a few metres away.

'Are you?' Amelia said, breaking into a dry cough.

'Ha! She's all right!' He yelled over his shoulder. Behind him, a woman slid from the van. She wore a long mauve dress, narrow straps over narrow shoulders. The woman stretched, two fists in the air. Her red hair shimmered, falling in a long, thick plait down her back. A man in a navy blue hat with a purple feather emerged too, lit a cigarette.

The waistcoated man approached Amelia with an extended hand. Lucy snuffled at his legs and Amelia held out her own limp hand.

'Jesus, you're a mess,' the man said. 'You all right?' He took her hand and shook so vigorously that her arm pulled in its socket. 'I'm Eddie,' he said.

'Any water?' she said.

'You got no water?' He looked her over with his hands on his hips, the hair in his underarms wet and hanging in strings. She blocked the sun with her hand and looked up at him; his eyes were vivid green and bloodshot.

'Well, shit,' he said. 'Come on.' He beckoned her with a scoop of his arm, then turned on his bare heel. She walked behind his long strides, followed the tinkling of his anklets. From the shade of a tree, the man in the navy blue hat nodded towards her and she nodded back. The red-haired woman squinted in her direction, then claimed the cigarette from the lips of the man in the hat. Lucy approached them and the man in the hat crouched to meet her; she walked straight past him.

Bedcovers with a rainbow print leaked out of the side door of the van. Eddie handed her a bottle personalised with cartoon stickers and permanent-marker figurines. The water was fusty and she gulped it down, catching drips from her chin and licking her fingers. She called Lucy over and she drank from Amelia's hand.

'You got any more?' Amelia said.

'There's more in the van, I think. We'll get ya sorted.' Eddie ushered over the two smokers. 'This is the band, Sven and Clare.'

'How do you do,' Sven said, a European accent curling around his words. Clare's crossed arms and narrowed eyes indicated that picking Amelia up had not been her idea.

'What's your name?' Eddie said.

'Amelia. That's Lucy.'

'Right, Amelia, do you know how to drive?' Eddie said.

'Yeah,' Amelia said. 'Why?' A cramp tightened beneath her shorts and she twitched, but did not wince.

''Cos we want you to drive,' Clare said. 'Obviously.'

'Go easy, jeez,' Eddie said, giving Amelia a wink. 'These losers don't know how to drive, you see.' Clare shoulder barged him but he was unaffected, keeping his eyes on Amelia.

'I don't think that's a good idea,' Amelia said. 'I'm not really feeling right . . . and I've never driven a van.'

Clare dragged on the cigarette, lowered it to her side between two fingers. 'We need a driver, not a passenger,' she said. She piled her hair on top of her head, a few strands remaining stuck to her neck. 'Eddie's tired.'

Amelia took a deep, secret breath. 'Where are you going?'

'Melbourne,' Sven said.

'The big smoke!' Eddie yelled, then hooted. Lucy walked over, blinked slowly. Keys came flying towards Amelia and she let them fall to the ground.

'That's the spirit,' Eddie said, then disappeared into the back of the van.

'Do you mind?' Sven said, eyes pale and serious, the blond hairs of his top lip caught in the sunlight.

'She's fine,' Clare said, slinking into the back of the van behind Eddie.

Amelia bent to pick up the keys. She stood up too quickly,

leaned against the kombi's metal as her head spun. The others were laughing from within the van.

This is it.

She walked around the front of the van and pulled herself up behind the wheel. The van smelled of old cigarettes. Springs stuck into her through the seat. She pictured the stains she'd make on the material, the blood she was leaving behind her: a trail to Sid's door.

Her fingers sank into something wet and spongy as she adjusted her seat. Sven sat in the passenger seat beside her and Lucy squeezed into the footwell in front of him. Sven handed over a bottle of Mount Franklin. 'Drink as much as you want.'

'Do you have any painkillers?' Amelia said. She held a sip of water in her mouth, let it trickle down her throat.

'Clare?' Sven said. There was a rustle, then a metal packet flew between the front seats. Sven popped out two pills and Amelia held her hand out; dirt darkened the lines in her palm. She threw the pills in her mouth and swallowed more water, tracked the gurgle of it as it moved through her.

The van puttered out onto the highway. Its sides trembled as she reached the height of each gear, and by the time the speedometer hit one hundred, the whole thing threatened to dismantle. The rag was squishy between her legs, fresh blood wet and warm; the earthy smell of herself escaped each time she moved.

Sven was quiet and he let Lucy rest her head in his lap. Clare and Eddie giggled from the back seat, and it was only a matter of minutes before laughter turned into murmurs and kissing sounds. Eddie moaned and Clare shushed him; there was a flicker of movement in the rear-vision mirror, a flash of skin, an arched back, then Clare's arm emerged and yanked a mustard-coloured curtain across.

Amelia watched the road with quick glances to Sven; he was stony and stared out his window even as Eddie's muffled groans were matched by Clare's higher-pitched panting. As a sign stated there were three hundred and fifty-two kilometres to Melbourne, the slap of skin on skin was sharp and steady.

Amelia gripped the sticky wheel, listened. Clare's gasps were filled with a pleasure Amelia had never known.

The kilometres passed in a blur; she drove and couldn't recall anything she'd seen for stretches of time. The painkillers kicked in and softened the edges of her cramps. The passengers all fell asleep. She fell asleep, too, and was woken by the wheels bumping over markers on the side of the highway. She corrected with a jolt; Sven woke up, looked around, then went back to sleep.

Aeroplanes gave the city away; they circled and swooped, or escaped in straight, sure lines. The late-afternoon heat brewed with exhaust fumes and was channelled between lanes of traffic. Amelia negotiated tailgating, speeding and unpredictable cars as they headed towards the claustrophobia of the impending city; it rose in glimpses as she rounded bends in the road, black and grey buildings piercing the sky, swallowing the light.

Amelia slowed the van to a stop behind lines of blocked traffic. The van sputtered as it idled and was slow to respond when she accelerated, creeping forward in the queue. The sleepers stirred. Lucy's tail thumped against the floor as Sven woke up. He inhaled deeply and stretched, cracking his back from side to side. Eddie opened the curtains over the back seat and poked his head out, hair at angles, pillow marks up one cheek. He gave her a thumbs-up.

'Nice job,' he said.

She waited for Clare to reveal herself and was surprised when she popped up, radiant, her eyes bright and clear. There was no evidence of invasion. Clare rubbed her nose with the palm of her hand, put her slender feet up on the back of the seat, completely unmoved.

They crept along, bumper to bumper. Amelia put her window down, let in the hot, metallic wind of traffic. Grit caught in the hairs on her arms. A plastic bag bashed itself against the cement road barrier, finally finding its way over and under the wheels of oncoming vehicles.

An ambulance picked its way through the grid of traffic behind them; cars turned at angles and squeezed together to let it through, metal tickling metal. She struggled to manoeuvre the van, bunny hopping towards a taxi; the siren screamed and the ambulance stopped right on her tail, unable to fit past. It tooted its horn, red and blue lights colouring the van's interior.

'You gotta move up,' Clare said. 'You're blocking it.'

The taxi edged forward and Amelia followed suit. The ambulance workers shook their heads and glared at her as they moved past, only centimetres between them. Lucy cowered at Sven's feet, her ears pinned back on her head.

The siren rang in Amelia's ears well after it was gone. Eddie knelt on the seat and his top half disappeared out the window. 'That shit doesn't look good,' he said, bending in from outside.

'What is it?' Clare said, her face to the glass.

'There's a truck that's lost its trailer . . . looks like it spilled boxes of fruit,' he said. 'A car's wedged under the side of it, totally squashed.' He pulled himself in and dropped back onto the seat. 'Shit,' he said.

The faces of the surrounding drivers were defeated: a woman all done-up, a turquoise hat balanced on the side of her head; a man tapping his fingers on the steering wheel, pushing up in his seat to look ahead for better options. He took a gamble, flicked on an indicator to move to the next lane of halted traffic.

Sirens converged, seeming to come from every direction. Amelia wiped her upper lip. Her thighs were sweaty. She was jittery, the city closing in on her. She scanned for escape routes; the best option was the nature strip a hundred metres down the road. She and Lucy could bolt, make a run for it before they entered the tunnel and were trapped.

Another van eased past, branded in graffiti. Two sets of brown legs hung out the window, both crossed at the ankles.

'Oi!' Eddie shouted. He lifted his shirt and pressed his nipple against the window. The van tooted its horn and Eddie laughed.

Lucy scampered up onto Sven and pressed her nose against the window, panting. A ute with a mastiff in the tray moved ahead of them in the next lane. The dog paced back and forth, unchained and restless, without a place to shelter from the sun. It saw Lucy and stood on the edge of the tray, leaning out towards her, barking. They overtook the ute and Lucy scampered over the console and into the back seat, barking her reply.

They sidled up to the graffiti van again, and the dangling legs were replaced by middle fingers from the women within.

'Rock'n'roll!' Eddie yelled, launching out of his seat. He slid the van door open and hung outside, fist extended to the sun. Lucy's paws scrabbled for traction on the seat and she was gone, the white tip of her tail streaking out the door.

'Lucy!' Amelia yanked the handbrake on and opened her door. A motorbike swerved around her, the air of it grazing her skin.

The traffic moved forward as she ran against it, following Lucy. Horns beeped. She saw a flash of fur up ahead, weaving between a silver bull bar and the hood of a red sports car.

'Lucy!'

Amelia darted through cars, pressing into their hot bonnets, dodging side mirrors, exhaust searing her calves.

On her tiptoes, her chest tight, Amelia searched for Lucy amid the haze of fumes, the glare of sun bouncing from metal surface to metal surface. There was a hive of horn-honking ahead and a gap in the traffic; Lucy stood facing a car, ears back against her head. Her tail was between her legs and she was lowered onto her haunches as the driver leaned on his horn. When Amelia reached the spot Lucy had been, there was no longer any sign of her. The traffic continued snaking ahead.

A black-haired woman had her window down, tapping ash from her cigarette. 'Did you see a dog?' Amelia shouted. 'Did you?'

The woman inched her car forward, avoided eye contact. Amelia pushed herself off the vehicle and kept running. She caught a glimpse of Lucy four or five cars in the distance, but she disappeared under a Land Rover.

'Lucy!' The air was sharp in her lungs. Her legs burned. 'Shit, shit, shit,' she said, approaching the stopped Land Rover. Its tyres were huge. She bent beneath the vehicle, looked for the familiar fur . . . and there was nothing.

'Better run,' the man said through a gap in his window. He pointed behind him with a thumb.

Amelia saw her a few metres away, poised with two paws on the barricade, preparing to leap. On the other side, the traffic going in the opposite direction rushed past, four lanes of vehicles escaping the city.

'Lucy, stay,' Amelia said. She raised her hands, pushed them gently down. 'It's all right, girl,' she said. 'It's all right.'

Lucy looked at her; her pupils were large, her body trembling. Amelia was still, everything tense. Lucy stared, and Amelia stared back. 'Easy, girl, easy.'

Lucy slid her paw down the barricade, began to retreat. A siren started up very close by and, in a flash, Lucy jumped. With a clear, graceful leap, she disappeared over the other side of the wall.

Car tyres screeched. A white hatchback jerked out of its lane. Amelia ran to the road barrier and threw her top half over, the cement grazing her stomach as she peered at the other side. Down the road, Lucy cowered against the barrier, her ears plastered back. Her mouth was open and she yelped, high-pitched, confused. Amelia couldn't tell if her dark coat concealed blood or injury. The traffic hurtled past. As Amelia ran, a piece of wire tangled between her legs and she almost fell, hands out, face angled towards the ground. Then she was there, at the barrier, reaching over and grabbing fistfuls of fur. She dug her fingers into the scruff of Lucy's neck and yanked her up over the concrete, scooping her hind legs up beneath her. She collapsed to the road, her back to the barricade. She cradled Lucy on her lap, running her hands along Lucy's body searching for sticky blood, squeezing limbs to test for broken bones, found nothing. Amelia buried her face into fur and it zapped her cheeks with static.

Fast footsteps approached, but she kept her ear down, listened to Lucy's heartbeat bashing her ribs but starting to slow. A figure blocked the sun and when she looked up, it was Sven, out of breath, his hands on his hips.

'Is she okay?'

'I think so ... I don't know, she's so frightened.' Amelia buried her head again in fur, breathed in dust, sweat and skin.

The traffic driving into the city surged forward; an extra lane had been cleared of debris up ahead. Eddie approached at a trot. 'Great catch,' he said.

'What the fuck did you do that for?' Amelia said.

'Do what?' he said, hands open to the sky.

'The door, man,' Sven said, still quiet, still calm.

'Well, I thought she was trained, I just –'

'She is trained! She got worked up and you just let her out onto the road!' Amelia said.

Eddie kicked at a spot on the road barrier. 'It was an accident,' he said, shrugging. 'This is no place for dogs anyway.'

Amelia gripped Lucy tight. She couldn't tell which trembles were her own and which were Lucy's. She leaned back and the hard, warm barrier took their weight. Vehicles gathered pace. Down the road, the van was stationary, blocking the lane. Music blared from a passing car, a deep bass vibrating plastic and metal. 'Get off the fucking road!' the driver yelled at them out the window.

'Let's go,' Eddie said. Lucy squirmed in her grip, restless and no longer willing to put up with being squeezed. Eddie held out his hand to her. Holding on to Lucy's collar, she refused the hand, pressed herself up from the asphalt so that little stones dug in to her skin. Her legs were shaking and she rested her fingers on the barrier. She scooped Lucy up into her arms and walked behind the others, in single file, towards the van.

Clare was sitting in the open door of the kombi. 'Are we done?' she said, jumping to her feet. A bus groaned as it edged closer to the back of the van. The traffic in the lane beside it was unyielding. Sweat prickled down Amelia's neck and her arms itched where Lucy's fur bristled against her.

'Let's go,' Sven said, placing his hands on the back of Eddie's shoulders, steering him towards the driver's seat.

'Righto, righto,' Eddie said, dragging his feet.

Amelia and Lucy had the middle row of the van to themselves. Clare sat in the front seat, Sven in the back. Lucy's paws dug into Amelia's thighs and Amelia hugged her neck; Lucy shook off the clinginess and stuck her head out the window.

Eddie insisted on dropping her where she wanted to go. If she'd bled onto the seat, he showed her mercy and did not mention it. They cut through the city, passing servos and fast-food joints on the outskirts, finally making it to the leafy streets of Kew.

'Just here, please,' Amelia said, pointing to the car park of the local shops. The van rolled to a stop and Amelia sat for a moment, waited for relief to rise up through her, for the familiar surroundings of the shops, the hanging baskets bursting with flowers, to make their impact. The others seemed to wait, too, seeing what she would do.

When nothing came, she took a deep breath. 'Thanks,' she said and slipped out of the van, keeping hold of Lucy's collar.

Sven climbed down, too. 'Here,' he said, leaning back into the van, clicking something. 'Take this.' He handed her a long black strap. 'So she doesn't run.'

'Right,' she said. 'Thanks.' She looped the strap through Lucy's collar and held on to the ends.

Eddie got out of the van to give her a hard pat on the back, then accelerated off with two beeps of the horn. Clare looked out from the front window, curled up with a pillow. An elderly lady flinched, put a hand to her chest as Eddie howled out the window. Once recovered, she continued to shuffle her walking frame up a ramp.

The heat of the pavement seeped through the thinning soles of Amelia's shoes. She tied Lucy beneath a supermarket awning; gold and silver tinsel weaved around the pole. Amelia dragged over a white tub of water that read *Doggy latte* in black texta. Lucy lapped at it, splashing Amelia's legs with the sun-warmed water.

The lady with the walker moved towards them; when she was a few steps away, she stopped and met Amelia's eye. Lipstick was painted above her mouth, decorating lips that weren't there. Despite the heat, she wore a huge knit cardigan in Christmas greens and reds. She stared with a vacancy that suggested her body was also only a design for a person no longer present. Amelia smiled at her quickly and tied another knot in Lucy's new leash.

'Darling, Merry Christmas,' the woman said in a wavering voice. 'I hope Santa looks after you . . . But only if you've been a good girl.'

'Thanks, you too,' Amelia said.

'Have you been a good girl?'

Amelia closed one eye against the sun and looked up at the woman. 'Dunno,' she said.

The woman nodded. Her arms shook as she held the rubber grips of her walking frame. 'As long as you've tried your best,' she said. 'That's all a young girl like you can do.'

The woman worked her way over a lifted paving stone, leaving a scent of talcum powder behind her. Lucy's tongue hung from her mouth as she panted. She looked up at Amelia, all the wildness of earlier gone.

'Stay,' Amelia said, holding up her palm.

The supermarket doors slid open and closed for customers, releasing bursts of cool air. Amelia walked inside, into fluorescent lights and polished floors.

The aisles stretched out ahead, full to bursting. Cash registers beeped. Someone bumped past, caught her shoulder, another rolled his eyes as she stepped out of the way of his trolley.

A teenage boy unpacked a stack of cardboard boxes, shoving bags of chips into place with fast hands. The sanitary products were one aisle over; packets of pink, purple and yellow rose before her. She grabbed a box of heavy-flow tampons and scratched open the plastic wrapping while pretending to browse. She lifted the box to the shelf and, under the cover of the neighbouring products, tipped the tampons into her hand. Feigning close interest in a packet of pads, she put her fist into her pocket and let the tampons fall in. When she looked up, the chip-packing boy was watching her from the end of the aisle, eyes wide. With a new cardboard box of chips in his arms, he returned to his station, her partner in crime.

In the bakery section, a gluten-free orange and almond cake sat alongside a Victoria sponge. She fingered the two-dollar coin in her pocket, looked at the security camera watching over the cakes. Her lips were dry and swollen; she caught a thread of skin under her teeth and dragged it downwards. There was the sting of it, the taste of blood.

A basket sat in the corner with a 'Specials' sign in bright orange; it was full of a mishmash of products shunted from the shelves as they neared their use-by dates. Rummaging under a mountain of vegan beetroot and sweet potato crisps, she spotted a packet of sponge fingers: $1.75.

She joined the queue for the checkouts. People shifted their weight, flicked through magazines. Some of them looked at her and quickly looked away when she caught their eye.

'Next please,' the cashier sang out. She wore a crisp blue apron tied over a yellow shirt.

Amelia's shoes screeched on the linoleum. 'Found everything you need, darl?' The woman had a yellow name badge: Rhonda. Make-up was caught in the lines on Rhonda's forehead. Her eyelashes were black and clotted.

'Yes thanks,' Amelia said. 'Just these.' She flopped the sponge fingers onto the counter. Rhonda scanned the item and, upon seeing the price, examined the package.

'You probably don't want these, love. They're out of date.'

Amelia took the packet from her, pretended to examine the date for the first time: the expiry was the day before. 'Oh well,' she said. 'I don't mind.'

'Can't sell 'em, love. Not allowed to. Health regulations, you see. 'Cos if you buy these from us and get sick –'

'It's fine, really. I'm not going to get sick.'

'It'll be stale, darl. You won't enjoy it,' Rhonda said.

'Stale maybe, but definitely not deadly.'

'I'll have to call Mark, darl,' she said. 'You can fight it out with him.'

'Please don't call Mark,' Amelia said.

The woman held the sponge fingers out in front of her, squinted at the label again.

'There are nice cakes on the shelves, hun, why don't you grab yourself one of those. You don't have to queue again.' Rhonda winked.

'I don't want those cakes.' Amelia slid her two-dollar coin across the counter.

Rhonda's eyes darted down the growing queue. 'Take the bloomin' things then,' she hissed. 'But I tell you something, missy: never shoot the messenger.' She opened the till and gave Amelia her change. 'Need a bag?'

'No, thanks,' Amelia said, and she couldn't look at Rhonda as she snatched up the packet and was spat out into the heat by the sliding doors.

She squinted, adjusting to the glare. Lucy's tail wagged as Amelia approached. Amelia cupped the side of her head in her hand.

'Right,' she said. 'This is it.'

Lucy moved her head, licking the space in front of Amelia's face. There was a new addition to Lucy's collar: a knitted Christmas tree, bright green with red baubles. It was tied on to her collar with twine. No one was nearby to take credit for it; she scanned the car park for the cardigan woman but didn't find her.

Amelia walked around the back of the supermarket and followed the walkway to Sid's house. Dry grass reached out to itch her calves. The plastic wrapping of the sponge fingers rustled as it bumped against her leg.

Sweat gathered along her hairline and upper lip. A row of tall bushes lined the path and she tucked in behind them. Backed by someone's fence, she twisted open a tampon, undid her shorts, and shoved it up into the warm mess inside her underpants. Her hand came out strung with blood. She wiped her fingers along grass as best she could, some darker bits of blood settling beneath her fingernails.

Her heart was quick as she passed the houses she knew, as she recognised the children playing in a sprinkler, their same old dog barking from the window.

The place was more magnificent than last time she visited, though perhaps she hadn't appreciated it properly then, during a few days of respite enforced by her mother. Japanese maples matured with grace, the wisteria worked its way higher and thicker on the pergola, the azalea bushes were fuller, as if puffing out their chests. Sid was a born gardener. Unlatching the gate, walking under an archway, it was suddenly obvious that she would end up here, with Sid and the sanctuary he'd grown.

Lucy knew exactly where she was; she tugged on the lead, anxious to go ahead. After double-checking she'd closed the gate, Amelia held the sweaty plastic of the sponge fingers in her mouth while she untied Lucy; as soon as she was free, she launched down the garden path, leaving a wake of flying stones.

Amelia stood under the shade of an oak and tried to take it all in, the splendour of it, the fact that she was there. Sid had finally got the fountain working, a big elaborate white thing with rounded cherubs' bums, water splashing against the stone basin. Even amid the neighbours' ornate gardens with trees cut into balls like poodle tails, Sid's work was impressive. Colour was woven through so that the garden looked grown, not designed or built, as if each plant had chosen to be in a relationship with those around it. She knew it was important to him that she see the meaning of what he was doing, and she did.

He was there – visible only in fragments – between bushes on the far side of the garden, up a stepladder. Lucy would soon give her presence away, but Amelia was glad for the few seconds to take in her best friend. His calves were straining, bigger than she remembered, his toes exposed in thongs, in danger as a branch fell victim to his pruning. It was unlike him to not wear his proper boots; he'd been so proud when his never-there boss, the owner of the property, had bought him a pair with steel caps in them.

His legs were going down the ladder then, and eventually a forearm was revealed, more defined than when she last saw him, muscles of the kind she didn't think him capable of growing. The tone of brown to his skin was new as well; despite working outdoors, he didn't tan, unless you counted his freckles joining up. But despite the differences in him, she knew this person, every piece of him familiar. He was down off the ladder, ducking under the branches that obscured his face, bending to talk to Lucy; she stopped briefly to sniff his hands then burst through to the other side of the foliage.

It wasn't Sid after all. It was Zach. And that too shifted into place somehow, as if every step she'd taken had been leading her here; the previous weeks all shrivelled up to this meeting, this moment, standing face to face with him in the yellow afternoon.

'Hey,' he said.

He was a few metres away, too far to touch her or to be touched. The beating of her heart was too fast for the way she waited, staring. He paused too and they were animals sizing each other up. A dragonfly flew close to her face, and she didn't flinch at the buzz of it, nor at the tiny movement of air its wings created at her cheek. Zach pushed hair out of his eyes, wiped sweat from his face with the back of his hand. It wasn't too late to run. She could leave now – walk down the path, beneath the archway, back out the gate she'd just stepped through – and this meeting could be erased. And yet she was still. He'd always been able to do this, to lock her up inside herself.

'How are ya?' he said. He put his hands on his hips. There was a slight curl of his mouth: he was laughing. She managed a step back because suddenly the distance between them was much too close. His hands dropped off his waist. Somewhere down the street, a lawnmower false-started, tried again. Choked.

'Hey,' she said.

She dropped her head. Muddy sediment went up over the toes of her shoes, her shins were a collection of scrapes and dried blood, her knees two bulbous, dirty circles. She became aware again of the cloth and leaves, a soggy mess of blood between her legs. And the sponge fingers, her only offering. But feeling his eyes on her as they moved over each scrape, ache and bruise, the injuries pulsed as if speaking to her; she could take him on if she had to.

'You okay?' he said. She had no answer, just the start of that warm feeling, but as she looked at him it spiralled away from her, water down a sink. She focused on the packet of sponge fingers, straightened the thin plastic out; he took a step towards her.

'Meels?' That was Sid, coming out from around the back of the house, seeing her and breaking into a trot. He crunched down the path in green overalls with tears all down the legs, and no shirt, teasing Lucy, who jumped and snapped at his finger-tips. 'Surprise, surprise,' he said, holding out his lean arms, bony chest bared to the sun. His smile was brighter than the bottle-brush beside him; it secured her feet to the ground, ending the desire to retreat. Zach slunk off into the shadows of the garden, where Amelia could no longer see him.

She stepped towards Sid, and she was smiling too, the sensation strange on her furry teeth, her tightened, burned cheeks.

'Hey,' she said.

'Hey, you.' She let him bundle her into his arms. 'God, there's not much left of you,' he said, moving his hands up her back. He nuzzled into the crook of her neck and shoulder. 'And shit, you're ripe.' He held her out at arm's length and she put her hands on his wrists. She took in his eyes, the same dark tunnels as always, let them flicker over her own, decoding. 'Has something happened? Don't you have any stuff?' He was looking past her then, as if trouble might be waiting at the front gate.

'I had to leave it,' she said.

'Are you okay?' He squeezed her shoulders.

'Yeah,' she said. She looked down, focused on the neat cut of each blade of grass that bordered the footpath. She pressed into him again.

'I didn't know you were coming,' Sid said. 'He's been helping me out over the summer.'

'It's okay,' she said, her words muffled against him.

'He just turned up out of the blue, you know? He said he went to see you, at your mum's, that you had a good talk.' He was doing his nervous rambling.

'Right,' she said. Zach had always been a committed and convincing liar; she once heard one of his and Sid's uncles say that Zach would lie about what was on his sandwich if you gave him the chance.

Sid held her out from him again, patted down her arms, tugged on her fingertips, as if to make sure each piece of her was there. 'Do you want me to send him away? Just say the word and I'll do it, no worries.' He squinted, his summer freckles twitching along the ridge of his nose.

'Let me have a shower,' she said. 'I need to think about it.'

The concern in his eyes was palpable. He rubbed a hand up the back of his neck.

'What's this?' she said, swiping at the little bun he'd grown, collected in an elastic high on his head.

'Just a new little friend . . . I missed you. I grew it in your honour.'

He pulled her in again, and she held his middle, hard and narrow. Lucy barked, circling around them.

They walked down the path, her arm linked through his. Two lorikeets flitted out of their way, taking cover in a nearby fig tree. Sid's shack was at the back of the garden, behind the huge house he maintained, where a wattle tree kept it in constant shade. He unlinked his arm, and Lucy trotted with him over to the hose.

Zach was in front of the shack, smoking a cigarette. He sat on a battered, yellowing surfboard that acted as the front porch. His eyes were closed, head resting against the tin wall. A can of beer sat on his thigh, nestled loosely in his fingers, and he took a swig. For a brief moment, he was just an average guy, his small pot belly sticking out, a blotchy red shaving rash down his throat.

He opened his eyes and acknowledged her with a small lift of the chin. 'Pull up a pew.' He scooted along to make space. The way he smiled, the wet inside of his top lip sneaking out, made him nineteen again. And his thick-knuckled hands: they were the same, too.

'No thanks,' she said.

At the corner of the shack, Sid sprayed water into a plastic tub with 'Lucy' spelled out in shells. Lucy snapped at the jet stream, leaping up as Sid angled the hose higher. The scene blurred at the edges. As Amelia stepped up to Sid's door, a breeze stirred the eucalyptus leaves above, the sea air blowing in from off Port Phillip Bay. She closed her eyes as its coolness hit her cheeks, lifted loose strands of her hair, sprinkled goosebumps up her neck. Sid was calling out to her, but it was muffled by the creak of the door closing behind her, sealing her into the quiet, dark world of indoors.

Her vision was fuzzy while her eyes adjusted to the deep red glow of the lamps in the windowless room. The smell of Zach's cigarette followed her inside and mixed with the scent of men's deodorant, filling her lungs as she took a breath. The air was stagnant and close. She leaned against the wall. The flimsy tin thing was not enough of a barrier; he was only inches away, on the other side. It was impossible that he was there, skin and bone, and so was she.

When her vision cleared, she saw them: trails of her postcards, crisscrossing the walls of the shack, above the mattress shoved in the corner, stuck to the kitchen cupboards, the fridge, the bathroom door. Dozens of them to her left, to her right, everywhere she looked, travelling over the cushions and beanbags that furnished the room. She shuffled around and examined them. Some of the cards had her coded message face side up, others she plucked off and turned over to read. She found the first one she'd sent from the road:

I've left home, gone on a trip. Need space and air, I think. I'll write.

She'd signed off with the three stars for missing, wishing, thinking. It was from a town two hours away from home, a picture of vast arable land, taken before the region was gripped by drought. She skipped along a few cards, recognising the sunset almost exactly as she used to see it from the white room by the coast.

You'd like it here. People move slow (like you), and the waves are rough, real dumpers. I'm staying for a while.

But she hadn't stayed, not for long enough. And another one, from when she had first arrived in the Northern Territory. It was stuck on a cupboard above the kitchen sink, and she stood on tiptoe to read it.

I'm heading into the desert. Hope you're keeping that grass alive.

Some of the places she couldn't remember being, others she could only recall the scrap of time spent writing the postcard by a road, in a park, or tucked up in a doorway. There was one she'd spilled gravy on, one she'd drenched, forgetting it was in her pocket as she ran into the ocean. Each one was a sliver of her progress, trapped and observed like insects on a pin board. Displayed in that way, the postcards seemed to make the last months count for something, though she had no idea what.

There was a bang against the wall, which reverberated around the metal shack; she scurried across the floor to the bathroom.

The bathroom was dark. She moved her hands over the walls in search of a light switch. Frustration rose fast and fierce in her chest as she traced cool tile after cool tile and found nothing.

Finally, she caught hold of a string and tugged it. White light revealed the border of dolphins diving around the room. Black mould crept up the base of a light-blue shower curtain.

Zach had probably stood exactly where she was, naked.

With a few deep breaths, she summoned the bravery to unbutton her shorts. They fell, circling her ankles. The skin was a lighter shade at the tops of her thighs where it had been protected from sun and dirt. She stepped out of her undies and, after bundling them up with the rotten cloth and leaves, placed them in the corner of the room.

She examined her face in the toothpaste-flecked mirror on the cabinet above the sink. The skin below her eyes was loose, hanging in light grey sacks. She leaned in closer and even the colour of her eyes – the dark green ring around the iris and the deep-water blue – was matt, as if switched off; her eyes gave nothing away, like an open book sitting in darkness.

Inside the cabinet was a crusty bottle of Betadine, two boxes of painkillers and a packet of cheap razors. She took one of the razors from the open pack and sat down on the edge of the bath. For a few moments she held it, then pressed it against the skin of her inner thigh. She snapped the three metal blades out of their plastic frame then lined them up in a neat row on top of her thigh, equally spaced out. The pleasing symmetry of them was deceptive; it was as if they would never dream of sliding through sad flesh.

Amelia picked up each blade and placed them in her hand, cupping them delicately as if they were a moth. The metal was cool in her palm. She sat, nursing the blades – blocking out the noise of the boys playing with Lucy outside, focusing instead on the distant bell of a tram – until she was able to let them go.

She ripped off a strip of toilet paper, folded it into a wad and placed the razors on there. Hovering over the toilet, she pulled out her tampon and added it to the pile. There was a bin stuffed with tissues and earwaxed cotton buds; she buried the package deep within this other mess.

She slid the shower curtain across with a scrape and stepped into the grimy bath, turned the taps. The water was freezing cold and it left her breathless as it pelted onto her back and ran down her clammy skin. She stuck her face in it and scrubbed, dead skin rolling up in little parcels beneath her fingertips. Heat kicked in. The jets pounded the top of her head, and she leaned back, letting water seep into her scalp. A twig was trapped in one of her knots and she wrenched at it, losing a clump of hair in the process. The twig and hair swirled around the drain, a strange, lost ship.

A bar of white soap sat in a dish, but it might have been all over him, in every secret crease and fold, sliding over the places he'd pressed her hands, the parts of himself he'd put inside her. She would not use the soap. She would not look at it again. It shouldn't have been there, so near, so slippery and unpredictable, so tainted.

She shuddered, and there was a wave inside her, sucking her in, pulling her under, tossing her over. A gasp ripped up from her throat, too loud, and she swallowed it. She held the tiled walls for balance then lowered to a crouch, jets of water still finding her. Her chest was heaving, more gasps escaping, the sound of them foreign to her, and she tried desperately to silence them but the only way was to hold her breath.

She wrapped her arms around herself, pinkened skin touching pinkened skin. The water from her eyes was hot and full and she could feel it moving down her cheeks, slow and salty compared to the shower stream. She stopped fighting; it was quieter that way. As she sat on the floor of the bath, knees to her chest, the sediment dislodged from her body, mingling with blood and tears. She stayed sitting there, hunched in a ball. She was there when the water went cold, and stayed longer still, shivering, the shower curtain sticking to her back.

Sid knocked on the door. 'You right in there?'

She hadn't heard anyone come inside.

'Yep.' She clambered to her feet and held her face up to the cold water.

'Kettle's on,' he said, knocking again in farewell.

She stepped out of the shower and pulled a beige towel off the hanger; when she pushed her face into it, it smelled of Sid, the way his bedroom had always smelled, his school uniform, his favourite shirt. She sat on the edge of the bath, staring at the tiles on the floor, the places where grout had come loose and mould lived there instead. She didn't dry herself, just sat with water from her hair travelling down her back. With each breath her shoulders grazed against the towel, and she filled her lungs slowly, again and again.

She started to count, willing herself to get up when she got to ten. When she couldn't manage it, she counted again, dragging each number out. On the third attempt, she stood, finally, setting her head spinning. In the mirror her eyes were red; bright webs of veins lit up, giving away the workings within.

She rescued the stolen tampons from her shorts and inserted a fresh one. With the towel wrapped around her like a dress, she collected her dirty clothes in a fist then opened the door a crack, releasing a little cloud of steam.

'Sid?' she said. 'Can I borrow something to wear?'

*

Dressed in a big orange T-shirt and basketball shorts, Amelia stepped out of the bathroom. Her dirty clothes were bundled away in a plastic bag in the bin.

The boys were waiting for her at the coffee table. She crossed her arms over her chest in an attempt to conceal her braless breasts.

'Cup of tea's here,' Zach said, and she couldn't look at him, only vaguely at the space he occupied. He was in a beanbag on the floor, knees high in front of him.

'Right, thanks,' she said.

Three steaming mugs of tea sat on the table. A row of the sponge fingers was laid out, a matchstick stuck in each of them.

'Shall we light 'em up?' Sid said, sprawled on his back across cushions, head resting on his arm.

'Let's do it,' Zach said.

'What a party. Few days late, but worth the wait,' Sid said. Lucy lay along the length of him, accepting a belly rub.

Amelia knelt at a distance, in the dark at the edge of lamp-light, as far from the table as she thought she could get away with. Her toes were flexed behind her, ready to get up in an instant, if required.

Zach lit the matches. As they burned down, Sid initiated the singing of 'Happy Birthday', orchestrating the song by moving his index fingers from side to side. Amelia stared into the fast-dying flames as her flat voice melded with Zach's. A hot flush came over her and she dragged the cool, wet ends of her hair over her forehead, her cheeks, the back of her neck.

Sid blew on each match as they faltered, plucking the black-ened corpses out of the inadequate birthday-cake replacements. Amelia wrapped her hands around her tea, the mug hot in her palms. Zach grabbed a sponge finger and took a big bite, jaw clicking as he chewed. There was a staleness in the way it broke; crumbs scattered on the table.

'Nothing a bit of tea won't fix,' Zach said, taking a sip. 'Brews like a champion, this guy.'

There was silence, and they all sipped from their mugs.

'So, you've been adventuring, huh?' Zach said, tilting his head at the wall; a postcard over his shoulder featured the Big Pineapple.

A chain of mug rings were stained into the table, and Amelia traced the loops with her eyes, round and round and back again. 'Guess you could say that.'

'Got any stories for us?'

'Not really,' she said.

Zach leaned forward into her field of vision and caught her eye. She looked away and concentrated instead on postcards on the wall behind him: Emerald, Jericho, Winton. Julia Creek, Cloncurry, Mount Isa.

'You must have something to tell,' Zach said, quieter now.

Over in the kitchen: Borroloola, Daly Waters, Katherine. To her left, inside the front door: Kununurra, Purnululu, Fitzroy Crossing. As she moved her head to the right she caught the end of a look, a nod from Sid to Zach towards the door. On the wardrobe: Carnarvon, Shark Bay and, when she narrowed her eyes, Kalbarri.

Zach slurped from his tea, then put it down hard on the table. 'Well, I'll get outta your hair for a bit,' he said. 'Will I see you later?'

Sid looked to Amelia. She shrugged. 'Guess so.'

'Do you want to go down to the water or something?' Sid said, still looking at her.

'Sure.' She pressed her fingers together, the pads wrinkled after her long shower.

'We'll probably be at the usual spot,' Sid said, looking from Zach to Amelia then back again.

Zach lingered, stooping under the low roof. Amelia picked up near where she'd left off: Geraldton, Green Head, Cervantes.

'I'll catch you in a bit, then,' he said.

He spent a couple of minutes lifting things, patting his back pockets, then lifting more things. When he was out the door,

Amelia stood; her knees clicked as she did so, and her body was stiff as she walked over to Sid's bed. The familiar tea spills and brown ripples of bodily fluids were all there across the mattress on the floor. She pushed aside a set of socks and his bird book, and folded herself down. The pillows were hard and flat, but lying there on her back, she could have been floating. She closed her eyes, but then Sid groaned and bounced with sudden agility from his knees to his feet. Lucy's tail wagged in adoration.

'Meels,' he said, stretching as he walked over to her, his collarbones jutting out. 'What's the deal?' She shifted over so he could sit on the edge of the mattress; he picked at foam through a tear in the fabric. 'I thought things were okay between you two.'

She put her arm out, wrapped her fingers in the seam of his shirt. 'I don't think anything about him is okay,' she said. The furrows between his eyebrows moved in and out of focus. 'Can we talk later? I need to sleep, just for a bit.' Her eyes were already closing.

'All right, but you've got me worried,' he said, patting her leg. 'Real worried.' He puffed out a breath and she knew he was frustrated. He pulled the musty sheet across her, said nothing more.

*

She woke to spots of pain flaring up her leg. Sid perched over her, pressing in the bruises on her shins.

'Wakey-wakey,' he said. 'Remember we're pretending it's my birthday? I don't wanna spend the whole time watching you sleep.'

She stretched, her spine convulsing for a second as it unfolded. 'Sorry Siddy,' she said, croaky and softened from sleep. He was fresh from the shower, smelled of soap; her heart kicked in as she scanned the room.

'He's still out,' Sid said. He was on his knees on the mattress and she curled around his legs, her eyes heavy. Another pain in her leg; he pressed harder this time. 'Oi,' he said. 'You gonna tell me what's going on?'

She sat up, rubbing grit from her eyes, then wiped her hand over her mouth. Dried blood gathered in places where her lips had split. She scratched it off, setting the cuts stinging.

'Water,' he said, passing over a mug of it. 'So?'

She took it and drank, moistening her lips, the taste of it tinged with blood.

'What do you want to know?' she said. Her insides sounded hollow as the liquid moved within her; Lucy listened, ears twitching.

'Whatever you want to tell me.' Sid squished right up close to Amelia so their shoulders were touching as they leaned against the wall. He shoved her gently, splashing a bit of water from the glass onto her lap.

'I don't know where to start,' she said, tucking her knees to her chest. A postcard from Jugiong fell from the wall behind her; she tried to conjure the rolling hills of that place, to take herself there.

'Right,' he said. He reached across her and picked up the postcard, ran his thumb over the symbols she'd written. 'You can talk to me, you know. I get that you needed to go off and be alone and whatever, but you can still tell me anything. Even if it's about him.'

Lucy picked her way across the mattress and squeezed into the space between their thighs. They both rested a hand on her back and she lowered her head, blinking slowly.

'I feel sick about it all. He makes me sick.'

Sid exhaled with force, shaking his head, and Amelia was grateful she didn't have to look at him.

She continued: 'I know him not being around was hard, that you're mates, cousins, whatever. And you must be happy he's finally willing to spend some time with you,' she said. It was too abrupt. Sid tensed beside her, and she instantly wanted to fix it. 'I don't want to ruin your relationship or anything.'

'You won't ruin anything, Meels. I just want you to be okay.'

Amelia tugged on the loose material of the shorts Sid had lent her.

'You hearing me?' Sid said.

'Yeah.'

'I can tell him to leave. You don't have to see him again. We don't have to meet him later.'

Amelia turned and looked up, tracking more postcards: Toowoomba, Dalby, Chinchilla. 'It's fine,' she said. She searched, then, for the lighter-burn scars in the web of her hand, the little gifts from Zach. Some of them rose in small bumps and she traced back and forth across them. 'It's just that . . . I think I might want to say something to him.'

He paused, taking her hand in his. 'Sure?' he said.

'Sure.'

'Let's get you out of here then, get a beer. Have some fun.' He was on his feet, the mattress recovering from his sudden movement.

'Two minutes,' she said, closing her eyes.

'One and a half.'

Sid got dressed in his going-out shirt: short-sleeved, collared and bright with wildflowers and vines. He went to pump up the tyres of the spare bike. Amelia dug through her drawer in Sid's dresser, found a singlet and bra.

They cycled towards the bay through residential streets, Lucy following close behind. Amelia didn't bother with the lead; she wanted to forgive and forget Lucy's mistake on the highway earlier.

Amelia got off her bike as they reached the back roads of St Kilda. She walked slowly, peering into the windows of houses for too long, mesmerised by the flicker of televisions.

Sid linked his arm with hers, and they each managed their bikes with their outside hand. 'C'mon, straggler.'

A woman leaned back on a street lamp. When a car rolled up, she went to the driver's window, then walked around to the passenger seat, dragging her hand along the car bonnet. Lucy went up close to a driveway gate; she taunted the terrier that was in captivity, setting it yapping and growling.

Sid wanted Amelia to talk and she glossed over the devastation of Pops's abandonment, speaking instead of her days in the white room. She tried to describe the different birds whose song woke her each morning, how fiercely the wind moved the trees outside her window, the rainless storms that lit the sky. Then she wanted to hear him talk instead, to hear every detail of the days, weeks, months that had passed.

'It's all the same with me,' he said. 'I've just been working, sleeping and missing you.'

Once they reached The Esplanade they locked up their bikes. The path widened and people walked slowly, taking in the last of the sunset over Port Phillip Bay. The sea breeze picked up and Amelia sucked in the air, which was laced with salt and fried food.

'Just felt like seeing the water,' Sid said. 'You know?'

'Yeah,' she said, resting on a railing beside him, a road buzzing between them and the beach.

'Even though it's this shitty bay, and there are all these shitty people around, it's still the water; it's still big and scary and strange.'

'Not that scary,' she said. 'Biggest thing to fear on that beach is broken glass.'

He scoffed. 'I know, I know. But you get what I mean.'

'Yeah,' she said. 'I do.'

Kitesurfers cut through the water, coloured sprinkles across the horizon. Unmoved by the view, Lucy sat with her back to the bay, sniffing the air as people passed. A couple walked by, in no rush; a woman wore a striped maxi dress and gripped her partner's biceps. He leaned in, kissed her on the forehead, and she raised her chin to collect a second kiss on the mouth.

'Stop staring!' Sid said, stern but quiet. The woman met Amelia's eye before she quickly looked away.

'Don't realise I'm doing it,' she said.

'Doesn't make it okay. Weirdo.'

'You look too, don't you?'

'Not sure. I think so, but I'm much better at it. Maybe it helps me to have brown eyes. Your eyes are so bloody bright and big. Lovely, of course, but it's so obvious when you're looking at someone.'

'Righto, righto,' she said. 'Told me a million times.'

'You gotta be more stealth,' he said. 'Like this.' He kept his head still but his eyes followed the path of two teenage boys, skateboards tucked under their arms.

'That side-eye treatment is so much worse,' she said. 'You look like a creeper.'

'But at least no one notices.'

'I reckon they probably do. But they're scared of you so they don't dare look back. At least my way it might look like I'm just thinking hard or something.'

'I doubt they think that. It looks like you're judging them and that you're absolutely disgusted.'

'I didn't think that couple was gross,' she said. 'I thought they were nice.'

'They'd never have guessed.'

'Who cares, anyway? Everyone's looking at everyone. That's how it works in a city.'

Sid looked out to the water, reaching across his body to scratch his shoulder. 'You're right, as usual,' he said. 'Who cares. Stare all you want.'

'Thank you. I will. Can't help it.' She stared at him then, at his soft cheeks, hairless where he'd always longed to be able to grow a beard. He smiled, still looking out over the water. 'What?' she said, her lips cracking as she smiled, too.

'Nothin',' he said. 'Just that . . . I know you're not okay. Feels like you're still far away somewhere. But I will make you talk to me. You can't shut me out. You know that, right?'

Amelia nodded, then bowed her head. 'Yeah, I know.'

Sid shrugged. 'But this breeze,' he said, 'the whole night ahead of us . . . I dunno. I'm just excited you're here.' He picked up her wrist and gave it a gentle shake before letting go.

'Me too,' she said, and she was smiling, closing her eyes in the breeze. The last light of the setting sun was warm and soft, somehow massaging around the pit in her stomach, the part of her that kept formulating words for Zach then deciding against them.

They stood for a few minutes, quiet. The railing was warm beneath Amelia's arms and she tucked in next to Sid as the air cooled, felt his breath go in then out, his heart buried shallow in his slight frame.

Bars and restaurants lit up for the evening. 'Time for a drink?' Sid said.

They wandered further down The Esplanade and an outdoor table freed up as they approached a bar.

'Beer?' she said.

'Beer,' he said with a single nod. Lucy lay flat beneath the table, resting her head on her paws.

'Your shout, I'll queue,' Amelia said.

Inside, the line for a drink was three rows deep. A glass smashed, followed by shouting. A group of men took shots at the bar; one of them shook his head then beat his chest, letting out a loud roar. Amelia took a deep breath and chose what appeared to be the shortest route to the bar, behind two women with sleek hair.

'You'd be much prettier if you smiled.' A man's voice from somewhere beside her. She scanned the faces and found him, saw his lopsided grin, his drunken gaze, loose and wet. She smiled without meaning to, only for a second. 'That's better,' he said. Amelia crossed her arms over her chest, wished herself back into Sid's giant T-shirt.

'No need to be so narky, sweetheart,' he said. 'You're so pretty . . . it's just a shame, that's all.' There was a surge from the bar and rows of people stepped back onto each other. One of the women in front trod on Amelia's toe with a dagger heel. She sucked in her breath, closing her eyes briefly as the pain flared. 'Anyway, what are you up to tonight, sweetheart?'

'Trying to get a drink.' She turned her shoulders away from him, moved up in the queue. He sidled in next to her.

'You here with friends?' He leaned forward and searched the faces around her. 'Boyfriend?'

A woman sloshed her way between them, spilling cold liquid down Amelia's back. 'A friend. A boy who's a friend.'

'Ah,' he said with a nod. 'It's complicated, huh?'

'Not at all.'

'Friends with benefits then, is it?' he said, nudging her with his elbow. His arm was sticky, the hairs hard with sweat or spilled drink. 'Got time for another one?' he said.

As she tried to get out of the crowd, she had to push right up against the guy, chest to chest. 'Look out, she's a feisty one,' he said as she squeezed past. She shouldered people aside as she made her way to the exit, ignoring their exclamations, needing fresh air.

Sid stood as she stepped out of the door and Lucy was ready, too. 'Let's go,' Amelia said.

'Too much?' he said.

'Way too much.'

Sid popped in to a bottle shop and came out with a box of goon.

'Ten bucks!' he said, lifting it proudly onto his shoulder as they walked across a bridge and down the stairs to the beach. Coloured lasers flashed across the sand from a nightclub perched on the boardwalk. They continued making their way up the beach till the dance music dulled, Lucy kicking up sand as she ran ahead. A couple of metres from the edge of the water, Sid sat on the goon box and began punching in the cardboard opening.

Amelia unlaced her shoes.

'You're brave,' Sid said. 'Still pretty druggy round here.'

She shrugged and pulled her shoes off. 'Live a little.'

She walked to the water and curled her toes in the wet sand. Small waves tickled the tops of her feet. Boats drifted far out at sea, their lights flickering like tiny candles.

'Oi, come give me a drink,' Sid said, patting the opened goon box. 'Like the good old days.'

She turned to him and as she approached, he fell to the sand on his knees, mouth open. She picked up the box, held it high over his head and squirted the liquid into his mouth. It came out in a powerful stream and his mouth overflowed; he lowered his head as he choked, and copped the stream in an eye. They both laughed, and hers came from deep in her belly, from the same muscles she hadn't realised were sore from crying in the shower earlier.

Lucy ran over to join in, bouncing around Sid, snapping at the air and growling in excitement. He rubbed his eye, still smiling. He remained on his knees, threw his head back again.

'More,' he said. Amelia pushed the lever and squirted him in the neck and all down his front. 'Jesus,' he said, laughing again, collapsing onto his back in the sand, clutching the wet spot as if it were a wound.

They built an elaborate sandcastle while they worked their way through the wine. Amelia concentrated on moats, arches and bridges while Sid finessed turrets and collected debris to use for decoration, taking Lucy with him to scavenge. When they were finished, Amelia sat looking at the sky; the glow of the city lights shrouded the stars. The crowds had slowly dispersed from the beach as the night went on, and it felt like just the two of them and Lucy still out there. Amelia picked up the goon box and squirted herself a few mouthfuls.

'Wanna walk to the pier?' Sid said.

'Sure,' she said, willing herself up.

He grabbed her hands and pulled her to her feet. With his arm linked through hers, he dragged her along the beach, her steps laboured.

At the pier, she tightened her arm against his, not trusting herself near the edge, which wobbled as she walked. Sid was unsteady too, and, clinging to each other, they made their way to the end of the pier in zigzags. Lucy trotted ahead, her paws clicking along the wooden planks.

The smell of salt was stronger out here and the breeze had force behind it, pressing her clothes against her skin. A pelican sat alone on the pier's last pole; it stayed for a few moments after they arrived, then jumped and flapped away over the bay. Metal railings signalled the drop into the water, which swelled below. Sid climbed up on the railing and sat with his legs dangling; once he was set, she passed him the goon sack and climbed up beside him, wrapping her legs around the poles for security. Lucy curled up nearby, a fuzzy mass in the darkness. Sid cooeed and the wind swallowed the sound, so he did it again and again, his own echo. He held his head back, the skin of his throat taut and illuminated by the moon, then drank from the goon bag.

'This is the life, eh?' he said. He slurred his words in the way he always did after too much drink, and his voice was croaky from all the yelling at the bay. 'You and me.'

'Yeah,' she said.

'It is, right?' he said.

'Yep, it is.'

He looked wild, closing his eyes to the wind, a smile stretching across his face. The alcohol was having the opposite effect on her; she had been energised for a while, but now her arms and legs were heavy and her mind was slow, taking too long to process the things that rose within it. She tried to steel herself for when Zach met them there, while also preparing for him not coming at all. If he came, she would look him in the eye, she would keep control of herself, stop the shaking, the rising heat. She took the goon bag from Sid; her head spun as she gulped.

'Get it in ya!' Sid yelled. He was playful, elbowing her so she snorted, the wine stinging its way up and out of her nose. She shoved him and he grabbed the railing to keep himself from falling in the water. 'Easy, easy,' he said.

She drank more to get rid of the sting, gulping till she thought she'd vomit, seeking whatever buzz Sid had.

'Were you angry at me?' she said, and she'd been wanting to ask all night but hadn't quite managed it.

'What?'

'That I did it without you?'

'Did what?'

'You know, just set off. Without saying anything.'

He took a deep breath, smile gone, his forehead creased with seriousness. 'When you've been through what you've been through, you get to do whatever you need to do.'

'I didn't plan it or anything. I would have told you, if I knew.'

'Honestly, you did what you had to do. You're brave, much braver than me. I would have held you back.'

'No, that's not true.'

Sid looked out at the water, swiped beneath his nose and sniffed, the way he did when he was contemplating something big. 'Has it helped, all that travel, all that freedom?'

'I don't know . . .' she said. 'Didn't feel like freedom, exactly. But there was a lot of time to think.'

'Good thinking time or bad thinking time?'

'I dunno. Maybe both?' She swung her legs back and forth beneath her.

'And do you know where you wanna go next?'

'Well, I know that I'm done . . .'

'You wanna go home?'

'No. I don't want to live in that house. Not without Mum.'

'Not ever?'

'Not ever.'

'What do you wanna do then?'

'I dunno. Something different.'

'You could stay here,' he said.

'Nah,' she said. 'This is your place.' Looking out at the choppy water, feeling the buildings of the city creeping up behind her, she knew she wouldn't live there. 'Let's jump,' she said.

'You serious?'

She dropped off the rail onto the pier behind her, then pulled her singlet over her head and stepped out of her shorts.

'What are you doing?' he said.

'What do you think?'

She climbed back onto the railing, but stood this time, balancing on the metal with her toes, using Sid's shoulder for support.

'Wait for me,' Sid said, sliding out from underneath her. She wobbled, arms out to either side, unsure if she'd last until he returned. Then he was there, teeth flashing. 'Ready?' he said. She grabbed hold of his hand and yanked, taking them both over the edge.

The fall was longer than she'd expected, so long she wondered if she'd been wrong about the presence of water – the waves, the reflection, the smell only an illusion. Then her body landed with a slap. The water was thick around her as her momentum dragged her deeper and deeper. Before she'd finished her descent she was out of breath and she kicked to the surface, face pushing forward, lips ready to open to fresh air. Once there, she searched for Sid and tried to recover. He squirmed beneath her feet, pinching at her skin like a crab, then surfaced, gasping.

'Yiew!' he called. 'It's so good!' The water was cold and dark, blending with the night sky. Sid slunk beneath the ink with a dive. Lucy barked from the pier, and Amelia could just make her out, peering over the edge.

'You're all right, Luce,' she called, still catching her breath. Lucy stopped barking but paced the width of the pier, her face popping over each side.

When Amelia dipped below the surface again, there was a new sound; it was Sid, calling out beneath water, the sound long and mournful like the howl of a caged animal. She blew out bubbles, emptying her lungs so that she sank, then screamed with all the yearning and muscle she had. Beside her, Sid slithered to the surface, and she stayed below, screaming, opening her eyes in the swirling darkness. It felt good, that time, to be completely out of breath, and she wanted to stay down there, underwater. Her legs had their own will, though, and kicked towards air. Breaking through the surface, she was greeted by the sound of a drag race roaring down the nearby road. Her hair dripped into the water. Sid was right there, spluttering as he caught his breath, eyes wide and bright. They bobbed there for a few moments, staring at each other. She submerged again, and was glad when Sid didn't follow to hear her next howl. She yelled so hard that white light flashed across her closed eyes, stayed down there till the very end of her breath. When she reached the surface, Amelia spat, wiped her nose with her hand. Water licked at her neck and face as she kicked to stay afloat, catching her breath.

She forced herself to lie back, as Sid was doing, and drift. There was a ticking underneath the water's surface, a mechanical noise that had her surrounded. Her body drifted into Sid's, and it was easier to be still and calm with him next to her. Their bodies separated then lapped against each other again, at the mercy of the current. With her eyes closed, she could have slept, the rocking of the waves taking her softly out of that world. She wondered if sleeping bodies could still float, and whether she was tired enough that she might sink too deep before waking and be unable to resurface in time. Except Sid wouldn't let that happen, and anyway, she didn't want him to have the job of diving down to retrieve her, of dragging her limp body back to the beach.

Sid splashed beside her. She straightened up and he was saying something, but she couldn't clear her ears of water fast enough.

'What are you doing?' she called. 'Oi!' He was already a few metres ahead and swimming further away, his freestyle smacking the water. 'Oi!' she called, louder this time.

'Beat ya to the buoy!'

'Yeah, you will.' She splashed in his direction, the splatter making fleeting white dimples on the water's surface.

In the bay ahead, she could just make out a buoy shifting in the waves. She flipped over into backstroke but quickly grew tired. Breaststroke was easier, but her limbs were jelly, barely driving her through the water.

The buoy wasn't getting any closer and she had little left to give. Sid swam ahead. He was doing breaststroke too; she could hear the rhythmic spray of his exhales, and could just make out the back of his head. Lucy had blurred into darkness though she barked every now and then, agitated. Amelia wanted to turn back, but not with Sid out there alone.

The wind picked up as she moved further from the shore and the waves became more aggressive. Some of them had little white heads that curled and barrelled into her, others swelled, full, lifting her up and propelling her away from her goal. There was turmoil beneath the water, though she may have imagined the kick of it. Her arms numbed, her shoulders exhausted.

'Almost there!' Sid called from somewhere out in the deepening blackness. She could no longer hear Lucy, nor make out her shape on the pier. She imagined a huge shark jaw coming towards her when she put her head beneath the water. The waves around her transformed into fins and she was encircled. There was definitely something moving towards her, and the glint of white flesh. It drew closer and there was a flash of orange too, then the intake of breath. A swimmer moved past her a few metres away, goggles covering her eyes. Amelia waited, unnoticed. It seemed important to hide, to not draw attention to herself nor disturb this ritual of the early hours. As the swimmer disappeared, Amelia continued her strokes, digging deep, seeking a second wind. But the current grew stronger and each wave swept her along like driftwood.

There was a hoot from the pier, she was sure, the human sound carrying over the water. Silence for a few seconds, then a splash. Her heart set off and it would have skidded across the bay to the ocean if it could have escaped her chest.

'Hey,' Zach called. 'Wait up.'

She didn't. She swam, moving her limbs faster than before. Her chest was tight, but breathing was no longer important; distance was all that mattered. She kicked hard, as if in defence, and she dared not turn around to see where Zach was, or even take a minute to ensure she was on target to hit the buoy.

Despite pushing with everything she had against the current, she was suspended in the action of swimming, getting nowhere. It was loud out there at the collision of wind and water, and her panic fed off the noise.

He caught her, pulled at her ankles, spun her to face him. As she gasped for air his face furrowed in worry.

'Hey,' he said softly. 'Hey.' He lifted her hands onto his shoulders. It was a relief, at first, to relinquish the battle against sinking. His skin was soft; her thumbs dipped into the ridges of his collarbone. He caught his breath too, both of them panting. He reached out to her, wiped hair out of her eyes, neatened it behind her ears. He held her head, pushed her cheeks in with his palms. 'It's all right, it's all right.' Spray flicked towards her as he exhaled and she could smell the breath of each word.

They bobbed in the water, and there was the force of his kicks below, keeping them both afloat, and the rise and fall of his shoulders. In the moonlight, she examined the details of him: the eyebrows that had grown thick in the middle, the nose that had been broken and decentred on his face, the ears with their small lobes, the boy inside this man. His hand moved down her face, his thumb running over her mouth, pressing in gently on her bottom lip, then moving down her neck.

'Don't touch me,' she said, lifting her hands from his shoulders, her legs working again beneath her. His hands were still there on her skin, and she gave him a moment more to let go, but he didn't. She said it again, each word slow and standing alone: 'Don't touch me.'

He released her then, held his palms open as if she needed proof they were off her. He paused, watching her, and she held his eye till he turned. His legs brushed against hers as he swam away; she endured the contact because he would never touch her again.

The thump in her chest slowed. She swam to match it, a soft kick of the legs, stroke of the arms, dip of the head, through the waves, concentrating on each of the movements, synchronising them so she could feel the glide of progress.

'Meels?'

She could hear Sid but not see him. 'Yeah?'

'Over here.' She turned a full circle before seeing the flashes of his arms, signalling her. He was laughing, now only ten metres away. She swam over, keeping the same rhythm: legs, arms, head, repeat.

'You made it,' he said. He had the buoy wrapped in his arms. Its base was gooey and slippery as she wrapped her own arms around it, too.

'Made it,' she said.

'I'm a better swimmer than you,' he said.

'I know.'

The buoy squeaked as Sid adjusted his grip; reverberations reached her through the hard rubber.

'Zach was there, in the water,' she said.

'What happened?' Sid said. 'Are you okay?'

'Yeah, I'm good.' She waited, catching her breath, counting each one, then she said it: 'What he did to me . . . I was too young. It wasn't right.'

The waves slapped against the buoy and she leaned in closer to Sid, needing to hear his response.

'Oh, Meels. I . . . I didn't know it was like that.'

She pressed her head against the rubber, allowed water to play around her lips. 'It doesn't matter that I cared about him . . . I didn't understand.'

'I'm so sorry,' he said, and there was the push of water before his hand reached her, rested for a while on her back.

It didn't seem possible that she could be there, then, with those words outside of her; beyond the land, with the smell of mould rising from the underbelly of the buoy, far away from people but not too far, and with Sid, close. She looked out further across the bay, only able to separate the horizon, black on black, by the light of boats in the distance, knowing that Tasmania was far beyond them, the Overland Track holding the imprint of her and her mother's footsteps, and after Tasmania, more water, water, water. Her mother was there in the waves; they were the suck and release of her breath in the night, the gurgle of her stomach before breakfast, her first evening sip of red wine, held in her mouth for a few long moments before being swallowed.

'Is there anything I can do?' Sid said.

'Just this,' she said. 'I've missed you.'

'Missed you too.'

They stayed for a long time, many slow breaths of time. Her mind took her far, across her travels, back to the desert, and further, to her and her mother snuggled up in a beanbag beside the heater, too much cream squirted on hot chocolates, to her and Sid, sneaking into his neighbour's house to swim late at night, the smell of chlorine from the swimmers hidden beneath her pyjamas. Her mind went forward too, and some of the blank spaces had movement and colour, and she had a feeling, only fleeting, that she'd like to be *there*.

'Let's head back,' Amelia said. Half-submerged, her shoulders and chest to the air, she was cold. He shivered too, teeth clacking.

'Righto.'

She took one last, long breath then kicked off towards the shore.

They cycled together back to Sid's place. Mansions adorned with Christmas lights glowed and blinked as they made their way through the streets of Kew. She told him she wanted to stay with him for the night, but that she wouldn't stay with Zach too. She told him she was leaving in the morning. She told him he should come and see her, spend some time, and she told him she would be all right. He said okay, okay, okay, and as they walked down the garden path her footsteps were light, somehow, beneath the weight of his arm.

The night sky had lifted to reveal a band of dark blue, and the first morning birds were singing. Zach was nowhere to be found. Amelia flopped down onto the mattress and pulled the sheet up to her chin. She rolled over onto her stomach. The mattress shifted as Sid lay down on the opposite side; Lucy pawed herself a nest at the base of the bed.

*

She woke fresh and sharp, despite the wine. Sid was already awake. He wore last night's clothes, legs tucked up to his chest, a paperback bent over itself in his hands.

After a cup of tea and some cereal with out-of-date milk, she stood at the door of Sid's old Corolla, Lucy already loaded into the front seat. Sid stood watching her. They'd already said their goodbyes; it was just up to her now, to open the door and get in. The tank was three-quarters full, he'd said, which would get her off to a good start, and he'd lent her some cash to see her through the next few weeks.

'See you soon,' she said.

'See you soon.' He raised his arm in a wave, and she could tell he was trying hard to give a smile she'd believe.

She opened the door, lifting it on the hinges a little because she knew it wouldn't budge if she didn't. The smell of it was just right. No one could stop her as she hit one hundred kilometres an hour, the car rattling with the struggle.

After a few hours signs sprang up directing her back home. She didn't follow them, and when the final option to turn off had passed, she was relieved. She would return, eventually. She'd strip the beds, cut back the garden, sort out the finances and her mother's things; it all had to be done sometime, but not then.

She kept her window down the whole way, and she was sure she could feel the air grow stickier as she moved from inland to the coast. She drove past the cafe where she once treated herself to breakfast, past the ice creamery, the post office, the supermarket, then up the steep hill where shops began to peter out into houses.

The art shop was open. She stepped inside, where stock was piled high and deep. The same woman was there and Amelia either had never known her name or had forgotten it. She wore a purple scarf around her head with a strawberry print spread across it, the same eyeliner as always arcing out from her eyelid. She was stitching something and it was close work, a patch of material held up to her face.

'Hi,' Amelia said, and the woman's face transformed from crinkled concentration into recognition.

'Well, hello there,' she said, resting the material on the counter. 'You're back.'

Amelia returned the woman's smile. 'Yeah.'

'Had a feeling I might be seeing you again.'

'The room, is it . . .?'

'There's no one in it, hun. Rent's the same. It's yours again if you want it.'

'Yeah, I want it, please. I really, really want it.'

The woman pulled open a drawer beneath the counter and fished around, holding the sewing needle between her lips. She found the keys and handed them over, then removed the needle from her mouth. 'Happy to let yourself in?'

It seemed like the room hadn't been touched since Amelia was last in it. There was a haze of dust turned golden by the sun. The bed was crumpled with the same grey sheets she'd used and there was the damp smell, but she could fix that. She'd air the place out, perhaps get up and clear the gutters. Lucy remembered the place, barely needing to investigate before opting to curl up in her favourite spot by the window. Most importantly, the walls were the same: stark white, bracing themselves for the light show of sunset about to begin. Amelia threw the keys on the bed. She pulled open the sheer curtain, unlocked the window then popped the screen out of its frame. Laying it carefully against the wall inside, she climbed out and hung her legs down the building, felt the familiar bite of the windowsill against the backs of her thighs.

The ocean was showing off as the sun lowered. It crashed over and over on the shore, an insistent child tugging on its mother's skirts.

Acknowledgements

My deepest thanks to:

Varuna, the Writers' House, and Limnisa community of writers, for the hours, the food, for the rooms with views. And to the writers I met at these places, for the conversations into the night.

To Ellie, Seren, Richard (and Lincoln!), for the time taken to read drafts, for your honesty and for your wisdom. To Lesley and Suzie, for the writing group meetings, talking words and beyond.

To Anne Meadows, for your warm and astute comments, which I returned to over and over.

To Philip Hensher and Tessa Hadley, for your guidance, encouragement and the generous sharing of your experience. To all at Bath Spa University who engaged with my work and allowed me to engage with theirs.

To my agent, Emma Paterson, for being there since the beginning.

To all at Penguin Random House Australia, particularly Meredith Curnow and Kathryn Knight, for responding to this book with such heart, attention and grace.

To Charlotte and Pam, for your generosity in early reading and in each sharing your skills in healing; for the pep talks and for your belief.

To Jill and Sue, for your interest in my work, your acceptance of me, and your openness. For sharing your home as a place for rest and discussion, and as a place for me to read, look out windows, and write.

To my friends all over the world, too many wonderful ones to name, for the joy you add to my life, for asking about this book for longer than you thought you'd have to.

To my best friend, Jacci; thank you for finding me and thank you for sticking with me. You'll always be the one I call.

To my late father, who was proud of this book; thank you for fostering my inquisitiveness, for letting me write during our road trip, for helping me to swim out beyond the breakers, for reading to me.

To Nan, for always asking about this book, for assuming it would be one. For the Froot Loops, the hidden bags of lollies, the school holidays.

To Natalie, for being a big sister worth following, a person worth aspiring to. To Tim, for your loyalty and understanding. To Erik and Eleanor, for being the wildest, most welcome distractions.

To my mother, Annemaree; because of you, I have always known what it feels like for someone to have my back. Thank you for loving this book before reading it (and afterwards, too). Thank you, for everything.

To Bridget; your patience, kindness and gentleness have eased me through the making of this book, and through so much else . . . thank you. We laugh . . . and may we keep doing so.

About the author

Kathryn Hind was born in Canberra and has now returned there after living for five years in the United Kingdom. She's published essays and short stories in various Australian journals and collections, and has had a poem published on one of Canberra's Action buses. Kathryn began her first novel, *Hitch*, while studying in the UK, and in 2018 she was awarded the inaugural Penguin Literary Prize for the manuscript.